The author, perhaps quite understandably, has chosen to remain very coy on any details pertaining to him or her.

The Peregrinations
Of
Pablo's Penis

Pria Pims

The Peregrinations
Of
Pablo's Penis

Vanguard Press

ISBN 978 184386 969 6

*Vanguard Press is an imprint of
Pegasus Elliot Mackenzie Publishers Ltd.*
www.pegasuspublishers.com

First Published in 2015

Vanguard Press
Sheraton House Castle Park
Cambridge England

Printed & Bound in Great Britain

To life.

Acknowledgements

Life's experience.

Storyline

This is the story of the Bernsteins, a family who have emigrated on account of the Holocaust. They live in England, initially in London, and then in Shropshire. The story is told from the point of view of Harry Bernstein's penis. It chronicles its experiences from three months pre-natal, babyhood, the toddler stage, kindergarten, infant school, junior school, grammar school (where he obtained the nick-name Pablo), university, graduation as a doctor, liaisons, marriage, family, old age, death, and a triumphal rigor mortis.

Part I
Spring

(Age minus three months to twenty years)

Far away and long ago in a distant Teutonic land, poverty and misery was the lot of the masses consequent upon the Treaty of Versailles and reparations to the victorious Allies. A scapegoat had to be found, and as is well known, Mr Hitler chose the Jews. Anyway, they knew they were the chosen race, though they had rather it had been by God, not Hitler. Ethnic cleansing reached its zenith in the Holocaust, but fortunately some were able, by selling all they had, to escape. Some went to South Africa, some to Shanghai, others to South America, and some to England.

Among the last mentioned were the Bernstein family. Dad (Sol) short for Solomon, Mum (Martha), daughter (Brenda), whose original name was Brunhilde, and after arrival in England, baby Harry. Sol had been a director in the family's shipping business, and the family enjoyed a luxurious life-style. They had a cook, a gardener, and a chauffeur who transported them around Breslau in the Maybach. (To those not expert in the history of motoring, a Maybach was the equivalent of a Rolls-Royce). After *Kristallnacht*, (November 1938, when Nazis destroyed many Jewish premises, the quantity of broken glass giving the name for which this infamous time in history is remembered) they realised the writing was on the wall. Sol was forty, and beginning to get thin on top. His face bore a scar incurred during a fencing bout when at university in Darmstadt. Martha was petite and very house proud, particularly about the new gas cooker. Both had worked hard at their English, but as might be expected, still had marked accents.

My story begins a long time ago. Oh, I feel I should explain. You may find this hard to believe, but I am Harry (later nicknamed Pablo) Bernstein's penis. He was my master, and as such is named in my story. I wasn't actually aware of my existence, and neither were my owner's parents. Had their son been born sixty years later I would have been demonstrated by an ultrasound examination by the fourth month of pregnancy. It would have fallen to the technician to indicate my presence as no more than a blob, but like a rocket on the radar, my presence would have been detected. And five months later, I landed on planet earth, attached to my master. I had a pretty rough time travelling down the tunnel of love, stop, go – I wish they would make their minds up. Though of course I didn't know it then, but come physical maturity I would be spending a large part of my life attempting a return journey.

Finally I emerged into a blinding, cold, noisy world. Someone said, 'You have a lovely little boy.'

I wondered who they were referring to – was it me? Or was it the master? They seemed to pay me no attention whatever, but I hit on a plan.

One day, during a curious ritual called 'changing baby's nappy' I felt a sudden warm urge of pressure and was able to squirt a good cupful of lovely warm wee straight into his Dad's eye. I must say, my aim was uncannily accurate. I don't think he was any too pleased. But, well wrapped in a terry towel nappy, I was warm and secure, though always terrified of the proximity of the dreaded safety pin. As company, I had two round bits (Bill and Ben) always hanging around and whose purpose I could only wonder at for many years. Anyway, life was great, what with all the billing and cooing of parents, friends, and the curious and possibly envious gaze of my master's sister, Brenda. Life adopted a routine, my master feeding at his mother's breast, which left me curious as I never got a look in at a breast, and wouldn't for many a long year.

The first week on planet earth settled into a routine of nappy on, nappy off, my master glugging at the aforementioned, or sleeping. I was getting accustomed to this until just into my second week, we all got into a car and were driven off to a large place which I later discovered was a synagogue. We had an appointment with a Mr Mohel, and people round about me were muttering weird incantations, and something about a 'bris'. It is at this point that I would advise the squeamish reader to turn over the page. On the other hand, for those of a sadistic nature, or possibly fond of sexual perversion, or whatever, what next happened was to leave me scarred for life.

My master was given a little wine (would you believe it – I thought you had to be at least sixteen), on some gauze. If any reader seriously believes this to be an anaesthetic, let me assure them it isn't – all it does is salve the consciences of the doting audience. I know now how the bull feels in the bullring. Mr Mohel had a cloak and hat, somewhat different from that of a matador, but the game started with a little to and fro sparring. Whenever he tried to grab me I would sway first to one side, then the other. (Remember, I'd had some practice dodging the safety pin.) I think some guy called Bizet in a far distant land set the scene to music. Anyway after the first attempts, the guy in the cloak brought in the picador who made several stabs at pulling my hood off. Eventually he succeeded and pulled my hood down to my knees. For me, this revealed the world as I hadn't seen it during the eight days I'd been on it. For my master, sod the 'anaesthetic', he was bawling his head off. Mr Mohel and the others were chanting all kinds of (to me) meaningless stuff. Worse was to follow. Scissors! Horror upon horror, I feared my short life was at an end, cut off in my prime, detached from my master, and destined for the bucket! However, doubtless realising the enormity of the injury he had inflicted, Mr Mohel full of remorse (at least that is what his mutterings and incantations sounded like), repaired the damage with some admittedly deftly applied, dressings. Then it was back home by car, with the aforementioned bullring spectators drinking coffee and eating cake. I suppose the 'anaesthetic' or whatever it was, was by now beginning to work, as I felt very tired and together with my master slept soundly for the next eight hours.

I expect by now you will have guessed that my master's family was Jewish, and that the aforementioned ceremony was circumcision. So now I'll fill you in with a little background.

His family came from Breslau in Poland, nowadays called Wroclaw. I must admit I owe my master's life to their emigration, as many people in their neighbourhood were being targeted by the local Nazi enthusiasts. It was 1937 when Hitler decided that all parents must bring up their children according to Nazi ideals or face the consequences. That was enough to convince the master's parents that it was time to leave. Those who didn't mostly died in concentration camps. I wasn't yet created, thankfully, but owe my existence to my master's parents' celebration of their arrival in England and lodging with a well-to-do uncle who had left five years earlier, and was managing a successful hosiery business in Edgware. My life was undoubtedly saved by the move to England. And one week later after my tremendous ordeal, I was healing well and getting used to my face-lift – or should I say, loss of face!

I was now three months into my attachment, when things took a turn for the worse. All I know about it is that I changed colour from pink to red, as did Bill and Ben my hangers on and all the immediate surroundings. A doctor was called, who visited the house and declared my master to be the victim of nappy rash. We all survived as a result of various creams, and once more life settled into the routine. But one night in 1940 our peace was shattered by an enormous explosion that shook our house to its foundations. I later learned that a bomb had been dropped into a house only a quarter of a mile away, killing five people including children. My master's parents and family became very worried, as it appeared the threat of a Nazi invasion loomed. And if it did, where else could we go? Suffice it to say, I was not affected, in fact my master was thriving and in addition to his daily glugs from the jugs, he was now getting to grips with the bottle.

As the months went by, I became aware of a sort of dragging sensation. I was being stroked by something outside my nappy. All was made clear when, on a rare moment, my master was naked on the lounge carpet, and it was then I realised he was moving forwards. This time it was the same stroking sensation, only stronger. I felt quite elated, and responded by vigorously peeing into my aunt's shoes as she lifted me up, initially with a look of adoration, but which didn't last long. It seemed as though whenever I attempted to express myself in public, it brought on disapproval. Somehow I never felt in control, my actions being determined from some centre situated elsewhere in my master.

Many years would pass before his brain took the occasional trip down to where I hung out.

The master was growing, and soon I felt the force of what I would later realise was gravity. He was by now beginning to stand up, and gradually move about by holding onto things, or (very frequently), sitting down with a bump and resorting to crawling. It was 1941.

Bath time was fun. It was quite sublime being free from those horrible nappies, and being nice and warm and being waved around as a consequence of the master kicking his legs. The master's sister was often present. I noticed her looking at me in a sort of fascinated way. She asked his mother what I was, and why she was made differently.

'It's called a willie, and girls don't have one, because only little boys have willies.'

I wasn't sure how good an answer that was, but it seemed to satisfy Brenda – at least at first. Then followed, 'Can I have a willie for my birthday?'

Brenda had reached the inquisitive age.

'Why has Harry got one – I can do wee-wees without a willie?'

'You'll learn about it when you're older, and please fetch me the talcum powder.'

This was all the response she got. Later that evening I heard my master's mother talking to her husband.

'You'll never guess what Brenda said today?'

Sol lifted his eyes from the Jewish Chronicle.

'What?'

'She asked why Harry has a willie.'

'What did you tell her?'

'I told her only little boys have willies.'

'Well that's not really answering her question.'

'All right, Sol, you do better, you tell her exactly tomorrow.'

Next day, a Tuesday, Sol felt it was time to put the record straight.

'Brenda, your mother told me that you asked her why Harry has a willie, but you do not.'

'Yes, Daddy, but I already know. Miriam told me when we were skipping in the back yard last night. Willies are made into Wieners, and you can buy them in the delicatessen. When willies grow bigger, you go to the deli, and have them removed. Her mother said she wished all men had theirs chopped off; those who escaped caused no end of trouble. What kind of trouble, Daddy?'

Sol chuckled.

'Don't you worry your pretty little head about it. Go and fetch me my pipe, my little princess.'

When I overheard this conversation I visibly shrank with fear. As if I hadn't already suffered enough, now, at some uncertain time in the future I was destined for the delicatessen, to be made into a Wiener. What could possibly be worse than that? And if by some stroke of good fortune, I were to escape that fate, I would be the source of all kinds of trouble.

The future was looking grim indeed. However, I surmised that manhood was still some way off, and I needn't be too worried yet. But I could tell by the way Brenda took every opportunity to look at me enquiringly during my master's ablutions, that she was hoping my ascent into wienerhood was imminent. Then, one Thursday, my master's mum casually announced we were having wieners this evening. I almost disconnected myself, and would have had it been possible. But there was no escape. Come supper time, and Brenda tucked into hers with gusto, then asked for more. Just before bath time, I had the opportunity of seeing a real wiener as I was carried through the kitchen, and comparing it with myself. There was, possibly, a passing resemblance, but no more. Things would have to change radically if I were to grow to that size, and develop such a smooth contour, because, as a result of the bris aforementioned, I looked different. I would live to fight another day!

I think it's time to fill you in on a little background. After all, you don't really want to read about me all the time. OK, so I'm very self-centred, but my repertoire at this stage was somewhat limited, and I can perceive in you a slight touch of boredom. You've seen one, you've seen them all. OK, that may be so, but we willies have our own lives, our own stories to tell, our own feelings, the good times and the bad.

Times were hard, and my master's mum did sewing for a clothes shop based in Kilburn. One day, I could hear her crying, and the use of a strange word 'internment'. It seemed that Sol, recently escaped from the Nazis in Poland was now regarded as an alien in England, and therefore would have to be interned somewhere in the Isle of Man. He was not alone, and lots of mums were bemoaning the same fate. Mrs Bergman, Mrs Silberstein and Mrs Horowitz were frequent visitors to our house; or me plus master in pram in theirs.

'My Jakob, such a wonderful husband, I don't know how I'll manage without him. Ach du lieber Gott, what shall I do?'

A different point of view was expressed by Mrs Goldfarb.

'I'm quite glad actually, my Werner is so demanding, I need some peace – three times a day, no wonder we were decreed a day of rest.'

These are samples of the varied exclamations, not all of which I was able to understand at the time. Days and nights went by, punctuated by snippets about the war, food and clothes rationing, and the nightly air-raid alarms. Initially, they all marched off to the local air-raid shelter, but eventually our family's response was to pack my master in his cot under the staircase. Quite how this would guarantee protection against a large bomb was never made clear. Certainly the sounds of the V1 'doodlebugs' became ingrained in my master's memory all his life. The sound was characteristic, and if it passed overhead and reduced in volume, then you were safe. If it was approaching, however, and the sound abruptly stopped, it meant your number might be up in about five to ten seconds. My master's dad, Sol, was by now away, and all that was heard from him was the occasional censored letter. My master, whose name incidentally was Harry, was thriving, all systems functioning well, and gaining weight. By now, gravity had a regular hold, as he was just able to walk. Instead of pointing up I was pointing down. Then one day, to our amazement Sol appeared in army uniform! He announced he had been discharged from the Isle of Man and had the honour of being a British soldier (actually a private in the Pioneer Corps stationed at Catterick, Yorkshire). He further enlightened us by telling us that his contribution to the war effort thus far, involved constructing latrines (he was a qualified civil engineer with a German university degree), and margarining hundreds of slices of bread. Using his knowledge of engineering to the full, he invented a new technique for same, namely melting the margarine, and applying it with the aid of his shaving brush! Thus equipped he could easily cover five hundred slices in an hour. It was ingenuity on this scale which doubtless helped us win the war. Strangely, he had been a wireless operator on the German side at the end of the First World War. Wars are funny things; I guess few people directly involved know precisely what it is they are fighting for.

By now my master was toddling about, frequently crashing into things. Luckily I never got hurt, which was one (to me) advantage of wearing a nappy. And on occasion, my master was sat on a potty, which afforded me a new view. Though for the most part I weed into the thing, I considered it good sport to direct the jet in a graceful arc, which startled our cat when it landed in his ear as he slumbered in front of the black anthracite stove.

By now Brenda was going to infant school, which meant that during the day, my master was the unopposed apple of his mother's eye. Occasionally there was more excitement when Sol came home on leave. Then one day, it was announced that we were all moving out to be nearer to him. We were accommodated on a farm with the Pickersgills, in Yorkshire. We travelled in a rattly wooden carriage from King's Cross. After what seemed an age, we disembarked at Catterick, and caught a bus to the farm. Mrs Pickersgill was a large jolly lady who soon made us feel at home. I noticed the difference to life in London immediately. It was so quiet. No air-raid sirens, no sounds of traffic (except now and then), but more especially the cold. There was a biting cold wind. My poor master's mother and Brenda complained frequently. I wasn't bothered as I had my nice warm nappy, which I could make even warmer (for a while) by weeing into it.

Every day we all went down the road to the bus stop, from where Brenda together with some other children got on, and went off to school in Cuffley. Then, one day, a strange thing happened. But first we must go back about six weeks.

The farmer had cows and sheep, but what interested my master more, were the pigs. I suppose it was the noise they made, or perhaps their smell. By now, he was toddling about within our share of the farmhouse, or the farmyard. I suppose the event to be described started when he first saw Bess, a large sow with her litter of piglets. They were all thriving, except one, who was referred to as the runt. This little fellow was taken into the house by Mrs Pickersgill, and fed similar stuff to what my master had been drinking from a tin with a picture of a cow and a gate on it. He watched with fascination as the little snorter glugged energetically. Piglet, as he was by now known (not much imagination to my mind – yes, penises have minds you know, not all one track), was becoming quite tame, and took a liking for my master. Wherever he would go on his peregrinations about the farm, Piglet would accompany him. But what was more interesting was the fact that Piglet took upon himself the role of minder. Whenever my master ventured into any danger, such as for example the ditch at the end of the yard, or the road nearby, he would interpose himself between the danger and my master. Unsurprisingly, they became best pals, but unfortunately from both their points of view, they were not allowed to share the same sleeping arrangements. My master had been given some crayons with which to unleash his artistic talents. These were freely exhibited on pieces of paper, the walls, the furniture, and even attempted upon Piglet (without success). But all this was to change when the master discovered paint.

Bert Appleby had been asked by Farmer Pickersgill to paint his fire buckets red. I suppose the War Department's thinking was that the Luftwaffe might at any time decide to bomb a quiet Yorkshire farm in case the British happened to be hiding some weapon of mass destruction (this kind of thinking would amazingly be repeated by a future British prime minister). So the decree went out that these buckets had to be painted red. And so it came to pass one day, Bert having gone for his tea-break, that my master (who had been watching Bert's skills with rapt admiration), took it upon himself to have a go. Unfortunately, Piglet sensed the danger, and duly interposed himself. Thus it came about that my master's first 'canvas' (so to speak), was Piglet. Piglet bore his role with equanimity, emitting encouraging grunts, and wagging his tiny tail. The master was having a whale of a time, and before long Piglet was invisible to anyone when interposed twixt viewer and painted fire bucket. The master then turned his attention upon an unpainted fire bucket, but soon gave up when he realised he didn't possess the skill of Bert Appleby, who at that precise moment having finished his tea-break, emerged from the farm kitchen. He let out a guffaw which sent Piglet running around the farmyard like a demented banshee, clearly enjoying the attention. In the course of his artistic efforts, the master had succeeded in painting his hands and arms, but I thought I had escaped until he decided he wanted a pee. Thus it was that I received my colours (well colour) of which I felt proud. After all, there aren't too many chaps on the planet with a bright red painted willie!

Meanwhile the war was continuing apace, though we up in Yorkshire were well insulated from its effects. Animals were still being fed, fields ploughed, though of course there was plenty of talk about it, and the dreadful blitz on London. We had to be especially vigilant for spies, according to posters like 'Careless talk costs lives', and 'Your country needs you'. Quite why my master's country needed me wasn't made clear, though I nevertheless felt patriotic, and would do whatever to help the war effort. There were no notices to this effect such as 'Penises, do it for England'. I would have felt a patriotic thrill and would certainly have been up for it. In that event poor Brenda would have missed out, because, according to my master's mum, she didn't have one. At this terrible revelation, she burst into tears.

'But, Mummy, why haven't I got one? Can I buy one?'

'You, my dear, should be proud to be a girl, because one day, you will be able to have babies, which boys never can.'

Unfortunately this didn't placate our Brenda, who developed a sullen expression whenever she saw me as I was being washed when my master was having a bath. Once, when his mother had to leave the bathroom for a short time because Mrs Pickersgill was at the door with some eggs, she started soaping my master, but suddenly took a flick at me. This she repeated three times – I was rigid with anger! How dare she? My anger however, only served to fascinate her, but by good fortune Mother returned in time to resume the master's ablutions. Not before she had observed the evidence of my indignation, at which, for some reason unknown to me, she chuckled.

'Brenda, please go and fetch me a towel,' she said.

'But, Mummy, you've already got one, why do you need another?'

I got the impression she wanted Brenda out of the bathroom, and for some reason it had something to do with me. By now, my sense of indignation had subsided, at which point Mum said, 'Of course, how silly of me.'

Later that evening, we were all excited because Sol returned from the army base at Catterick, with lots of tales to tell of the other refugees he had met there. Some were famous artistes, musicians, engineers, doctors – in fact all sorts. Even a penis could surmise that this was a great waste of talent, but then, ours is not to question why. And so, the war continued with us out of it. But not for long. Sol was being transferred to Ilfracombe, so a few weeks later, it was a tearful goodbye and off he went. Some time after, we were travelling there to meet him. In the train compartment, thick with the aroma of Woodbines, we chatted with some soldiers, who got off at Bristol. It was about seven o'clock on a dark November evening. Suddenly there was an air-raid warning siren – something we never experienced in Yorkshire. All was dark – I suppose the lights were switched off. Then we heard the droning sound of the bombers as they flew closer. And then, the rumbling and ground shaking, which was clearly felt inside the train, as the bombs fell around the station. Our train pulled out and just a few seconds later there was the most almighty explosion. Later we read that the station had taken a direct hit, and many soldiers who had shortly before disembarked from the train, had been killed. My master's mum was clearly upset, and wept whilst telling our landlady (we were in digs in Ilfracombe).

'We had just been chatting to them, such nice boys, it seems so hard to believe that a few minutes later they died.'

She was a courageous woman, and times were not easy. Food rationing was a major source of conversation. Eggs were not to be had, but instead we had dried eggs, and something called

Spam. This was not to be confused with the annoying version to be found on the internet seventy years later. My master clearly enjoyed eating Spam. He was a sturdy little toddler. I was happy too: Brenda seemed to have forgotten my existence (thank goodness). I still had the discomfort of a terry towel nappy, except on occasions when I was free as a bird, in the garden with my master running around pretending to be an aeroplane. When it came to pee time, he had great pleasure in pointing me whatever which way and playing with various combinations of water-aerobics. There was the direct squirt, with its resonance against an upturned bucket, the graceful sweeping arc for maximum range, the attack on poor little Ernie, the chap from next door who once came to play, but not again.

Came the summer of 1942, and I remember visiting the Bloch family who lived at the other side of town. It was a glorious day, and we caught the bus to the stop on Vicarage Road from where it was a short walk to the Bloch home. Mr and Mrs Bloch were, like my master's family, refugees from the Nazis in Europe. Mr Bloch was an excitable little man who enjoyed playing dive-bombers with my master. Mrs Bloch, a chubby jolly lady brought out her home-made cake which they all enjoyed.

Then came my adventure. The master's parents had forgotten his potty, and, as the Blochs had no children, there was little likelihood of them possessing one. So when the time came, the master was deposited on the toilet seat by his mother. Just at that moment, the phone rang. It was the hospital in Shrewsbury with news about her sister who had recently been admitted with a heart attack. So understandably she became extremely anxious, and abandoned the master. Young Harry was faced with a bit of a dilemma. First, was the urgent need to pee. Second, his little arms were getting tired supporting him, and he was terrified of disappearing down the gigantic cavern that was known to others as the toilet pan. So he compromised by allowing a gradual downward slip to be accompanied by releasing the bladder floodgate. The result, as can be imagined was an ever increasing arc that started with the lower part of the toilet door, and gradually ascended via the frosted glass pane to the ceiling. By now the poor master was about to disappear into the toilet. Fortunately at this moment his mother appeared. She stared aghast at what beheld her, then, full of remorse, rescued the poor master whilst praising him to the hilt at having used a proper toilet for the first time. Little did she know of the preceding aquatics. The master was then duly rewarded with an extra large slice of the aforementioned cake. I felt quite chuffed at our adventure plus the recently acquired skill of squirting as a sort of art form. I wonder if, suitably attached to a paintbrush I could have taken the world by storm – perhaps the great Penisso.

Eventually, it was the master's third birthday: 1943. Much excitement in the house. His mum, Martha, had baked a birthday cake, using wartime margarine. Not easy as the margarine was very hard. Several of his little friends were invited from the neighbourhood. None of them came from Jewish families, and it had become apparent to Harry that their parents spoke English differently from his. Mary, a little girl of the same age, took his eye with her ringlets. Jimmy was somewhat on the fat side and spent most of the time hoovering up whatever food he could lay his grubby little hands on. Jonathan ignored him altogether, preferring to chat to the various parents. He looked intelligent, and would eventually have a public school education, attend Eton, then Oxford University, join the Foreign Office and, along with his gay friends, become involved in a notorious scandal involving the security of the nation. But, back to the birthday party. Patrick was Harry's chum, and together they decided to chase the girls around the house with the intention of pulling their hair. At the table they tucked in to their food. Spam sandwiches went down well, as did jam tarts. This was followed by jelly, and then birthday cake. Of course everyone sang 'Happy birthday' after which Harry dutifully blew out the three candles. Jimmy grabbed two portions of cake, and soon reached out for a third. Harry and Patrick disappeared to the loo, where each could demonstrate their recently acquired expertise at weeing. It was then that they realised that Patrick's counterpart and me looked different. But both were able to perform, most of it into the toilet. They then ran back to the party where Jimmy was being sick on the settee.

'Patrick's willie is different from mine,' shouted my master, anxious to attain everyone's attention. At this, Brenda's face emitted a spark of fleeting interest, before she was summoned by Harry's mum to help clear up the sick. I must admit I was curious about my different appearance to Patrick's willie. My curiosity was further wetted when I attended kindergarten soon after. There I soon realised that I was in the minority, though I was comforted by the fact that Ben Goldfarb and Mo Hussein had identical ones to me. Kindergarten was fun. The ladies were nice to our masters, and that is what they expected when eventually they started school.

Something very exciting happened – 1945: the war was over! Everyone was very happy. Harry remembered the sound of bombs falling, including the V1s or doodlebugs. Out in Ilfracombe, he hardly heard any, except when the Luftwaffe was paying Bristol a visit. By now, we had moved back to London, living in Greencroft Gardens. We had lots more visitors who spoke German, or German-sounding English. Harry found them all to be ever so friendly, yet later in life, when he heard German being spoken by people who had not had to move out of Germany he couldn't understand his parents' antipathy towards them. Harry and the rest of the family piled into Uncle Erich's Vauxhall, and drove to the West End, where people were singing, dancing, and cheering. It was a carnival atmosphere. Anyone in uniform was being hugged or kissed, some more than others – Harry had never seen men with lipstick on their cheeks and collars before. He was told that from now on there would be no more air-raid sirens, and soon, food rationing would end. Sol and Martha enjoyed a celebration dinner at home later that evening with Gertrude, Sol's sister and Ernest her husband. They had three children. Renee, the eldest who was twenty-two years old, and in the Auxiliary Territorial Service, known as the 'ATS'. Then came Ricky, and Hermann, who was the youngest, at eighteen. The dinner was a very jolly affair, consisting of chicken soup, followed by Spam fritters with dried egg and potatoes. The finale was Gertrude's cake. She had managed to acquire (don't ask me how) some plums, so we had plum cake – delicious. My master entertained the party with his imitations of doodlebugs, until he was hushed as everyone listened intently to the wireless for a speech by the prime minister. From now on, it appeared, we faced a new dawn, rationing would end, and the task of rebuilding our nation would begin.

September arrived, and my master started infant school. There was much excitement, clothes (second-hand) were obtained, patches applied, socks darned, and off he marched clutching his mum's hand. The school was situated up a steep hill, off the Finchley Road. He noticed a bombed out department store, with but a solitary hat left in a window.

'Look, Mummy, Hitler forgot that hat,' he exclaimed much to his mum's amusement, a tale to be recounted to numerous friends and family over the years.

At the school, he was introduced to his teachers, and lots of children. A visit to the loos was arranged, with segregation of the boys and girls. This seemed odd to my master, as before, at home, and in other people's homes, this was not the case. It made him wonder if girls, (who apparently didn't possess willies, according to Brenda's peer reviewed information), had some other device with which to carry out the task. This was to remain a mystery for many years. The teachers were very nice, except one who was very strict and feared by the children. Miss Braithwaite was stern, devoid of any semblance of kindness, and delivered her words of wisdom to a silent and utterly subjugated audience.

'Children should be seen and not heard, except when spoken to, and a reply expected.'

How jolly! Mrs Brown was totally different, and my master's class was much more relaxed with her. Miss Simkins was younger and very pretty. My master didn't seem to notice, but I did. In general he and I communicated, but sometimes I think I was ahead of his game. Lessons consisted of learning the alphabet by rote, and writing some of the letters in pencil. On Wednesday afternoons, it was painting, and here my master felt he had more experience than his peers, recalling his porcine adventure. But before he got into the routine of the school, Sol announced one evening that the factory where by now he was employed as a draughtsman was moving from Uxbridge to Shropshire. It should be realised by the readers that German qualifications didn't carry weight in England. After all, what did the Germans know about engineering. Our Spitfires beat their Messerschmitts, and our Rolls-Royces were better than their Beetles, and on top of that, we had won the war, which proved we were better. The same applied to my master's uncle, who had a German law degree, but had to make a living in a shop in Edgware. Subsequently, some years later, he bade farewell to England, returning to Germany, and became a Supreme Court judge for the Americans in occupation as well as Grandmaster of the Freemasons. In England, the best he could have achieved was to be a shopkeeper.

So the Bernstein family moved to Shropshire in 1946, and lived in a small village. At school, my master found a difference among his classmates to that which he had experienced in London. There were no girls in the class; their school was separated by a high brick wall from his. Because his surname was Bernstein his classmates, having told their parents about the thin, weakly new boy, returned proclaiming him to be German, and therefore needed to be pushed around, and forced into fights against his will. On one occasion, the master tried to escape a bigger boy in the playground, and fell down hurting his knee. As he sat there crying quietly, two other boys sat down next to him, and tried to cheer him up. As part of this exercise in rehabilitation, the first boy, Johnny Onions by name, proudly exhibited his deformed arm, the consequence of a previous fracture which had been very poorly re-set by a local GP in his surgery with a whiff of ether. The master almost puked, but this was followed by Jimmy Smithers pulling out his glass eye, the consequence of having been struck by an arrow whilst playing at Robin Hood with his mates. The master forgot his grazed knee, and was given a little sparring practice with his new friends. He did quite well – in fact, being small and nimble, he soon found that he was quite good at fighting. Consequently, he enjoyed scrapping and found that he was no longer the butt of the other children, but quite popular, though everyone still thought his name rather odd.

My involvement was relatively small, though for the first time, in the boys' lavatories, I was expected to pee against a dark brown stained stone wall. The school was Victorian. School meals were interesting – there was no dining room or kitchen. Meals came from a van, and were partaken with plates delicately placed on the angled desk-tops. For three years, this school was Harry's source of education, which consisted each day of reciting the times tables from two to twelve. Writing skills were acquired using pens dipped into inkwells each of which were recessed into the desks, and covered by a sliding brass plate. These the children would polish every week, and receive marks for it as well as their general tidiness, including fingernails. Punishment consisted of being struck across the hand with a ruler. The master and his contemporaries became literate and numerate – it was hard not to be. This was before decimalisation, so he learned that twenty-two yards (the length between the wickets) was called one chain. Twelve pence to a shilling, twenty shillings made a pound, twenty-one a guinea, sixteen ounces to a pound, fourteen pounds to a stone, twelve inches to a foot, three feet to a yard, one thousand seven hundred and sixty of which made a mile. The number twelve was referred to as a dozen, but a baker's dozen was thirteen.

School milk was received daily in bottles containing one third of a pint. The milk tops consisted of round card, which were highly sought after. They were a surrogate currency for another playground game. This consisted of the first boy flicking one milk top about three feet. The second boy would attempt to project his milk top to at least partially cover that of the first boy, in which case, he would retrieve and keep both tops, and so on. Some of the more business minded children would set up stalls, in which they would sit down with their backs propped up against the wall. One milk bottle top would be placed down, and any passing boy would be invited to gamble as to whether he could flick his milk top and cover the target.

'One and your own one back,' was the standard shout, though occasionally when business was very competitive, and for a limited time only, one might hear, 'Two and your own one back.' This chap would one day head a famous bank in a land where kilts were traditionally worn, and bring it crashing into bankruptcy.

Behind the school, was a railway line, and Harry and his mates were avid collectors of train numbers. At precisely a quarter to four in the afternoon, a Stafford bound train would puff away, and its number (often 49726) would be duly recorded by pencil in Ian Allan's book of trains. To the modern day sane, this would appear to be a pointless exercise, as trains in the twenty-first century, at least in Britain, are places of distress, overpriced, overcrowded and often, over time. The experience then of the heady mix of Woodbines, St Bruno, and sagging upholstery in the compartments, plus the soot and grime on the windows, but most of all, the overwhelming majesty, and living breathing of a large steam locomotive, as the ground shook upon its arrival at the platform, was something that fascinated little boys (and also, sad old men). Nowadays, sitting cramped in a modern day rail coach, watching the countryside slide noiselessly by, the only sound being that of mobile phones, informing all who cared, that the asking price of a house was too high, or that these or those shares should be bought, or that Daddy loves you. The master and his friend, Barry, would go train spotting. All I got out of it was peeing into nettles that adorned the railway embankment. Barry's willie was unlike mine or those I remembered possessed by Mo and Ben. Any sense of inferiority was soon dispelled when I outperformed Barry insofar as peeing range was concerned. Then, back to the embankment, notebook ready, as a train rounded the curve, and Freshford Manor (number 7813) with its entourage of eight blood and custard coaches rattled past, bound for Birkenhead. A favourite game played by my master and Barry consisted of placing a one penny coin, or a halfpenny on the rail. After a train had passed over it, it would be twice the size and half the thickness (though no use as legal tender).

One day, during playtime, the master became aware of the frequent use, mainly by the bigger boys, of what later would be referred to as the 'F word'. Initially this aroused no interest, after all 'bloomin' was meaningless, 'bloody' didn't refer to blood, neither did 'flippin' refer to overturning. However, after some weeks had passed, and hearing the F word being used to qualify the otherwise unimpressive word that represented the place where all wicked people would go to in the afterlife, the master enquired of its user, what the F word meant.

'I haven't got a f**** clue,' was the reply.

As a consequence of this tautology, the master was none the wiser. After a while he felt that rather than being thought ignorant, he would start using it himself. It was a rather special word with an onomatopoeic property which rhymed with 'stuck' and 'muck' and therefore the master assumed it referred to something vaguely agricultural. This was all very well, until he pronounced one day after supper at home, when as a special guest, the vicar had accepted an invitation to join us (probably with the intention of converting the family to the teachings of Christ), that in his opinion, the dessert was 'f**in' good. A look of horror appeared on Ma and Pa's faces, the vicar turned a redder shade of crimson, and Brenda smirked.

'Where on earth did you learn that word?' the vicar asked.

'At school,' replied Harry, then feeling somewhat desperate for no reason he could fathom, decided to embellish his story a bit.

'All the teachers use it all the time – to describe the food, our reading and writing, and when describing the headmaster. And by the way, what does 'twat' mean?'

No explanation forthcoming, the conversation turning to whether John Cordle would defeat Ivor Thomas in the upcoming election (he didn't). However, one day in the school playground, the master asked John. John was in the senior class which was taken by the headmaster for those boys doing time until they could legally leave school and go into the wide world, having failed to get into grammar or secondary modern schools. John told him what it meant (within the limits of John's somewhat limited knowledge but which had the essential aspects of the process correct). The master was horrified, he felt sick, and consoled himself by picking a fight with a smaller boy, and cutting his lip. Later, he tried working it out. Firstly, if the beastly thing was done, how could a willie get into a wee-wee hole?

Secondly, how in God's name could that make a baby come? At home in the bath that night, he picked me up and stared wonderingly at me. I felt strange – he had never seemed in the least bit interested except in target practice. He surmised that perhaps girls, sorry, ladies, after they got married, had a stock of very tiny babies stored somewhere within. So then, when the ghastly act was committed, the sheer revulsion would somehow release one, boy or girl, which would have to grow somewhere until ready to – what? How would it come out? He had heard tales of doctors delivering babies from their little black bag, and even more unlikely, by babies being brought by a stork.

The master asked his mother some days later. She informed him that babies were carried inside Mum's tummy until ready to come out. In fact, she confided, she had one inside her which was expected to arrive in seven months' time. He thought this a little odd. How could his mum be so sure about the time it would take? Was he going to have a baby brother or, horror of horrors, a sister like Brenda?

'Mum, what makes babies start?'

'Start what?' came the reply.

'Well, do they come when God wants them to, or does Dad have anything to do with it?'

'Oh, Harry, ask your dad when he comes home.'

'Daddy, Mummy says she is going to have a baby. Did you have anything to do with it?'

'Of course, my boy, I love your mummy very much.'

'So how do you make her have a baby?'

'Well you see, the baby is inside her tummy, and when I love your mummy, it makes it start.'

Harry felt a surge of triumph. He had got it right. Daddy's willie when he put it there made Mummy so sick, (in fact she seemed to be sick most mornings) that it triggered the baby thing. But another problem loomed. Would it be a boy or a girl?

'I don't know,' his dad replied to this question.

The master reasoned that it was due to pure chance which one tumbled out first, and sometimes two came out, called twins. Perhaps that was the consequence of an extremely hard willie stimulus and the undoubted revulsion it would cause.

But another question reared its ugly head. The Kumars at number twenty-four were a mixed race family, Surjit having married Eileen Jones. According to Harry's willie theory, Mrs Kumar's babies were already there awaiting the willie trigger. So why, given that Eileen was white (in fact very pale), were their children sort of half white, in fact they looked as though they had just come back from holiday in Blackpool (which they hadn't as he discovered on quizzing Mrs Kumar).

'Mrs Kumar, why are Rohit and Arahdna sort of, well you know, brownish? Have you been to the seaside on holiday?'

'No, Harry, we can't afford a holiday, as Mr Kumar is on short time at the moment.' (Perhaps the start of Britain's industrial decline.)

'So why are they browner than you, but not as brown as Mr Kumar?'

'Well, Harry, it's due to Mr Kumar's genes. They combined with mine.'

(Mrs Kumar had passed her School Certificate in biology.)

'Sorry, Harry, I've got to go now, I've got some buns in the oven, I mean cakes.' Mrs Kumar hurried away.

Harry was now more puzzled than ever. What was it about jeans that determined the colour of a baby? He had heard of colours coming out when clothes were washed, and if by some chance Mr and Mrs Kumar both wore jeans (though he had never seen them doing so), then if the colours mixed whilst in the wash, somehow this would affect the babies she had had, and might in the future have. He then had a flash of inspiration, and thought he would ask clever clogs, Brenda. At first she appeared puzzled too, but then piped up, 'Well jeans are very sexy you know. The girls at school think Johnny Ray is ever so sexy in jeans. And men go crazy about Marilyn Monroe.'

'What does "sexy" mean?'

'Harry, you're too young. There are lots of things you don't know about, like periods.'

And with that, she scooted off chuckling. The master was left totally bemused.

One day his mother explained to him that soon she would be having a baby, perhaps a brother or maybe a sister. No one knew which. Harry pronounced his urgent preference for a brother, as having a sister like Brenda was unthinkable. His mother said she would do her best. The master turned his mind to statistics. This was not a subject he had encountered at school, but with an innate degree of intelligence, he thought that the preceding gender sequence of the Bernstein offspring had thus far been girl, boy, and so the next would be likely to be – oh horror, a girl!

It was now becoming clear that Mother was developing a bump in her tummy. The master wasn't that interested, recalling with horror what must have happened to bring this about. But when he was invited to feel the unborn baby kicking from inside Mum's tummy, he became very excited. The prospect of a little friend with whom to play football made the whole thing worthwhile. Perhaps Mum would go on to produce a whole team, if she got a move on. Brenda was fascinated and took up knitting, at least for a while, until she got bored. However, should the baby eventually be born legless and armless, with a poorly developed chest, then Brenda's efforts might be of some use.

However, God was merciful, and in due course, Martha gave birth to a healthy little boy, whom his parents named David. He was a healthy bonny chap, who clearly enjoyed his liquor, naturally administered. The master watched these proceedings with great interest. Breasts were fascinating, now he understood their purpose, which hitherto had been something of little interest, though the other boys at school would often go on about them, commenting frequently about Cynthia Hardcastle's, which attempted to burst through her blouse. Aficionados of this sort of thing would later in the master's life be known to him as 'tit men', but at this moment in time, his interest was purely nutritional. Because the Bernsteins lived away from any Jewish community, and because they weren't particularly religious anyway, they dispensed with circumcising David. All went well, until the day when the Bernsteins and the Goldfarbs (another Jewish family who were passing through on their way to Liverpool, and who had been friends in earlier times in London), were enjoying lunch. Martha had secured a chicken, which was a great luxury. Mrs Goldfarb was entranced by David, and asked who had done his circumcision. Sol replied that it hadn't been done, and that David appeared none the worse for it. The Goldfarbs appeared none too pleased. Brenda then butted in her observation that David's winkle looked different to Harry's and surely there must be some reason for doing the operation. It seemed that at this moment in time, David's winkle was outnumbered around the dining table by three to one.

I sensed that I and my fellow-phallics were being discussed. How could I tell them what a horrible experience it had been? I wondered how Mrs Goldfarb would have felt if something of that nature had been performed on her when she was a baby (though what that would have involved I hadn't a clue).

In May 1948, the master's parents were very excited about some news that had been broadcast on the Midland Home Service. The Jews in Palestine had proclaimed a new state of Israel. This didn't mean much to Harry, whose knowledge of religion was mainly what he had learned in school (a Church of England school). He knew about Jesus, and that Jesus had said he was the king of the Jews, so it was a bit of a puzzle why he would eventually have a gruesome death according to the Bible, which the master and the other kids learned in school. On the brighter side however, was Christmas, with carol singing (the master liked carol singing, but no one in their right mind liked the master carol singing). The British had a mandate (whatever that was, but it was mentioned in the news – was it a male form of date he wondered), and this involved leaving Palestine. This was followed by fears of a new war, between the Jews and the Arabs. Harry wasn't too worried as long as it didn't mean bombs (he remembered the sounds of his earlier days in London).

However, a month later, grown-ups were talking about the Russians blocking Berlin, and the possibility of a war against Russia. This very real danger was illuminated to the master one playtime by Charlie Daniels, who clearly had more than a passing interest in politics. Later in life, he would become a journalist with a bright future, but unfortunately would die of leukaemia in his twenties. Another thing that struck the master was that whereas you previously had to have some money if you wanted to see a doctor now you could see a doctor and get medicine absolutely free. It was called the National Health Service. Very soon, doctors' surgeries were packed out with patients going to see their doctors with lots of ailments for which previously they would have waited a bit longer, because most things got better anyway. Not now! A bottle of medicine of assorted colours was the usual outcome. The worse it tasted, the more likely it was to do you good. Back at school he was due to go up into the next class, which was the one before the class that prepared you for the examination to go to the local grammar school. The summer term ended, and his parents were discussing what to do regarding the holiday. Sol booked the family into a hotel in Rhyl.

One fine day early in July, they all caught the train. As they left Rhyl railway station, it began to rain. It was a short walk to catch the green Crosville bus, which deposited them two miles down the road. They were booked into a small private hotel, run by a jolly lady called Mrs Whimshurst. The hotel called itself 'Shangri-La'. They had arrived in time to be shown to the shared bedroom, and there was a toilet and separate bathroom in the corridor, shared with the other guests. After unpacking, the master, Brenda and Mum went down to the dining room. It had five separate tables, each seating up to six people. This meant that we had to share with another family, the Joneses from Lampeter. Baby David was parked in his carrycot, and kept himself to himself, having been fully refuelled upstairs a short while ago. Mr Jones was a bus driver, and he and Mrs Jones had a precocious daughter, Jane, aged thirteen, like Brenda. The two hit it off straightaway, and left Harry to his own (lonely) resources. Supper was brown Windsor soup, followed by fish and chips. The Joneses generously offered to share their Vimto with us. The master's mum, Martha, chatted away with Mrs Jones who expressed a keen interest in what had happened during the war. Apparently lots of children from our cities had been evacuated to Lampeter to escape the attentions of the Luftwaffe. Brenda and Jane talked about boys. Harry discussed buses with Mr Jones. The master had always been interested in cars and buses, and asked Mr Jones what make of bus he drove.

'Well, I usually have a Bedford, but I prefer driving the Dennis. It's got a separate cab, so I don't have to listen to the tittle-tattle of the passengers, and I can smoke my pipe in peace.'

'Which is the fastest?' enquired the master.

'Well, I've had the Bedford up to forty-five miles an hour on an excursion, not sure what the Dennis will do.'

The master felt the need to wee, so excused himself and went to the toilet. Brenda and Jane, having finished their meal before him, were in the corridor. They giggled as he went past.

Later that evening, all the guests gathered in the lounge to read newspapers, and listen to the radio. It was the Pickles show, called *Have A Go*. People would be asked general knowledge questions and, if they got them right, Wilfred Pickles would instruct his assistant called Barney, to 'Give'im the money Barney', which became a nationally recognised catchphrase. Among the other guests were a schoolmaster and his wife, the Posthlethwaites. Mr Postlethwaite looked rather knowledgeable, and volunteered most of the answers, all of which were correct. The master deduced that he was obviously very clever, so decided to test his theory about human reproduction by running it past him.

'Mr Posthlethwaite, do you mind if I ask you a question?'

'Certainly, my boy,' he replied.

'Suppose a black man marries a white lady, and then they have a baby. I think it would be sort of half coloured I mean half way between black and white. Is that right?'

'Well, my boy, it probably would be, but it isn't always so—'

'Well, what I don't understand is how their jeans would cause this to happen,' interrupted the master.

'Harry, I teach English and Arithmetic. I never could understand much about genes, though I do believe there was once an Austrian monk who found it all out using sweet peas.'

This explanation completely floored my master. How could sweet wee-wee determine the gender of a baby? Possibly sweet wee-wee made girls, who were considered the sweeter sex (sugar and spice and all that). The master badly needed the toilet, having ignored my signals for the past thirty minutes, so engrossed was he with the Wilfred Pickles show, followed by what had seemed a great opportunity to clarify his jeanetic theory. Five minutes later, duly relieved he ran down stairs with the intention of quizzing Mr Posthlethwaite further. However, the holidaying schoolteacher sensing this made a quick excuse and, together with his wife, announced that they would be going out for an evening walk along the shore.

Brenda and Jane came across. Jane said, 'Why did you ask about babies? You obviously know nothing. I bet you've never heard of periods.'

'Yes I have. Sam Eastham who goes to the grammar school was telling me last week that after the French lesson on a Thursday they have a free period for private study in the school library.'

'Girls have periods every month, so there,' retorted Jane.

'Come on, Jane, we're wasting our time,' said Brenda urging Jane to look at something she had found in the *Picture Post*, which someone had left on the armchair. My master and I decided to go out for a walk, as he was getting bored and Brenda was no use. As we walked he put his hand into his pocket and gave me a sort of reassuring squeeze, probably to make me realise that we were a team, who together would eventually sort out the mystery of human reproduction, from education. This meant lectures from teachers. The master had heard that if one got into a grammar school, they also had practical classes. This might one day deliver the answer.

Next day, they awoke to sunshine and after breakfast headed off to the beach. The tide was out, and the sand was clean and powdery until one walked about a hundred yards towards the sea. Mrs Bernstein and Brenda had come prepared to bathe. They had their swimwear under their clothes, but for some reason the master hadn't been told to wear his. He realised as they were leaving the Shangri-La, but was told to pick his up and hurry. He did as he was told, but clearly, changing into it was going to be tricky. His mum showed him how to wrap a towel around his waist folding in the upper edge. Thus protected, he took off his trousers and underpants, then pulled on his trunks. So far, so good. The water was cold but they all paddled out until it came waist high. The master received his first swimming lesson from his mum, with instructions how to float on his stomach. He quickly mastered it, and I felt somewhat odd moving in a horizontal position, and by now blue with cold. Suddenly I realised that my services were urgently required. He asked his mum what to do, where was the nearest toilet.

'Don't worry, son, just do it into the sea. Pull your trunks down first – no-one will see you.'

This for my master and me was a totally new experience (except that I'd been doing it before he was born, but that was not into the sea). For him, it was a pleasurable experience accompanied by a temporary sensation of warmth. After about half an hour they all returned to their blankets spread out on the beach. Mum brought out the Thermos, and they all had a mug of tea. Just then the Jones family appeared, and Jane and Brenda started chatting away. Mum told the master to apply his towel as before and reverse the process and thus get dressed. He applied the towel as previously instructed and then proceeded to pull down his swim trunks. Unfortunately, being wet this proved difficult. Gradually, however, he was successful, or so he thought, but at the last moment, his towel came away. This was much to the amusement of the girls, but he was mortified. He hadn't realised how blue with cold I was. Neither did the girls expect to see a dark blue appendage attached to a shivering little boy. Eventually, however, dignity was restored, and the families walked up the slope to the road.

'Ice creams, anyone?' asked Mrs Jones.

'Yes please,' the children piped, (oblivious to the fact that I was freezing and in danger of gangrene), and then they caught a bus into Rhyl. The bus was quite warm and I soon recovered – surgery to remove the gangrenous appendage would not be required. Roy Rogers was on at the Rialto, and the master asked his dad whether they could see it.

'Certainly my boy,' he replied. 'Anyone else want to come?'

The girls and Mum weren't for it, so in the afternoon Sol and the master queued up to get in. The programme started with advertisements for upcoming films, then the 'B' movie. This starred some unknown called Ronald Reagan as a cowboy sorting out some bank robbers. Not very convincing. Next was a Mickey Mouse cartoon which had everyone laughing. The master was fascinated when he looked backwards and saw all the cigarette smoke twirling about in the beam of the projector. At last, the Roy Rogers film, called *Apache Rose* with a beautiful lady called Dale Evans and Trigger, Roy Rogers' horse. The film was action packed, with Roy Rogers protecting said Dale Evans from being robbed of her fortune of gold.

On the way back to Shangri-La, they passed an amusement arcade and went inside. The master was very excited when he succeeded in winning a monkey by throwing a small hoop. He asked his mum for a drink and was bought a small bottle of Vimto. This was followed by an iced lolly. The Shangri-La was still about a mile away, and he needed the loo. He and Mr Jones went into a public toilet. I hadn't seen one of these before and was impressed by the large porcelain pillars in which the name Armitage Shanks was incorporated. I couldn't understand why it bore this name. Who was Armitage Shanks? It was far too precise to be an autograph of some previous customer. The master tried but I was unable quite to angle my stream to totally wet it from where he was standing, and he couldn't very well stand back to raise the angle of trajectory required, at least not with Mr Jones present. On the wall was a white plaque informing people that venereal disease including gonorrhoea was serious and gave the address of the nearest venereal disease department.

'What's venereal disease?' asked the master later that evening at the dinner table.

This aroused the attention of Brenda and Jane because for once they too were ignorant. Mrs Bernstein said she didn't know, as her English, though passable, wasn't all that good. She asked Mr Jones, who coloured visibly and said it wasn't a subject for the table. That ended the subject, but the master, being a determined lad, cornered Mr Posthlethwaite, the fount of all knowledge.

'Mr Posthlethwaite, you were very good when you got all those questions right on the Wilfred Pickles show, you remember on the wireless?'

'Yes, my boy, I think I can, in all fairness claim to have a broad range of knowledge over a wide range of subjects, including areas not generally known by the majority of the population. In fact, I received an honours degree at Durham University in 1934.'

'Wow!' exclaimed the master, in admiration. 'I bet you're a genius.'

'Not quite, Harry,' the Fount replied.

'Mr Posthlethwaite, what is venereal disease and gon...gonor...rowia?' asked the master quite innocently. 'Did they teach you that at university? Have you ever been to a venereal disease clinic? Are they fun?'

'Now, Harry, that is something you are far too young to know about. You should concentrate on the three 'R's': reading, writing and arithmetic.'

'Why did you call it the three 'Rs' when writing begins with a 'W' and arithmetic with an 'A'?'

'Harry, it's a sort of joke, by the way I have to go now as I'm studying equine performance.'

The master didn't know what that meant, and concluded that Mr Posthlethwaite was very clever and unfortunately that made him feel like a dunce.

Next day it was raining, so sea bathing was not on the agenda. Instead they played cards, Snap, and Strip Jack Naked. The master and Jane fought it out to the finish at Snap, the master finally emerging victorious. Jane thought him rather interesting, much to the chagrin of Brenda, who kept trying to pull her away on any old pretext. The three of them then had an arm wrestling contest, which the master again won, by cleverly stamping on Brenda's foot, and disclaiming any guilt afterwards. He noticed Jane's hair, which was prettily arranged in ringlets, in contrast to Brenda's pigtails which he frequently tried pulling until she slapped him. Came the end of the vacation, and after a vociferous farewell from Mrs Whimshurst, and Brenda and Jane promising to write to each other, the Bernsteins caught a train back home.

The autumn term beckoned with the master due to go into Mr Dryden's class. Mr Dryden's hobby was bird watching, so at every opportunity he would try to engage the pupils' interest. Some boys had tracked down bird' nests, and brought eggs into school. The unspoken rule was that it was all right to take one egg out of a nest that had four in it. The master was fascinated by the sight of a thrush's egg: pale blue with a few spots. Freddy Smedhurst demonstrated his skill at sucking eggs. This involved pushing a pin in at both ends, inserting a straw and sucking, then blowing. With a bit of luck, what emerged was egg yolk and egg white, unless the egg had developed further in which case it was bad news for the unborn chick. But for most of the time, class work involved reading, writing, and maths. By now the school had acquired a canteen, so the classrooms no longer had to double up for eating.

A worrying, and puzzling thing occurred one evening at home. As the master was waiting to get into his bath, on an unusually cold night, his mother came into the bathroom, unannounced. She looked at him, and a worried frown crossed her face. She appeared to be looking at me, and I wondered what was wrong. Then she called his dad in, and together they peered at Bill and Ben, my two hangers on previously alluded to. Except that there weren't two hangers on, only one. Ben had done a runner. They asked the master if he had any pain, he said no. In due course, an appointment was arranged with the doctor. The master duly dropped his trousers in the rather cold consulting room.

'Aha,' exclaimed the doctor, as he spied the offending hanger on who had mysteriously re-appeared, and then in front of everyone's eyes could be seen legging it skywards.

'Perfectly normal, Mr and Mrs Bernstein,' announced the doctor.

'It's due to an overactive muscle called the cremaster, but as long as the testicle comes down in a warmer environment, all is well. If not, call in again, it might need a small operation to correct it.'

Ben, I could sense was none too pleased at the thought of his cold induced perambulations being restricted. The master was bemused by the whole process, I was totally ignored. His parents were very relieved, as they got into the old Ford 8 and drove home.

School was fun, and the master was making good progress with the academic demands. This included reading *Robinson*

Crusoe, and doing addition and subtraction. Fractions were next and he found them rather difficult. Brenda was no use, or couldn't be bothered to help. Dad was great, and soon the master was more confident.

Near the Bernstein house on the estate lived the Vickery family. This consisted of Mr and Mrs Vickery, and their children Jonathan and Alice. Jonathan and the master played together, mainly kicking a ball around in the road which fortunately was a cul-de-sac. Mr Vickery drove the local bus. Mrs Vickery was a full time housewife, as were most wives then. She was a great cook, and the master and her children particularly enjoyed her jam roly-poly. The master was rather taken with Alice who, it must be admitted, was very pretty. He used playing with Jonathan as a pretext for visiting the Vickerys in the hope of seeing her. She was pleasant to talk to, and didn't put him down the way Brenda did. He was invited to Alice's ninth birthday party, which was attended by a total of twelve children. The food consisted of the usual sandwiches, jam tarts, jelly and ice cream, followed by Mrs Vickery's *tour de force*, the birthday cake. Brenda hadn't been invited, as she was much older and, in her opinion, more mature. She was actually two years older.

After tea, they played games, starting with 'Blind man's buff', followed by 'Pass the parcel'. This was followed by 'Postman's knock', which the master had heard of, but never played before. When a girl went out of the room, the boys left inside were each given a number. The girl then entered, and would say, 'I've got a letter for number—' whatever.

The lucky, or unlucky receiver of the letter would receive a kiss from the postman. The game would then continue with the receiver of the letter being the next postman. In order to prevent favouritism, the numbers allocated were changed each time, so in theory it was always a lottery who kissed who. When it was the master's turn to be postman, he entered the room in considerable trepidation. He viewed six faces, all excited at the prospect of being chosen, though not as much as when Ronald had gone out. Ronald was clearly top gun, his charm and freckles having the girls near to swooning. The master came a poor fourth.

'I've got a letter for number twenty-three,' he stuttered.

Number twenty-three was a rather jolly plump girl called Eva, who wasted no time in dragging him out, and giving him a generous kiss on the cheek. He blushed alarmingly, and I felt a tremor, about minus one on the Richter scale. He then walked back into the room. The next set of house numbers were agreed between the boys, and Eva's entrance reluctantly awaited. Numbers were again allocated, and this time Martin, a weedy nerdy little chap who enjoyed collecting frog spawn, and cutting up dead frogs was the 'lucky' object of Eva's desire. Many years later he would become a forensic pathologist. Outside the door, he met his fate with eager Eva. As he did so, I received a message on the turgor waveband which was our way of intercontinental as well as local communication. Quite clearly Martin was shaken as well as stirred, Richter scale three. So the game progressed, but despite the master's hopes of kissing Alice, fate decreed that it was not to be – at least not yet. When the party was over, the various parents arrived to collect their little treasures. He thanked Mr and Mrs Vickery after prompting from his mother. He politely said goodbye to Alice, copy to me. What was I meant to do?

And so the days and weeks passed, the master doing well in class, and by now well able to hold his own in the playground.

Jonathan occasionally came to play, and they would kick a ball around, climb trees (there were a few very old struggling apple trees in the garden). When required to play indoors, they would get out the master's clockwork train set which would clatter from kitchen door to bedroom door via the stove, the engine LMS red with two crimson coaches. On one weekend, Brenda, feeling she wanted to suck up to Alice in time for her next birthday party and thence the chance of being invited, invited Alice to play. She had brought a rather unhappy doll which she trailed around more or less because that was what little girls were supposed to be interested in. Brenda, however, was rather aloof, because Alice was too young to talk to about boys, and hadn't even heard of Johnny Ray, the current pop idol. Baby David was thriving, though his bawling at night when his lactiferous demands were slow in being delivered led to Martha discerning in him a tendency to impatience and demand for instant gratification.

At last Christmas time arrived. Mr Dryden's class had been well informed in regard to the Christian take on Christmas. The master never could understand what all the fuss about virgin birth was about. Anyway, what did virgin mean? He asked Brenda, who actually blushed and directed him to Mum. Mum said she didn't know what this strange word meant; she hadn't been very familiar with the Christian attitude to Christmas before she sought refuge in England. But to give her her due, she looked it up in the family's German-English dictionary. Now she was faced with a real problem, as she had never instructed him on the subject of the facts of life, assuming he would pick it up at school, either from other children or from the teacher.

'Well, Harry, when two people get married, they share their lives together, even sleeping in the same bed, and then babies just come. But Mary and Joseph didn't get much opportunity, what with all the problems with King Herod taxing them, and making them go to Jerusalem to be recorded, so it was a miracle that Mary found herself to be pregnant. Christians believe the father of her child was God himself.'

'Does that mean one day God got into bed with Mary, and got her pregnant?'

Before Martha could answer, he went on, 'What if Joseph had caught them?'

Mum had no answer to this. In fact the whole Christian community find this a somewhat taxing question. The master's understanding of human procreation was at this time understandingly not understood. Particularly as jeans hadn't been invented in ancient times, at least not from what he could gather from any of the illustrations he studied in children's' illustrated Bibles. Another thing which he found puzzling was why Jesus, who seemed pretty central to everything Christian, proclaimed himself to be the king of the Jews – in fact he was a Jew. Yet Jewish people with whom he came into contact when the family visited other family members in Golders Green, told him that Jesus didn't exist, or that if he had existed he was not important. The Messiah hadn't yet arrived on earth, but would one day. So the master was a very confused kid. At least arithmetic and English were things he could understand. He enjoyed reading Enid Blyton books. However, setting these matters aside, the Bernsteins had Christmas dinner, Mum having at considerable expense obtained a chicken from Mr Castle, who lived down the road, and kept a few in his back yard.

The master and Brenda watched mesmerised as Mum plucked it, then removed the giblets. The neck was used to make soup. The liver and kidneys were gently fried and tasted delicious. Dad had bought a Christmas tree, and the family decorated it with tinsel, and lots of small candles which were placed in tiny cups that clipped onto the branches. When the candles were lit, it looked (and smelled) beautiful, though it was clearly a fire risk. Came Christmas Day, and the master was given a Meccano set. It came in a large red cardboard box, with the number two in the bottom right hand corner. He was delighted, and immediately set about building a windmill. There was lots of preliminary screwing together with nuts and bolts. Although the finished model was rather short of realistic, nevertheless he felt very proud that he had managed to build it. Brenda couldn't understand why it was so appealing to her brother. She had been given a needlework set, with which she could make a doll's outfit by stitching the various pre-cut items together. It would have suited a rather disfigured and very asymmetrical doll, but it occupied Brenda for many a long hour.

Meanwhile Mr Bernstein was busy at work, designing steelwork for buildings. David by now had grown into a rapid toddler, and was much admired by friends and family alike. This didn't altogether go down well with the master and Brenda.

Came September, and he went up into Mr Owen's class. Mr Owen was quite a strict teacher, fair-haired and fond of brown shoes. As an aid to education, he possessed a ruler (for minor infringements, the application of which to the hands was moderately painful), but when a major offence was detected, e.g. talking when not to, or chewing gum in the classroom, his weapon of mass destruction was brought into play. It resided in a cupboard, and when required involved a slowly played out drama.

'Hold out your hand,' came the command.

With that, Mr Owen advanced slowly and deliberately in the direction of said cupboard. The weapon, a flexible and well run-in cane, was dramatically produced, and flourished. By now the whole class was giving the sort of attention every teacher craved. First Mr Owen would have a practice run, the whistle of the cane creating a grim sense of foreboding in the victim-to-be. One, or occasionally two swipes of the cane were then administered, and the recipient returned to his desk with a complexion not out of place had one just returned from a Turkish bath. By these various means was education administered, times tables were by now firmly ingrained, fractions were added, subtracted, multiplied and divided. Special coaching was offered for those determined to pass the entrance exam for the local grammar school. One particularly bright chap, Tony Bateman, was regarded as a cert to pass, but would eventually fail. The reason was that his parents had told him to, as they wanted him to leave school as soon as possible and get a job. Times were hard for many, not everyone had an indoor toilet at home, and as for possessing a car, that was very unusual. This would instantly make the child of such a family regarded as posh. The headmaster was Mr Brotherton, a large well-built man who taught those intent upon staying at school until they could legally leave. This included those who failed the eleven-plus, and those not interested, as aforementioned. The master never found precisely what form the lessons took, but one day was told that the mathematics theories were applied in situations regarding the purchase of cigarettes, including the unit cost for packets of ten or twenty, and the amount of change when the price for twenty was two shillings and eight pence, and a ten shilling note was proffered.

In appropriate instances, the applied maths was applied for the purchase of a pint of beer (about seven pence) and what was the change from half a crown. Across the road from the school was the fish and chip shop, financial transactions from which were also facilitated by the applied maths inculcated close by.

Cometh the hour, and the master caught the bus to the local grammar school, accompanied by his father in order to sit the exam. His tools consisted of a pencil, a rubber, and a ruler. The exam itself was pretty straightforward, consisting of no-brainers like 'divide twelve by three', or 'if three potatoes cost sixpence, how much would twelve cost, and what would be the change from half a crown?' In the afternoon, there was an English paper in which pupils were asked to re-write a passage converting the singular to the plural. Also, to alter a sentence from the present to the past tense. There then followed a composition titled: 'What is your favourite four-legged animal, and why?' The master chose a lion, as the idea of being the king of beasts appealed. Later that evening his parents quizzed him about the exam. They were a bit worried because Brenda had previously failed hers, though she was to be given a second chance as she was over thirteen years. The master felt pretty unperturbed as he had found the questions pretty straightforward. However, the next day he began running a temperature and feeling poorly. His face seemed to be swelling up, and this caused his parents to be concerned.

He was seen by the doctor, who attended him at home, and arrived in a large black Jaguar. The master forgot about feeling ill and offered to bring the doctor's bag in for him. When he opened the door of the car, he was regaled by the wondrous odour of acres of red leather forming the luxurious amazing seats, and a large walnut instrument panel. This inspired him one day to be a doctor. However, for the present, he was diagnosed with mumps. Unfortunately no one asked me about the goings on down below where Bill and Ben were also involved, in a most painful fashion. I was worried, but my abilities were not affected. The following week, the doctor announced that Harry had mumps orchitis. However, within a week Bill and Ben had settled down to their normal life, which at that time did not amount to much.

Summer arrived, after a cold wet spring. The master liked riding his friend's bicycle, as he didn't possess one of his own. Most kids at that time, were promised one if they passed their exam. I enjoyed it when he rode his bicycle, and to prove it I grew in size quite dramatically when he rode over bumpy ground. He didn't seem to mind, but this was not the case after the same thing happened whilst he rode on the local bus. When it arrived at the terminus, he felt embarrassed to stand up, as I was straining at the leash, and he would have to walk down the row between the seats.

'Come on, Sonny,' said the conductress. 'There are people outside waiting to get on.'

The master felt his face going red, but nevertheless, got up. The conductress clearly saw his predicament, and winked to the driver who by this time had turned himself around to see why the delay had occurred.

'Wish I had one like that,' he chuckled.

'I wish my Bert did too,' replied the conductress.

I felt puzzled by these phenomena, what could be bringing it on? One day, the master was reading the *Picture Post*, and was looking at a photograph of Marilyn Monroe in a swimsuit. Just like in the bus, I found myself enlarging and being strangled by the buttons on his trousers. Life was getting quite uncomfortable, at least once or twice a day.

Then, one night, a most incredible thing happened. All was quiet; he was fast asleep and snoring gently. It was about two o'clock in the morning. Now I know you won't believe this, but penises have eyes, and they can see through clothing. Which is why, I noticed the master's eyes seemed to be making rapid movements. I suppose he was dreaming. To my amazement, I again started growing, just like in the bus – but not a bus or magazine in sight. Worse was to follow. He started moving rhythmically, still fast asleep. Suddenly he convulsed, I shrank rapidly, and he woke up. He was clearly puzzled, and embarrassingly noticed he had wet himself, and felt rather sticky. He remembered that as he was waking, he had experienced a strange and fantastic tingling sensation, which was very pleasurable. Try as he might, he did not know how this had come about. He tried remembering what he had been dreaming about before waking, but couldn't. He dared not tell his mother as he felt very embarrassed. He certainly wasn't going to mention it to Brenda – how could she understand? And this new experience was repeated several times a week. A real mystery!

The exam results – Harry Bernstein had passed! His parents were very proud and pleased. They told their friends and relations. Brenda ignored him completely – but he didn't mind. Now he expected his dad to buy him a bicycle – which in due course he did. It was a Hercules, shiny black, with a square reflector on the rear mudguard. He was delighted. Off he went, down the track which passed the rear of his house, across the field behind Franklin's farm, then on down the slope to the pond, where he joined some local kids, who admired his new bicycle. One of them proudly showed him his catapult, made from a small V-shaped branch, and thick elastic attached to the wood by tightly wound string. It was quite capable of killing a small bird at up to fifty yards its owner claimed (though it never had), but had proved itself on two occasions as capable of breaking windows, necessitating a rapid retreat. Back home, there were several visitors who had come to praise the master's achievement. I felt ignored – he had his bicycle, and because he let his friends ride it, he was very popular. I tried to draw his attention to my presence by the previously described extension strategy when riding his bicycle or riding in a bus. Whereas the latter still worked, in the case of the former, he prevented my expression by standing on the pedals, leaving me suspended in mid-air. On one occasion though, having flown over a bump on some rough ground, Bill was subjected to a hard landing, which left the master clutching him in his hand for a few minutes, in pain.

Talk at the table in the evenings turned to preparing for grammar school entrance. Parents were told Harry would require a grey shirt for winter, and a white one for summer. Then there was the grey flannel short trousers, grey socks, and of course, the satchel. In addition, the school tie was needed, as well as the blazer badge emblazoned with the school motto: *Vitae lampada tradunt* (They pass on the lamp of life). Then there were the PT shorts and vest, plus plimsolls, and a towel for the compulsory showers which would follow the games sessions. Mr and Mrs Bernstein, like many others, found these requirements very expensive. But before going to the grammar school, there was the last day at junior school. Mr Owen wished all those boys leaving the very best, and invited any of them who wished, to visit him at home in the coming months. This sounded very attractive to the Master, because Mr Owen had a television (a Bush with a nine inch screen). On several occasions he would pay a visit, always being rewarded with tea and cake baked by Mrs Owen, and the offer to watch some TV.

Then came the summer holidays. The Bernsteins booked in to a small private hotel in Church Stretton, which would have been an excellent idea if the weather had been good. But it wasn't. In fact it rained every day during the six they were there, but the sun shone as they left for home. Also in the small hotel were two other families, the Gardners and the Evanses. Mr Gardner was a newsagent from Smethwick. Mrs Gardner was a full-time house-wife, with a jolly sense of humour, especially for Black Country jokes involving the legendary Enoch and Ayli with Enoch purported to have said, 'Thee costna see so good as thee couldst, cost?'

The master enquired for the English translation of this sentence originating from a far distant land known as the Black Country, of which he had never heard at school. Mr Gardner duly explained. 'Well, Harry, Enoch and Ayli (pronounced Aynock and Ayli) were two fictitious characters from said country, where they spoke in a strange tongue. The translation of the aforementioned was: 'You cannot see as well as you could, can you?' The master was intrigued. His language experience had up to now encompassed German English (as spoken at home, and by relatives), English (as spoken in London), English (as spoken in Shropshire), and now this peculiar language originating from the Black Country.

'Why do they call it the Black Country?' he enquired.

Mr Gardner explained and gave a potted history of Lower Gornall and the surrounding district. Jennifer, their teenaged daughter, befriended Brenda, and gave her some classified information about sex. (This I should add, was sex as practised at the time, in Smethwick). Whether or not it applied in the wider world Jennifer was not in a position to say, and certainly not as to whether it was practised by her parents. She was afraid she had been conceived naturally by her parents and would have preferred it if she had been adopted, because then she would have been spared the horrifying thought of their copulation. Brenda asked her experienced friend about bras and how to choose them. The master overheard their conversation, but was quickly lost in the technicalities involved with terms such as cup size, and number of inches. Their conversation moved on to tampons and towels, at which he clicked – at least when the word towels was used, but why towels came in tiny packets purchased from Boots he couldn't fathom out. However, he was delighted to find an old copy of a magazine devoted to cycling, particularly the advertisements quoting the specifications of various models, including his own. His main ambition in life was to acquire a Sturmey-Archer three speed, so that he could travel up hills more easily, and move faster along flat roads. Another item on his wish list was a dynamo so that he could have front and rear lighting without need for a battery.

Next morning, together with Brenda's newly procured friend, Jennifer, they walked down the hill to Church Stretton. It was a picturesque village, with a restaurant called the 'Orange Tree', in the square. Here Sol and Martha had coffee; the master and Brenda were treated to an ice cream. There followed a walk to the Carding Mill valley, Church Stretton's famed beauty spot. By lunchtime they reached the café, outside which were some strange looking machines, which required a coin to be inserted and then by turning a handle, one could observe a sort of picture show. There were two such machines, one was titled 'Holiday in Brighton', the other 'What the butler saw (not suitable for children)'. Sol put a sixpence in the 'Holiday in Brighton' machine, and invited the master and Brenda to watch in turns. Sol then invested in the other offer, and chuckled. Martha realised and pulled him away, exclaiming, 'Sol, you should be ashamed at things like that.'

Reluctantly Sol came away, but quick as a flash, a young acne ridden youth who was standing close by darted in to watch the remainder of the show. The master asked him if he could also watch, and was given permission to watch the last few seconds. To his amazement, what he saw was an almost naked woman sprawled on a couch, fanning herself, just as the butler disappeared behind a curtain. Then down came the shutter, and the machine awaited its next customer. I was curious because whilst he was briefly watching, something to do with him, perhaps his brain, paid me a quick visit leaving me at forty-five degrees elevation. (Later in life, I would learn that the brain is capable of migrating south, and in some men, takes up permanent residence there.) Brenda and Jennifer came out of the nearby shop, having gazed longingly at nylon stockings, in time to witness the end of the slot machine drama. Their gaze wandered from the machine which, being mechanical was of little interest, to said acne ridden youth, who aroused far more. He was wearing rather tight trousers, and had somewhat pointed shoes. His hair seemed to continue down below his ears, (sideburns as they became known) and his jacket looked amazing, with what looked like velvet lapels.

'I think he's a teddy boy,' whispered Brenda, who had seen photographs of this current form of masculine display in the *Daily Mirror*.

Jennifer's jaw dropped, as she experienced for the first time: lust. Yes, real, tummy cramping, in yer face lust. She couldn't understand this feeling, nor why she should be sweating when the weather was anything but hot. Brenda quickly realised the object of their passion was making towards them.

'Come on, Jennifer,' she said tugging her cardigan sleeve.

'No, no, let's speak to him,' answered Jennifer.

'Hi, girls, what brings you here?' it asked.

'We're here on a nature walk,' exclaimed Jennifer.

'Great,' replied the sexual Colossus, 'let me show you both some of the wonders of nature.'

Sensing danger, the girls made their excuses, and returned to the other Bernsteins. Later, at lunch, the girls remained quiet, clearly in a state of suspended animation, as they recalled the events. Sol declared that the Carding Mill valley was very beautiful, and that he would tell his colleagues at work about it. Mr Gardner agreed, but he and Mrs Gardner noticed how quiet their daughter had become.

'What's up with our Jenny?' enquired Mrs Gardner. 'Anyone would think you'd seen a ghost.'

'Oh, it's nothing, only I think we saw an actual teddy boy this morning.'

'Well my dear, that's nothing to worry about, I'm sure they're quite harmless, but better keep away from them, just in case.'

During the afternoon, they played Ludo, Snakes & Ladders, and listened to *Life with the Lyons* on the radio. The master gave me an outing, nothing special, Armitage Shanks again. Oh, and as before an invitation to the Venereal Diseases clinic.

'Harry, what were you looking at in the slot machine?' asked Brenda.

'Oh, it was a film called "Holiday in Brighton",' replied Harry.

'No, not that one, the other one,' persisted Brenda. "I saw you and that teddy boy. You both seemed pretty interested. What did the butler see?'

'It was a lady without any clothes on, and I think it was the doctor behind the curtain,' explained my somewhat embarrassed master.

'So, what did you see? Did she look any different to you? You know what I mean, it's no good being shy.'

He was mortified.

'She was obviously very hot, it must have been a hot day, so she took off all her clothes, and tried fanning herself. But that didn't help, so she must have called the doctor, who was carrying a tray with a bottle of medicine on it.'

I think it was more a case of the master getting hot, I could sense it.

Came evening, and supper was served. There was Spam salad, sandwiches with margarine, strawberry jam, cheese and marmite. The master enjoyed a drink of Vimto, as did the girls. Sol enjoyed a bottle of Wrekin ale, as did Mr Gardner, whilst the wives had lemonade. Afterwards, they retired to the sitting room, and listened to *Ray's a Laugh*, featuring Ted Ray who was very funny. Afterwards, as it was only eight o'clock, the girls asked whether they could go for a walk into the town. The master asked if he could join them, but this was declined. Brenda and Jennifer headed off, and enjoyed a leisurely walk down the tree-lined road, crossed the main road at the bottom of the hill, walked over the railway bridge with the station below, and into the parade. They gazed into the shop windows, then came upon one selling paintings. Their eyes fell upon a large one in the centre of the window depicting naked fat women sprawled on the ground with little cherubic children all sporting tiny penises, and a man with a malevolent eye bearing a spear. They wondered how things that were clearly rude managed somehow to be acceptable in paintings, which otherwise were pretty dull, with ships and fields and mountains, barges and cattle. When they got back to the guest house they asked their parents about it. Sol said they had probably been looking at a print of a Rubens, and that he was a very famous painter, whose main interest was in painting people who were well fed. Mr Gardner muttered under his breath that he thought the painter was probably a pervert, a remark overheard by the master.

'What's a pervert?' he enquired.

There was an embarrassed silence, interrupted by the clack of knitting needles wielded by the ladies.

'Never you mind,' was Mr Gardner's reply. 'You'll learn about these things one day.'

Next day they all ventured into the town, and as they passed the art shop the master exclaimed, 'There's the pervert's painting,' which was overheard by a group of rather serious students from the Shrewsbury Art College who had been admiring it. One of them, hearing the remark, made his way over.

'Why do you think the painter was a pervert?' asked James Poulter, a rather serious young man of eighteen.

'Because that is what Mr Gardner said when I asked him,' replied the master. He went on, 'Church Stretton is a funny place. The shop contains pictures of naked ladies, the slot machine in the valley also has naked scenes and, anyway, what is a pervert? Is it some kind of club?'

'What is your name?' asked James.

'Harry Bernstein,' replied the master.

'What school do you go to?'

'Next September I'll be going to the grammar school,' replied the master.

'Well, when you go there, you will have lessons in art, and you'll learn to appreciate the work of many great painters. They aren't perverts, and there is nothing wrong with the human body. It is nothing to be ashamed of.'

Mr Gardner coughed and spluttered, clearly not impressed. Sol smiled, but said nothing. The wives looked away clearly embarrassed. Brenda and Jennifer were intently perusing the cherub's penises. Brenda pointed out that her brother's appeared different, whereupon Jennifer admitted she had never seen one before. Brenda felt this was very odd, and decided upon a plan. This involved for a change being nice to the master.

'Harry, how would you like some of my chocolate which I brought with me – I know you like chocolate, don't you?'

The master answered in the affirmative, but was then instructed that the offer was dependent upon doing something in return. Brenda and Jennifer had been sharing a room, this arrangement having been agreed by their parents when making the booking.

'Come to our room after cocoa,' said Brenda. 'Then you will have your chocolate.'

By now it was nine o'clock, and shortly before bedtime. The master changed into his pyjamas, then quietly tiptoed to the girls' room. He gave a gentle knock, and entered.

'Now, Harry,' said Brenda, 'I know you would like your chocolate, but there is something you have to do first.'

'What is that?' he asked.

'Well, you see, you know when we looked at the Rubens painting today, with the naked fat ladies, and the babies, well Jennifer said she had never seen a real willie. So I told her I could arrange for her to see one. You don't mind do you? And then I'll give you a piece of chocolate.'

'What do you mean, a piece of chocolate?' replied the master. 'I would need at least a whole bar.'

'Half a bar is all you'll get,' replied Brenda.

'OK,' came the reply, and before I knew what was happening I was produced.

Close inspection by Jennifer followed, then, 'Yuck, it's disgusting, and any way, that's not like the willies we saw in the Rubens.'

At that moment, the door opened, and Mrs Gardner appeared with a tray.

'I've come to collect your cocoa mugs—' she said, before trailing off in horror at the scene before her.

'What is going on? Harry, put it away, what on earth made you do such a thing? I shall tell your parents. And, oh, before you do, is that what they look like after… what's it called? I've forgotten the actual word. I've never seen one before. How interesting!'

There followed a full five seconds of total silence, and I cringed. This resulted in Mrs Gardner exclaiming, 'Oh look, it's hiding in its whatever. How sweet, poor little thing.'

At this point, I was returned to my normal environment, and Mrs Gardner left the room. Next thing, Sol and Martha appeared.

'Harry, what on earth is going on? You should be ashamed of yourself showing people your willie. Is that how we've brought you up? Brenda, how could you let Harry behave this way?'

'It had nothing to do with me,' she replied. 'We were just drinking our cocoa, when Harry knocked on the door to ask for some chocolate. Then he just did it. It was ever so rude,' she sniggered.

The master went bright red.

'No it wasn't like that, Brenda. You said I had to show you and Jennifer my willie if I wanted the chocolate.'

'No I never did, I would never do that.'

During all this, the master, by way of distraction was quietly consuming his chocolate, then sidled away to the sanctuary of his bed. The incident closed, it was not mentioned again.

First day at the local grammar school, September 1950. Crisp new uniform, leather satchel with pencil, rubber, and a ruler. The new boys were marshalled to the far corner of the playground, under a venerable oak tree to be addressed by the headmaster.

'Good morning, boys, and welcome to the grammar school. Grammar is spelled gee are ay emm emm ay are, not ee are. I expect you all to work hard, do your homework, and obey the school rules. No eating outside the school when you are wearing your uniform. Don't forget your school cap. If you see a master in the town remember to raise your cap. No bad language is allowed. You are all first formers, and your lessons will include English, history, maths, geography, music and French. You will also have physical training in the school gym, together with football in autumn and winter, then cricket in spring and summer. After games, you will all have to shower – no excuses. Every morning we have assembly. You must not be late for school, or you will face detention.'

Then the school bell rang, and they all trouped into their classrooms.

The master quickly settled down and enjoyed school. There were new friends. The boys were far friendlier than they had been in the previous school, where he had learned to look after himself the hard way. In maths he had difficulty with algebra. His mind was fixated on the notion that a letter which represented a number, was obviously part of a code, and the object of an algebra question was to suss out the code, as they did in spy stories.

'If I buy a apples and b pears, how many pieces of fruit have I bought?'

He thought he had to discover the secret code, like perhaps a being the first letter of the alphabet, it stood for one (apple), and b being the second, would stand for two. So the answer would be three pieces of fruit. To his dismay, the answer strangely was 'a+b'. How stupid! 'If an apple costs a pence, and I spend one shilling and sixpence, how many apples do I get?' Answer, eighteen divided by a. Big deal, fancy telling your mum you had just bought eighteen divided by a apples. She'd think you were nuts! He really had problems with algebra. Geography was fun, especially drawing the shape of a mountain from its contours. History started by telling the story of Kufu of the Nile. Music wasn't much fun, as they were given three pages to learn of composers' names, date of birth and death, and country of birth. Nothing like Bing Crosby, and Johnny Ray, whose wailing was frequently heard on the radio. He discovered that some of the composers were to be heard on the BBC Third programme. He learned that Beethoven was probably the greatest of all composers.

Then games! Football! Real goal posts, not discarded jackets as had been the case at junior school. One day the master was thrilled to learn he had been picked to represent his school against another school. The field was at Shifnal, and was overlooked by an embankment containing the main railway line. For the master, much as he enjoyed football, it could not match up to the fascination of watching an express train powered by a Castle class steam engine go past, and thus he missed a golden opportunity to score his school's winning goal. Needless to say, this was the first and last time he was selected. Afterwards, there was tea, with jam tarts, and mayonnaise sandwiches. Delicious!

At other times, they had PT (physical training) in the school gym. The gym was beautifully equipped with a sprung wooden floor, and wall bars all around. No one was allowed to enter the gym unless they were wearing plimsolls. He greatly enjoyed PT, as he was very nimble, and could climb up the wall bars with ease, but climbing ropes suspended from the ceiling was more difficult. Then came the showers. All the boys had to undress and walk slowly through the tepid water. It was thus that I realised I was one among many, and that there were some that looked like me, though not many. Though my master was on the small size, there was not much variation in the height of the boys as a whole. But this was to change, and with it, herald some intriguing other things! Then towels and kit back into satchels, and return to the form room for history. Later that day, there followed the grand debrief at home. The master's parents were very interested in the academic content of the lessons. Brenda's interest was confined to the showering.

'Were you totally naked?' she asked.

'What did the other boys' penises look like? Were they like the ones in the painting we saw, or like yours?'

'There were both sorts,' replied the master, 'but most were different to mine. One boy had some hair growing above his – I've never seen that before, and his voice was sometimes normal, and sometimes deep, like a man's.'

'What a disgusting place to grow hair,' replied Brenda. 'If that happened to me, I'd shave it off straight away. Yuck!'

The master caught the bus to school every day, and en-route, it would stop to pick up some girls bound for the girls' high school. One in particular caught his eye. She was blonde, with blue eyes and a very pretty face. Her beauty took his breath away; he hardly dared look at her. She never noticed him. But she became the topic of conversation amongst the other boys, some of whom boasted that they had been out with her. How on earth could they manage that, he wondered. But several boys claimed they had girlfriends, though the evidence to support their claims was extremely sparse.

Homework was at first a novelty, but also a chore. Most of the master's friends hadn't passed the exam for the grammar school, so were free to play, whereas he was stuck with analysing the structure of sentences word by word, subjects and predicates, definite and indefinite articles, and triangles of various shapes. Winter turned into spring, soccer into cricket, mud into new mown grass, and post-PT showers that revealed more and more peri-penile sproutings. Soon, there were exams, and beyond that, summer holidays. And, wonder of wonders, on one Friday afternoon, the last week of term, guess who happened to sit next to the master on the bus going home? He could hardly believe his luck. Calm as you might, she of the blonde hair! Yes, yes, yes! The fact that the seat next to his happened to be the only vacant one was lost on him. He hardly dared breathe, and concentrated on peering out of the window. Finally, and breathlessly he asked her name.

'Carol,' she replied.

'Mine's Harry,' he responded. 'Would you like to come out for a walk this evening, that is if you haven't got too much homework?'

'All right,' she said.

The master could hardly contain himself, and I shared his excitement. This, for some reason didn't go down well with him, as I felt a restraining hand over me. Carol got off the bus two stops before him, and he rushed home. He couldn't eat much supper, made a quick excuse that he was going to play cricket on the local recreation ground, and rushed outside. It was then he realised he hadn't arranged a time or place for their rendezvous. So he walked back to where she had got off the bus, and hoped she might turn up. One bus came, then a second, then a third. He was about to walk back home when he heard a voice.

'Hi, you little weed.'

It was Brotherton, a pubescent Lothario of the third form.

'What are you doing here, Bernstein?' he asked.

'Oh, nothing,' the master stammered, somewhat concerned that he might get pushed around.

'Well,' said Brotherton, 'I'm here to meet my girlfriend. I doubt a weed like you will ever have one.'

Sure enough, Sally Titley, whose body and name conveyed a certain concordance, strode up, and, totally disregarding the master, said, 'What picture are we going to see? Grand, or Clifton?'

'How much money have you got on you?' asked Brotherton, 'because I'm not getting my pocket money till tomorrow. We could get the ninepenny seats at the Grand.'

'OK,' replied Sally. 'I think it's *Scott of the Antarctic*. Oh, who's this?' looking at the master.

'Nobody,' said Brotherton, 'I just found him here. Anyway, Bernstein, what are you here for?'

Before the master could answer, the Venus of the Universe, the most beautiful creature ever created, sauntered up.

'Hello, Harry, I didn't know what time you meant, but anyway, here I am.'

So saying, we (including the master) meandered off in the direction of the recreation ground.

'Christ, I wonder what the hell she sees in him,' remarked Brotherton, as he placed his arm round Sally's waist.

'Come on, don't waste time, if we hurry we'll be in time for the little picture,' she said. So saying, they went off in the opposite direction.

It was a beautiful summer evening, there was in fact a cricket match in progress, and they stopped a while to watch.

'Well hit,' someone said as the ball hurtled past the boundary. The master realised his chance to impress Carol and ran to retrieve the ball from the long grass, before hurling it back to the wicket keeper.

'Do you like cricket?' he asked, breathlessly.

'Yes,' came the answer, 'though I don't know all the rules. My dad's got a book all about the game, called *Wisden's Almanack*. He's always deep into it. Anyway, Harry, tell me about yourself. How come you've got a posh accent?'

The master then explained about his family, and that he had until recently, lived in London, where most people spoke the way he did.

'My parents came here from South Wales,' said Carol, 'but I was born in Broseley. Then my dad got a job at Sankeys, so we moved. Gosh, what time is it? My mum said I had to be back by seven o'clock.'

'Well, you'd better go, because it's five minutes to. Thanks for coming out with me, I have enjoyed the walk. Bye.'

And with that, they walked their separate ways. It was only as he flew home on cloud nine, that the master realised, he hadn't arranged to see her again.

'Did you enjoy your cricket match?' asked his dad.

'Er, oh yes, it was great, Frank Russell hit a good boundary.'

Summer holidays came. The master and Carol met twice, but then one day she told him she couldn't see him again, because she was going out with Brotherton.

'Why?' asked the master.

'Well, he's more mature, and his clothes are so smart. He gave me a cigarette – made me feel much older. Sorry, Harry, that's life.'

And with that, the master descended from cloud nine to ground zero. Such pain! Deep, deep pain.

'Come on, eat your supper,' urged his mother, but at first to no avail. Five minutes later his appetite returned, and he enjoyed listening to Jimmy Edwards in *Take It From Here*.

That summer, in May 1951, there was a school trip to the festival of Britain, held on the South Bank of the Thames in London. There was great excitement at school, and a special train was organised to take pupils to Paddington. Half the fun was collecting engine numbers en-route. The exhibition itself was amazing, leaving the master with lasting memories of John Cobb's Railton special, which held the world land speed record for a car, having achieved over 400 mph. Also on show was the latest steam locomotive, number 70000, named 'Britannia'. Whilst standing in the cab, he was amazed to see real bricks surrounding the firebox. Also, there were some amazing sculptures, including one that showed people with large holes going right through them. 'Reclining figure' stuck in his memory and was regarded as revolutionary at the time, the sculptor being Henry Moore.

In August the Bernsteins were off to Cromer. Sol and Brenda sat in the front of the Ford 8, with Martha plus baby David, and the master in the back. The car had no boot to speak of, so they had a roof rack on which was perched a pair of suitcases covered with a canvas sheet, and held in place by string. Of course it flapped wildly as the car reached its cruising speed (45 mph). It began to rain, which obliged Sol to switch on the practically useless windscreen wipers. Some genius in Dagenham had decided that in order to enhance road safety in inclement weather, the wipers would slow down or stop whenever the accelerator pedal was depressed, but perform wiping miracles as soon as the foot was lifted off the pedal. Brenda was totally bored (as per usual), and refused even to reply to the master's attempts at conversation. They had a pit stop in Lichfield, which permitted a nappy change for David, his soiled terry towel nappy being placed in a brown paper bag, on the floor beneath the driver's seat, awaiting soaking in a bucket of disinfectant when their destination was reached. Fortunately the aroma was competed with, and ultimately defeated by Sol's determined huffing and puffing on his pipe.

'Thank goodness for St Bruno's,' he chuckled to himself, narrowly missing a cyclist, the presence of whom was obscured by tobacco smoke. The other occupants of the car were by now fairly comatose. Finally, they reached their destination, and checked in to their boarding house. It was set on the road overlooking the sea, offering fine views of the rain that remorselessly continued.

'I'm afraid the gas is off, so I can't cook dinner for you all,' came the grim news from the landlady. 'Of course you'll get a refund. The fitter promised to come this evening, so hopefully breakfast will be as usual.'

Sol was tempted to enquire what 'as usual' meant, but refrained.

'OK,' he decided, 'we'll go down to the town and get some fish and chips.'

Unfortunately, in the excitement of reaching rain-sodden Cromer, they had completely forgotten the brown paper package under the driver's seat. This discovery would not be made until next morning. They walked down the road into the town. By now, it was lit up, and the eye was caught by the illuminated pier, with its theatre at the far end.

'Can we go to a show?' asked Brenda excitedly, seeing a poster advertising it with topping the bill, Max Bygraves.

'All right, if you are a good girl, and stop arguing with Harry,' replied Sol. From that moment, and for the next hour, Brenda was very nice to the master, who couldn't understand what had brought about this transition. Unfortunately, at that age, he was still naïve about the wiles of women, and was flabbergasted when she agreed to share her bar of chocolate. They queued at the fish shop, and emerged, each with their bag wrapped in newspaper, the contents liberally sprinkled with salt and vinegar. Shortly after, nature called, and Harry popped in to the local public toilet. Once more he spied the venereal disease notice, but was more taken by the artistry of the urinals, as was I. They were tall, elegantly sculpted, with the manufacturer 'Adamant' proudly displayed. The master made a valiant effort for my stream to reach the said inscription, but unfortunately the trajectory was somewhat misguided, there being no gyroscopic stabilising system, as a result of which the spray landed in the adjoining urinal. This didn't please its patron overmuch, who cuffed the master's ear with his free hand. As he emerged from the gents', with his sore ear, he noticed it had stopped raining, and the sun was making a belated appearance. Blue sky appeared over the sea, and in the distance could be seen a trawler, probably en-route for Grimsby. Down below the promenade, some brave stalwarts were walking along the beach, and some children were building sandcastles.

'Why don't you go and join them?' asked the scornful Brenda, addressing the master. By now the truce period had expired, as had his chocolate, and provided her parents didn't overhear, there was still a likelihood of Dad buying tickets for the show.

The master ignored the question, having spied a rather pretty girl, all alone, and clearly bothered by something which had got into her eye. He remembered that the best way to cope with this predicament was to stop rubbing the eye, and to pull down the eyelid, thus depositing the offending grit or whatever, on a handkerchief. He had learned this from reading an article on 'medical matters' in the local newspaper. Thus armed with a wealth of knowledge, Sir Galahad strode forth to assuage the plight of the stricken Lady Guinevere.

'I say, can I help?' he innocently asked.

'No, go away,' came the unexpected reply. At that very moment, said Lady Guinevere opened the offending eye, gave a smile and addressed a youth who happened to be passing.

'Hi, Dennis,' she said. 'Glad you came along. Please get rid of this creep who is bothering me.'

Dennis turned round to face the master, and cuffed his (other) ear.

'Why are your ears so red?' enquired his mother later that evening, as they were gathered around the radio listening to *Bedtime with Braden*.

'He realised he was no good with girls, and got his just desserts,' volunteered the ever helpful Brenda who had observed the (second) cuffing.

She then described, with several embellishments, what she had witnessed.

'You're far too young to be bothering with the opposite sex, Harry, isn't he Sol?' remarked Martha.

'Isn't he what?' asked Sol, who had been studying the *Racing Times*, with particular interest in the three thirty at Newmarket, scheduled for the next day.

'Well, he shouldn't be trying to chat to them, he's far too young. When did you first try to chat them up?'

Sol had never been asked this question by his wife, and realised the question might turn out tricky, as he had been a bit of a lad himself.

'In my day, we didn't have much time for girls, we were more into climbing trees, playing football, scrumping apples and riding bicycles like lunatics.'

He omitted to mention his first introduction to the female form by the precocious daughter of their friends, the Hertenbergs. It had happened in Krakow during the spring of 1913 when the Hertenberg family was having tea at the Bernsteins.

'Solomon's started collecting stamps,' his dad volunteered after the tea things had been cleared away.

'Oh yes,' Sol's mother added, 'he's specialising in German and Polish stamps.'

'That is very interesting. May I see your stamp collection?' asked Ludmilla, the Hertenbergs' daughter.

She was sixteen years old, with dark brown hair matching her eyes. Nature had been generous to her in such a way that, to put it politely, her centre of gravity was markedly for'ards of the usual level. Sol was aged thirteen at the time, and becoming acutely aware of changes in his physiology, such that at certain times his centre of gravity likewise was wont to migrate horizontally at the most inconvenient of occasions. Such was the case as they went upstairs. He awkwardly reached for the album situated on his bookshelf. To his surprise Ludmilla seemed disinterested as he explained the various special editions of German stamps, and the overprinting on some of them.

'Do you have a girlfriend?' she asked.

Sol blushed. He had never had the courage to ask a girl out, as it was pretty unique among his peers. Sure enough, Leopold Schwanz had, but his girlfriend was a timid thing with buck teeth, unkempt hair, and clearly overweight. Sol wondered what had attracted Leo – perhaps it was her huge breasts – and they were huge. Poor girl, later in life she would need to undergo breast-reduction surgery, but at the time, they were literally her biggest asset.

'No, I haven't time for things like that. Look, isn't this mint stamp a beauty?'

As he turned to show Ludmilla, he suddenly realised she had unbuttoned her dress.

'Would you like to see my breasts?' she asked.

Sol went from red to purple, and almost fell forward as a consequence of the aforesaid.

'I don't mind if I do,' he managed to say, as though this was an everyday occurrence, much like putting on his shoes.

Ludmilla seized his hand and placed it over her left breast. Sol affected an intense interest in the ceiling, as his hand circumnavigated new territory, culminating in the nipple region. By now Ludmilla was starry eyed, and breathing heavily. Sol became worried, rapidly withdrawing his hand and asking if she wanted a glass of water.

'No thanks, I'm perfectly all right. What's the matter with you, don't you like my breasts?'

'Oh yes, but I've only seen one.'

'Well, you'll have to wait for another time before I let you see the other.'

An awkward silence followed, during which Ludmilla fastened her dress, then went downstairs as if nothing had happened. Suffice it to say that by the end of that particular week Sol was absolutely petrified of going blind as a consequence of certain ministrations he felt compelled to carry out following the Ludmilla incident.

'Sol, what's the matter?' asked his alarmed wife, as he had seemed lost, eyes fixed on the ceiling, having time travelled fifty years to said incident.

'Oh no, I'm fine,' he replied, returning to the present.

'Well,' insisted his wife. 'When did you have your first girlfriend?'

'I can't remember,' lied Sol, conscious of the fact that further details of his subsequent explorations with Ludmilla were not exactly appropriate for present company. They had resulted in his counterpart to me being exposed, in a state of repose, but which had rapidly rallied as a consequence of the laying on of hands (Ludmilla's), culminating in an embarrassing genetic expulsion. Sol wiped his brow, before rapidly returning to the *Racing Times*.

The master reassured his parents that he wasn't really interested in girls, and that aeroplanes, and cars were his main hobby. In particular, he had fallen in love with a black Jaguar Mark V11, and fantasised that one day he would drive it with the beautiful but unattainable Carol by his side. Next day, after breakfast, (which thanks to the skills of the gas fitter) was really quite good, they were going to go for a drive to Hunstanton. But on opening the car doors, they were regaled by the aroma, not of a certain leather upholstered Jaguar, but by the forgotten nappy, secreted beneath the driver's seat of a Ford 8. Mrs Bernstein had to take it back to the guest house, and dunk it in a bucket of disinfectant, then rejoined the party in the Ford. David, now aged two, was a bit of a live wire, and very demanding of anything and everything. He was at his happiest when running about nappiless, but this, as might be expected, often had unfortunate consequences. Now, on the morning in question he was happily bashing his little plastic spade against the back of the driver's seat. This didn't please Sol too much.

Eventually they reached Hunstanton, and went for a walk along the promenade. Then the sun appeared, and they made their way to the beach. Brenda, David and my master paddled around, then begged for an ice cream, which was duly provided. On the way back to Cromer, there was a grating sound, and the car ground to a halt. 'We've got a puncture,' announced Sol.

The master watched with interest as Sol fixed it, replacing the punctured tyre and wheel with the spare which was located within its own housing behind the boot lid. Then back to Cromer, in time to catch the end of the pier show, Mrs Bernstein selflessly staying behind to look after David. The show opened with some pretty dancers, which obviously had an effect on the master who sent me a coded message which read 'prepare for action', but unfortunately on this and every occasion for the next eight years it would lead to nothing. It really was a kind of phoney war.

Came September, and back to grammar school. Grading was now in force, and the master found himself in form 2L. Those less academic were in form 2, without suffix. 'L' stood for Latin. In form 2 they would have woodwork, but the headmaster didn't feel that a suffix denoting this was anything of which to be proud, so plain '2' it was to be.

'Latin is a dead language, so what's the point of learning it?' was a question the master heard frequently, and to which there didn't seem to be any answer.

Someone mentioned that if one wished to become a doctor, one would need Latin. The master puzzled over this. Perhaps learning a dead language would be an advantage as one would come into contact with dead people, so it was possibly a form of introduction to the concept of death. Nevertheless, and without any intention to become a doctor, the recitation and rote learning of nominative, vocative, accusative, genitive, dative, and ablative, (the declensions as applied to nouns), was a sort of pleasant mantra.

'Mensa, mensa, mensam, mensae, mensa, mensa.' Mensa means table.

Meanwhile, the form 2 boys were learning about different forms of joining wood together, and the master for the first time in his life was fascinated, when talking to the lesser mortals, of mortise and tenon jointing. He wondered whether he could also do woodwork, but for some reason he was given to understand that it was impossible to countenance such a menial discipline when one's mind was concentrating on far more demanding intellectual tasks such as declensions. So when the form 2, and later forms 3, 4 and 5 were producing coat hangers, stools, coffee tables and even storage chests, the Latin boys were learning about Caesar's Gallic wars, pluperfects, subjunctives, and the accusative and infinitive form of sentence construction as applied to what some dude in times past had said.

Ah, the fascination of education!

Unfortunately, discipline was not always of the best, and some boys thought it great fun to throw brand new text books around. Others discouraged any form of collaboration with the enemy, i.e. the teachers, as this would make one a 'creep', or 'teacher's pet'. This was of course preliminary training for eventually joining a trade union, when the equivalent activity would make one regarded as a 'scab'. Whilst the master was hard at work, and learning other subjects, I felt rather left out, except in the showers after games or physical training. It then became clear that things were happening in my neck of the woods, though not to me. Bill and Ben's colleagues were obviously growing on some boys, as was my equivalent, and additionally, some were sprouting pubic hair. The showers were always set at lukewarm, or lower, the effect of which was to turn me into a 'hoodie'. Then back to classes, for trigonometry, the tanning of the poor boy, the cost of the boarding house, and the sign of the public house, referring to tangent, cosine and sine of an angle. Wonderful stuff! Pythagoras was a clever chap, all those clever Greeks calculating things, whilst their form 2L chaps were fighting their wars. Helen of Troy, whose face could launch a thousand ships (probably well-constructed with the aid of mortise and tenon joints – the ships that is), I thought she must have been a cracker. In fact, it wasn't only ships that she could have launched – I felt somewhat buoyant too.

The master was doing well in his class work but not excelling at games. The fact was that many of the boys were by now bigger and stronger, with hair appearing here and there, plus deepening voices. The master surmised that they possessed more 'masculinity mixture', a hypothetical masculinising liquid he imagined was of a brown colour. (At this time in his evolution, he hadn't heard of testosterone, but he wasn't too far off the mark, though he was probably wrong about the colour.)

Geography seemed pretty meaningless, except when applied to Great Britain, though it was galling to learn that our highest mountains were mere pimples when compared to the Alps, the Rockies, and the Himalayas. When it came to history, the same applied in regard to the politics (bore, bore, snore, snore), but hacked off limbs and decapitations were sufficient to awaken one from the afternoon's slumber, whilst fantasising about Carol. Speaking of which, or more correctly, who, she had appeared again on the bus that morning, and given the master a half-smile of recognition. This resulted in a most embarrassing blush on his part, and a jolt to me. Bill and Ben had rotated twenty degrees. The jolt resulted in me growing, and coming up against the resistance on the short trousers still worn by the master. This didn't matter too much, as no one could see, and he hoped I would return to normal repose before we reached his getting off stop. But, to no avail! I was now reaching forward to greet the morn, as he stumbled down the aisle. His saving grace was his satchel which he clutched in front of his bulging trousers.

Television came into the master's life. *What's My Line?* was a very popular panel game, chaired by the irascible Gilbert Harding. Many an evening was spent watching television at the expense of homework, and the master's ranking in class dived from being in the top five to the bottom ten. On the radio, *The Goon Show* was also very popular, and many of the master's friends, and the master himself would imitate the ridiculous characters portrayed. At home Brenda's appearance was changing. Much to her chagrin, she began putting on weight, but on the plus side, her breasts were becoming quite prominent, which she noticed, with some satisfaction, resulted in boys' sniggers and the occasional wolf whistle. She seemed to spend more time chatting to her mum, probably for reassurance. Martha was busy with David, now three years old, who was into everything, and being very awkward at times. Sol was busy at work, often bringing it home and spending till all hours designing. The master was disregarded most of the time, and felt compelled to watch TV.

At school, 'Prodder' Jenkins showed him a well-thumbed magazine called *Health and Efficiency*, which portrayed nudes. The master was very curious as regarding female anatomy, as well as the facts of life. Sex education as would be perceived in the 1960s was well nigh non-existent in the 1950s. Oh yes, lip service was paid to it, the boys sitting in hushed anticipation, being 'informed' that it was the supreme love of a man for his wife that would result in the baby growing within the stomach of the wife. The miracle of Christ's virgin birth wasn't mentioned, as the subject of virginity was not touched on, and the only reference to a hymen was to a genus of bees, the origin of the term being that of a membranous wing. God did indeed move in mysterious ways his wonders to perform. Same sex acts between men, totally unknown and totally abhorrent to the master, were at the time, considered criminal. But the times they were a changin'. As was the master.

Strange urges began to insinuate themselves into his mind. He allowed himself a chuckle at the thought of juxtaposing his body with that of a girl. It seemed 'rude' because 'naughty' parts of the body were involved. One day, he happened to witness a motley collection of dogs, all forming a somewhat disorderly queue with the intention of taking a vigorous ride on one other dog. It was obvious that certain anatomical rearrangements were taking place, though precisely what he didn't know. His previously taught facts of life were totally inappropriate. Why did it need a husband and a wife to have a baby? Animals who took rides like that which he had just witnessed, and which he was subsequently informed, would result in the lady dog having puppies, did not require holy matrimony. Although his friend, Martin, whose cat was forever having kittens, told him he could always tell when she was going to have more kittens because she had 'been married again'.

'How can you tell?' asked the master.

'Well, whenever she gets married, she loses a lot of fur on the back of her neck,' came the reply.

Clearly, Martin's mother had devised a clever way out of the embarrassing predicament she would otherwise have found herself in. As an aside, it may here be mentioned, that whenever the master saw Martin's mother, who had a mysterious habit of repeatedly smoothing her skirt over her shapely bottom, I would go into orange alert. So it was no particular surprise that on this night the master suddenly woke up, having experienced something totally electrical, and intense, and massively pleasurable. Problem was, he didn't know what it was, or how it had been brought about. He tried remembering what if anything he had been dreaming about but couldn't. He wondered whether, if he went back to sleep, it would happen again, but it didn't. Then, one week later, it did. Again he tried to figure it out, but couldn't.

Meanwhile at school his work was improving, largely as a consequence of a firm talking to by his dad, who strictly limited his hours of watching television. His interest in the arts was temporarily stimulated when it was announced that a visiting theatre company were to perform *Macbeth* in the school hall for one day only. This was great as lessons were temporarily suspended. What interested the master particularly was not so much the play (which seemed pretty gloomy, with witches and cauldrons and unimaginable things going into them) but rather the fact that the troupe arrived in vintage Rolls-Royce vans. They were probably ex-hearses, garishly redecorated with sign writing. On another occasion, the school was treated to a performance by an extremely famous string quartet, called the Amadeus. Little did they realise that this was probably the leading string quartet in the world. They were also given to understand that one of the performers had a Stradivarius violin, hundreds of years old, and extremely valuable. Now the master had recently signed up for violin lessons, and had been entrusted with an instrument which came in a black case, all provided by the County Education Authority. He assiduously learned the notes, G, D, A and E which were the notes sounded for each of the strings when bowed without any fingering. These didn't sound too bad, but whenever the master attempted to go up one, two, or three notes by fingering, the sound that emanated sounded like the catgut being removed from a still conscious cat. He reasoned that his problem would doubtless be solved if he had a Stradivarius, but unfortunately, none was forthcoming. He and his friend Robert would regularly meet on Saturday mornings to practise 'Drink to me only with thine eyes' with their violins. There is no doubt that their efforts would have brought tears to the eyes of any audience, of which fortunately, there was none. After a few months of intense practice they gave up. The violins were returned, doubtless to be re-distributed to some other hopefuls.

Art classes were interesting, the master, a Mr Jamieson-Crowther, MA (Oxon) being determined to instil some sort of appreciation into about seventeen adolescents more interested in Ruben's nudes than van Gogh's corn fields. But when he taught about Picasso's cubism, the master found himself tremendously interested, and actually produced a landscape drawing in pencil in cubism. This was regarded by Jamieson-Crowther as remarkable, and from then on, my master was nicknamed Pablo.

It was while chatting about things generally, that Robert one day asked him if he had ever had a wet dream.

'What's that?' asked the master.

'Well, it's when you suddenly wake up, and feel wet.'

The master pondered this, and remembered his night-time experiences, but they weren't always wet.

'No,' he replied, 'but I have woken up with a fantastic tingly feeling.'

'Yes, that's a wet dream,' said Robert. 'They start dry, then eventually become wet.'

And so it turned out for the master. Trouble was, when they turned wet, his pyjamas became stained and stiff, as did the sheets. The master turned his brain to this problem, and came up with an ingenious idea.

'Harry, why did I find a paper bag in your bed this morning?' asked his mother.

The master had taken the precaution of covering me with a paper bag each night, though this proved unnecessary, as nothing more happened for several weeks. Eventually, concluding that it was all a wasted effort, he gave up the paper bag idea. Of course, as you may have guessed, by Sod's law, the next night, I duly obliged with a genetic deluge. The master was also developing other things. I noticed the sprouting of a forest close by, and my master's voice took on a strange croak, oscillating between treble, alto and bass, all in one sentence. Many other boys who previously were in the school choir, found themselves ostracised for several months before their voices adjusted themselves. This didn't apply to the master, whose singing voice was never tolerable, especially as he was tone deaf.

A self-styled learned colleague, the aforesaid 'Prodder' Jenkins, one day informed him of the secret of procuring a wet dream. Interestingly, the dream part was superfluous. All it required was to regard me like the stem of a violin, going from G to top A in *allegro con molto vivace*. Eventually, this resulted in *cantabile*. Oh what ecstasy, oft to be repeated, until one day the master was told by the religious instruction teacher, Mr Pricker, that this act could lead to blindness. All the boys were shocked, and for a week, total pseudo-celibacy ensued. All except 'Wanker Wal', who disputed this threat, and assiduously continued this nefarious practice. The other boys watched with great interest, quizzing him daily as to his visual acuity. Wanker Wal seemed unperturbed, until one day he was noticed to be wearing spectacles. The whole class, who had initially resumed the 'violin playing' now again discontinued, greatly anxious. Then, one Thursday afternoon, during religious instruction, Wal asked Mr Pricker why he wore glasses.

'Because I need them for distant vision, but I can read without them.'

'Aren't you afraid of going blind, because of what you told us?' persisted Wal.

Mr Pricker turned scarlet, and quickly exited the classroom, making an excuse that he had just remembered he had an appointment with the headmaster. Gradually everyone resumed their 'violin practice' and I discovered that in so doing, I grew amazingly in length.

About six months before the master's thirteenth birthday, his dad informed him that he was going to have a bar mitzvah.

'What's a bar mitzvah?' I heard him ask.

'It's when you become a man in the eye of the Jewish faith.'

The master, i.e. Harry, alias Pablo, had forgotten that he was Jewish, though at some time in the past he had been told this. So a somewhat bemused master began attending Hebrew lessons in a large city, some thirty miles distant. He was introduced to some strange apparel, and its religious significance explained, but more importantly, he was coached on some recitation which, on the day appointed, he would have to perform in a synagogue. He was also told that the act of circumcision was essential for a Jewish baby, this being a covenant between God and man.

'What's a covenant?' the master asked.

He was told it was an agreement between Abraham, Moses, David, and God, and would serve as a mark of distinction for the Jews. All this seemed quite daunting, but the master rather fancied himself as a performer, having starred in the leading role at school in *Emil and the Detectives*, so his bar mitzvah recitation would be a piece of cake. When his dad told him there would be a big party afterwards, with lots of the family, and to expect many presents, the master prosecuted his Hebrew studies with great keenness. Came the day and everything went off smoothly, his presents including two cameras, a Brownie 127, and a Bilora box camera. Sol and Martha were very proud. The master was surprised that the men and women had to sit on different floors in the synagogue. Brenda told him he looked a 'right prat' in his garb, but he didn't mind, as the end justified the means. She asked if she could have one of his cameras, but he told her to '****off'. She feigned shock and horror, but it was altogether the master's day, and he played it to the full. He charmed all the relatives. Altogether, it was a good day's work, and he duly rewarded himself with a spectacular performance on the violin stem.

From now on, school work became more serious, with the prospect of the General Certificate of Education exams. Much to the surprise of all the boys, it was told that for some subjects their papers would be set by the 'Northern Universities Joint Matriculation Board', whilst for others, it was to be the 'Oxford and Cambridge Education Board'. The logic behind this was unclear until the teachers revealed that some boards marked more leniently in certain subjects, and by playing the field, better pass rates could be achieved. This totally non-plussed the master, whose head was still filled with ideology, that all exam boards were equal no matter which one was entered for. The way of the world was beginning to enter his mind, and prepare him in a way that no teaching would ever achieve, for the inner workings and machinations of society. Now his voice had broken, he sported a generous crop of pubic hair, plus a tiny sprouting of moustache. His fantasy world was largely populated by Jaguar cars, Carol, and the violin. As part of the educational process, the school organised a trip to another school twelve miles away to see a French play by Moliere: *The Miser*. However, although the master was 'good' at French as taught, he hardly understood a word, it was all so fast.

In 1954 the year started with the shocking news of a second crash involving the revolutionary Comet jet airliner. Yet another Comet crash soon followed, and they were all grounded, albeit temporarily. This was a serious blow to the British commercial airline manufacturing industry, and the master felt very sad about it. School work began to dominate. However, all was not lost, as the master became interested in building model planes, using balsa wood. They would be propelled by wound up elastic. The amount of homework was increasing, but so were the master's urges, and I found myself in great demand. I couldn't help wondering where all this would lead, and as far as the master was concerned, the fundamental mechanics and physiology of procreation were still hazy. As was the concept of heat in physics, water equivalents, calories, specific heat and so on. Magnetism was amazing, but puzzling. Sadly, the master was told he had to choose between history plus geography, or chemistry plus physics. For some instinctive reason he chose the latter, as the thought of becoming a doctor had occurred to him. In order to do medicine, he would need science subjects, plus Latin in case he chose to go to Oxford or Cambridge universities. He couldn't fathom out why doctors trained at Oxbridge needed to be knowledgeable in Latin. It wasn't as though the local population in proximity to these hallowed colleges all spoke Latin. He did wonder whether it all had to do with bones, because one of his school friends told him that he had had broken his *radius* and *ulna*. When the master asked him what he meant, he was told it was a broken arm. Further enquiry of his Latin master, Mr Lloyd, revealed that these were the Latin words for the bones found in the forearm. Anyway, the master assiduously pursued his studies, with the Mark VII Jaguar (and Carol), his ultimate target, (plus a career in medicine of course).

Another year went by, and the master was delighted to notice that he was now as tall as most of his colleagues. As he grew upwards, I grew downwards, except that sometimes, I also grew upwards when applying the violin stem technique, as previously demonstrated by 'Wanker' Wal, who it must be stated, did not yet possess a white stick. Brenda had acquired a boyfriend named Steven, a somewhat acne ridden specimen with a passionate interest in biology. One day he brought a dead frog to our house, and with the aid of a pair of scissors, dissected it, much to the disgust of Brenda. The master noted with interest the heart and lungs and subsequently learned that it only had rudimentary ribs, and breathed in and out by buccal pumping. He wondered at the phenomenon of metamorphosis, from tadpole to frog, and from larva to pupa to butterfly. He fantasised as to whether this might apply to humans, the fertilised egg going through various stages, perhaps resembling a tadpole at some stage, before gradually assuming the shape and structure of a baby. Whilst he was developing his inquisitiveness into the development of the human foetus, Steven was developing his interest in the structure and function of Brenda's breasts, evidence of which was revealed when the master happened to enter her bedroom where she and Steven were officially listening to Bill Haley's record of 'Rock around the clock'.

'Get out,' she hissed.

The master seized upon the opportunity for blackmail this presented, and was duly kept sweet by weekly bars of chocolate.

It was now 1956 and Brenda had succeeded in getting herself a job at a local hairdresser, where she worked hard in order to obtain the wherewithal to maintain her (self-perceived) standard of attractiveness. Meanwhile, for the master, school work was becoming more and more frenetic, with the GCE exams approaching. The master felt fairly confident, and was entered for seven subjects, including French. However, the exam included an oral test, in which he was asked to wait in a side room, and read through a short passage of French, after which, he would be asked a few questions about it. He was duly ushered into the room by an examiner, but before he could read the appointed passage, noticed a copy of *Health and Efficiency* left on his seat. No contest! For the next ten minutes he studied it from cover to cover, as did I, until the door opened and he was asked to enter the examination room. He said that he wondered if he could have a few minutes more, as he had a stomach ache and, luckily, by this means was given a period of grace. Unsurprisingly there were no questions relating to the contents of *Health and Efficiency*, instead questions relating to the experiences of Monsieur Duval upon arrival at the railway station.

Summer holidays, and the family was off to the Black Forest, in the tatty Hillman Minx, Sol's pride and joy, having replaced the totally wrecked Ford three months earlier. They had been invited by the Silbermans, who had befriended Sol Bernstein through contacts at work. The Silbermans were comfortably off, and had a country house in the Black Forest. The holiday necessities were duly packed, including jackets and ties, as was the wont in those days. This of course meant the boot was insufficient, so as before with the Ford, a roof rack was fitted, and the suitcases covered by a large plastic sheet, secured with string. As might be imagined, this resulted in loud flapping noises as the plastic fought the wind, at speeds of up to sixty mph (which was all the Minx could manage). This was much to the chagrin of the master, as many a Beetle zipped past at its maximum of sixty-five mph, and when it came to climbing hills, there was no contest, the Beetle was far superior. In addition,

98

frequent stops had to be made to replenish the water in the radiator, never the case in Beetles which were air cooled.

Any pride in English cars was soon ended upon arrival in the Black Forest, where they were introduced to the Kaufmans, who had motored down from Berlin in their DKW Sonderclasse. This car was astonishingly quick, and beautifully styled. But as far as the master was concerned, the only consolation was the equally crafted and beautiful Birgitte, their sixteen-year-old daughter. She quickly intimated to Brenda that she was heavily into boys, and that she found Harry (Pablo) to be quite cute. This naturally infuriated Brenda who accused the master of stealing her chocolate and five deutschmarks from her jacket, then retired saying she had a severe headache. The master wasn't unduly bothered as he knew about Brenda's shenanigans, and he thought he would try out his German (learned from his parents, not his school), on Birgitte. She was tickled pink when he used the second person singular, when proffering her tea, as this, to Germans implied endearment, family connection, or intimacy. Perhaps this was why, after dinner, she asked him whether he would like to go for a walk. Brenda immediately said she would like to come too, but Birgitte reminded her of her headache.

They set off, in the beautiful Black Forest countryside, undulating fields, and outcrops of coniferous woodland. The track was surrounded by cornfields. Birgitte appeared quite able to converse in English, though she pronounced all her 'th's as 'ze'.

'Ze countryside here is very pretty, not so?' she enquired.

'Ya, Birgitte, die landschaft ist zer schon,' replied the master, albeit with some grammatical difficulty.

'I like you, Pablo, which year are you in at school?'

At this point the master decided it was quite pointless speaking in two languages, and felt that the gentlemanly thing to do was to allow Birgitte to continue practising her English.

'I'm in the fifth form, and have just taken my exams. Next year, I'll be going into the sixth form to study advanced level chemistry, physics and biology.'

'Zat sounds very impressive. Vot do you vont to be ven you leave school to vork?'

'I think I'd like to be a doctor. Doctors drive nice cars, and I'd like to have a Jaguar.'

'Oh yes, zey are good cars, but not as good as Mercedes.'

'What will you do when you leave school, Birgitte?'

'I'm sinking of taking up nursing. Zat vey, I'll meet a rich doctor viz his Jaguar.'

They walked on and a silence ensued, which was palpable. Suddenly, Birgitte took hold of the master's hand. I hiccupped.

'Pablo, haf you ever kissed a girl?' she asked.

'Never,' replied the master truthfully.

'Well, let's try,' she replied.

And with that, she planted her succulent lips firmly over the master's. Not content with that, she began gyrating her mouth, and then, horror upon horrors, she put her tongue into his mouth. To my surprise, Bill and Ben began gyrating in sympathy, and I protested firmly. After what seemed an age, they disconnected. The master had turned scarlet. Birgitte to his surprise, produced a cigarette and lit it. She offered it to the master who automatically declined, then realised that was not the mature thing to do, so accepted.

'You are a good kisser,' she complimented. The master was still covered in confusion, and choking on his cigarette. Bill and

Ben had retired after their wake-up call, and I realised I'd leaked a bit. They walked on.

'Ze boys I've kissed in Berlin were not as good as you,' she said.

The master felt a sense of triumph, not only had we beaten the Germans in the War, we were also better at kissing.

They walked back, to be welcomed by Borach, the Silberman's slobbery dog. Brenda immediately cottoned on to Birgitte to ask her opinion on her shoes, which had been bought two weeks previously. The master returned to his room and gave me a good thrashing. Thus relieved, he joined everyone at dinner. The food was excellent, sauerkraut roasted potatoes, and bratwurst. The adults quaffed Pilsner beer, the others, including the master, Brenda and Birgitte drank *apfelsaft* (apple juice). The head of the house, a bluff mature gent of fifty years, Herr Silberman, regaled the guests with tales of the Black Forest, and especially the pleasure of hunting deer. By deer he meant roebuck, not the grand stags to be found in Scotland.

It was arranged that he and the master would go hunting next day, but would have to depart very early (five a.m.) in order to ascend a special viewing platform (or *hochstand*), from which the chosen prey would be shot, and eventually eaten. After dinner, the master was kitted out with a camouflage trench coat, boots, hat, and a rifle equipped with a telescopic gun sight. In addition, they would have two pairs of high powered Zeiss binoculars. The master was very excited. Brenda said how sad it was to kill these beautiful creatures. Birgitte informed her that it was necessary to cull animals for their own good, though she was unable to explain why this was so. Sol Bernstein said he had once eaten venison in Poland before leaving on account of the Nazis. He said it was rather gamey. Brenda said she would never eat it. Birgitte volunteered, 'It iss very good to eat vild. Zat is vot nature is all about. I look forward to it.'

So, at last, everyone retired.

Birgitte's bedroom was next to the master's, separated by a stud wall. Just as he was about to fall asleep, he heard a knocking on the wall. He thought she was playing a game, so knocked back. Unfortunately, he didn't know Morse code, though Birgitte did. Her message, had he but known it, was, 'Come to my room now, nobody will know.'

His reply, much to her puzzlement was, 'Hdnmmq,' about which she hadn't a clue. She knocked a few times more, but the master, thinking of the hunt planned for the following day, ignored the knocks, and eventually fell asleep.

Five a.m., and Herr Silberman knocked on the bedroom door. The master, quickly got dressed, and they got into the car, a Fiat 2300 with green velour upholstery. It was almost new, so it was a bit of a shame that it was driven fast along bumpy country tracks. They passed a little hamlet called Wolpadingen, calling briefly at a hostelry 'Zum Adler', a wooden chalet, dimly lit inside with a smell of old wood. Herr Silberman had a brief conversation with the innkeeper, then returned to the car, where the master was wondering what it was all about. Finally they reached a field on a raised outcrop, and spied the Hochstand. It was about twenty feet high. The master was cautioned about making the slightest noise, as this would frighten away the deer, which were expected at any moment. The two donned their binoculars and started combing the countryside. There was an early morning mist, and the views were breathtakingly beautiful. In the far distance, they saw a couple of roebuck, but they were about half a mile away, and beyond range. It was cold, and the master got a bar of chocolate out of his coat, but as he was tearing the silver paper, he was hushed by his host. 'You have to be very quiet, as they can sense the slightest sound, as well as smells.' Thus cautioned, the master very carefully extricated a section, folding not tearing the foil. He offered some to Herr Silberman who declined. Then, to the master's amazement, he got out a cigar and lit it.

'They won't smell it, as the wind is in the wrong direction,' was the given explanation.

An hour went by, the sun was now coming up above the hill in the distance, and they were both feeling pretty hungry.

'Well, I don't think this was our lucky day, so how about getting some breakfast?'

The master nodded his agreement, and they drove back to the inn. Rye bread with home cured ham, and a mug of hot coffee soon had the master feeling better. The innkeeper, Herr Rothenberg, appeared to be grateful to Herr Silberman, who explained to the master, that he had helped fund a joinery apprenticeship for Stephan, Herr Rothenberg's son. Stephan then appeared. He was a well-built young man, with blond curly hair, and a German accent which the master couldn't decipher. He and his father together with the master and Herr Silberman then left the dining room of the Adler, and went round to the back of the building. They came to an outbuilding, with a wooden garage like door. This was opened, and to the master's amazement there were three previously shot roebuck hanging from the wall. Herr Silberman selected one, which was promptly placed in the boot of the Fiat. The men shook hands, and Herr Silberman winked at the master, who was aghast at what he had seen. There followed a rapid drive back to the *Landhaus*, where the Bernsteins, Frau Silberman and the Hofmans welcomed them.

'Das ist toll,' and 'Wunderbar' were two exclamations which registered in the master's memory, though he felt terribly guilty. Brenda told him he was cruel and heartless, and ought to undergo the same treatment he had apparently meted out to the roebuck. Birgitte told her not to be silly, which pleased the master no end. He followed this up by stating that he had shot it straight between the eyes first attempt. I felt a strange twitch of guilt, but this changed to a 45-degree elevation when Birgitte fixed him with an admiring glance.

'You are ze English Lord on safari, and ziz is your first kill.'

Lunch was duly served after the roebuck had been hung in the garage. No one thought to enquire as to why it had already been gutted, or why it was so cold. The master thought better than to draw this to their attention. Later that afternoon, they played scrabble, using a mix of English and German, which made it easier, and more educational. Towards evening, Herr Silberman got out his binoculars and they found to their amazement, they could see the Alps in the far distance. The master felt a thrill at their magnificence at a distance of over fifty miles. Unfortunately this portended a change in the weather, and sure enough, for the next three days it rained. And rained. And rained. On the second afternoon, Frau Kaufmann asked the master to ask Birgitte, who was having a nap in her room, to bring her the book on Alpine flowers she had let her have the previous evening.

The master duly obliged, and knocked on Birgitte's door. She was lying on her bed, wearing only her bra and pants. At first she appeared embarrassed, but quickly donned her dressing gown. The master blushed frantically, then blurted out the purpose of his visit. She regained her composure and reached him her mother's book. But just before he could clutch it, she withdrew it with a mischievous gleam in her eye.

'Pablo, I would like you to do sumsing,' she said.

'What do you mean, Birgitte?' he asked.

'I've never seen a penis, except in paintings by the Grand Masters, so could you show me yours?'

The master started towards the door, but she beat him to it and quickly locked it putting the key in her bra.

'I won't let you out unless you show me,' she teased.

At this stage, I can tell you, I was getting hot. My surroundings were getting very crowded. The master realised he was beaten, and felt that no amount of reasoning would work with this very determined girl.

'All right, but just a quick glimpse, that's all,' he volunteered.

And with that, I was presented, like a blushing bride. I rapidly became a shrinking violet, covered with embarrassment. Birgitte approached me in a clinical sort of way, and before the master could protest, took me in hand – literally! The rest is a blurred memory.

Per manum ad astra, to misquote the RAF motto. Five minutes later, the said book on Alpine flowers was presented to Frau Kauffman, as I detumesced in a lake of my own making. Wow! This holiday would remain vivid in the master's memory for the rest of his life.

Before long, we were back in Blighty, and awaiting the GCE results. The master was delighted to learn he had passed in seven subjects, and would now enter the sixth form. One problem however presented itself. In order to enter medical school to study medicine, three A level subjects were required, of which one was biology. Unfortunately, biology was not taught at the master's grammar school. Biology, like domestic science, was something girls did. This came as something of a shock, as it involved a journey across town, to be the only male among four hundred or so females. A daunting challenge, and one which the somewhat self-effacing master would have to meet. If they all turned out like Birgitte, he would have a job on his hands – and not only his hands! Brenda softened the blow by telling him he was a puny excuse for a boy, and no girls would spare him a glance. Little did she know of his recent Teutonic adventures.

Monday through Friday, physical chemistry, physics (lenses, and prisms), biology (amoeba, paramecium, euglena, hydra, plant stems, xylem, phloem, cambium, cotyledons, nitrogen fixing root nodules – it was a new insight into the world). Quite what amoeba etc. had to do with medicine remained a bit of a mystery. A rat was dissected (pure white in life, and now smelling of formalin), it made sense (sort of), as it seemed a workable possibility that in some ways it resembled humans. Well, some humans in history were rats, especially young Adolf whose machinations had resulted in the master being British. But I have omitted the most important part. The girls! What a disappointing lot they were. Blue tunics, white socks, many wearing NHS spectacles. Not exactly the thing that got the pulse racing.

Birgitte, Birgitte, wherefore art thou?

But come Friday, things changed. Dancing classes at Corrigans Dance School, hidden down a back alley in the town. Upon entering, the master was amazed to find some of his contemporaries smoking cigarettes in a most grown-up way.

They all seemed so much more grown up than him. And more confident at breaking the ice with the girls. Then the proceedings commenced.

'Take your partners,' came the command from Rory Corrigan. The master wondered what precisely he was meant to do. Then he saw the more confident lads walking up to the girls, and asking them to dance. Quaking in his boots, he self-consciously walked up to a very plain girl (the others having been taken), and asked her if she had already been picked.

'Picked for what?' came her reply.

'I mean to dance,' he blurted.

'Then why didn't you say so?' came her reply.

'Gentlemen, place your right arm round the lady's waist, and hold her right hand aloft with your left hand.'

And in order to demonstrate, Mr Corrigan asked a most ravishingly beautiful girl, his professional assistant, obviously older than the schoolgirls, to show everyone what he meant. The master's jaw dropped, unlike me – I felt my altimeter needle rising. And so proceeded the dance class – slow slow quick quick slow, for the quickstep, forward, side, side together, side, for the waltz. Mastering this intricate set of instructions took the better part of an hour, during which the master had sufficient courage to ask others to dance. One in particular seemed quite attractive. She had reddish ginger hair, and was very slim. Her lips were quite thin, which the master liked – having an inner fear of being swallowed by some big girl with big lips, and who knows whatever else. He fell passionately in love, but hadn't the nerve to say anything other than 'thank you' at the end. And thus it remained for the next two years as far as she was concerned.

Love and yearning from a distance was to be his *'modus operandi'*, which unfortunately never did *'operandi'*.

It may come as something of a surprise to the reader that the master up to this point was somewhat ignorant in regard to female anatomy. It was clear that girls didn't have anything resembling me. And when he once caught a glimpse of his sister (who would have murdered him had she known), he was amazed at the sight (albeit transient) of what looked like a bottom, but with her head pointing the wrong way. So clearly, she must have the ability to pee through a tube which presumably was the same as the one which was first revealed to him by the 'f' word. But such a tube, if it was to accommodate the likes of me, would be difficult to function for peeing. By the application of Ohms law, translated into hydrodynamics, in order to squirt a couple of feet or so, a much narrower tube, i.e. with greater resistance would be necessary to achieve the required force, or voltage according to Ohm. This troubled the master for some time, until one afternoon, when the biology mistress, a smart slim, heavily made up, and clearly embarrassed lady, mentioned that *in addition to* a urethra (alias the pee tube), the rat, like humans, possessed a vagina (alias the tunnel of love) towards which I would be navigating for the rest of my life, at the behest of the master.

'Eureka,' now all is revealed. At the age of seventeen years. By analogy to the London Underground, when we already had the Pee line, and the Poo line, we now had the additional Vaginot line (with apologies to the French).

Unfortunately, all these feelings were condemned by the Christian faith. St Paul would have none of it. Such thoughts were sinful, but if uncontrollable, could be assuaged by marriage. Thus it became the most fervent quest for the master to get married so that his cataclysmic urges could be permitted. There was no other way. However, a career would have to interpose itself first, so he turned all his efforts into passing his A levels, in order to get into university, in order to become a doctor, and to marry someone, and finally to have sex. In the meantime, he had to make do with the skills taught him by 'Wanker' Wal. Chemistry consisted of weird processes in the laboratory, which involved bubbling hydrogen sulphide into a test-tube containing the chemical whose content the master was behoved to ascertain. How this had any connection with medicine was hard to follow. Nevertheless, the prize at the end of it all kept the master beavering away. Similarly with experiments on sound, and seeing, or rather hearing, the sound of an electric bell disappearing as the bell, inside a large glass jar had its atmosphere removed by a suction pump. Sound doesn't travel through a vacuum. Electric motors, magnets, coils, it was all peripheral to the task ahead. The wonders of light traversing concave and convex lenses, focal length, spherical and chromatic aberration, heat calorimeters, specific heat, water equivalent, latent heat of evaporation, and of freezing. Extraction of aluminium from bauxite, the wonders of the Bessemer converter, a visit to an iron foundry, hell on earth with Beelzebub at work. What did a doctor need to know about iron puddling? Or plant stems? But keep the faith, the prize would be there at the end of the day.

Next came the challenge to storm the citadel of medicine. Unfortunately the fast track straight in to the doctor's surgery as an apprentice, for let us say three months, before being unleashed on an unsuspecting public, and with a beautiful black Mark VII Jaguar, with a blonde in the passenger seat, and marriage with plenty of tunnel of love action, was not to be. First one had to be accepted at a medical school. This meant interviews, as well as passing A levels. Interview number 1. A well known London teaching hospital. Three distinguished looking white-haired men, with stiff collars and somewhat haughty attitudes.

'Why have you chosen to do medicine?'

'I didn't, medicine chose me,' didn't go down very well, though the master thought it sounded pretty good, and was prophetically inspired by something John F Kennedy would one day say. Eventually he was successful at being selected for a provincial university, whose identity will be kept a secret. But first the dreaded A level exams.

One day, in September through the letter box appeared an invitation by a Mrs Alderney, to a dance at the Malt House, in Atterbury. The master was puzzled, he hadn't ever heard of the good lady, but together with a sixth form pal, Tony Pond, he was driven to the venue in Tony's dad's Simca. The dance was a jolly affair, the girls were quite passable, and all agreed to dance when asked. There was a live band which banged out the 'hokey cokey' and other favourites of the day. Came the last waltz, and the master succeeded in dancing with Beryl. Beryl was a country lass, keen on riding, and had absolutely nothing in common with the master. But he feigned knowledge about 'riding to hounds'; though he kept the identity of the hunt he supported a secret. The dance proceeded, and the master attempted to hold Beryl a little closer. Beryl, however, knew how to hold the reins, and kept the master at a respectable distance. 'Cheerio' was her parting remark, and before he could interpose a suggestion that they might meet up for a coffee, she was getting into Daddy's Daimler Consort, and was gone. The Simca plus driver were waiting.

Tony hadn't had a particularly good evening, having been refused on two occasions, but did get a dance with Betty (known in Atterbury as 'Busty Betty'). In the course of legitimately waltzing with her, and keeping strictly to the protocol he had learned at Corrigan's dancing class, he had indirectly become well acquainted with the feel of the mammaries. He confided to the master, that it had resulted in him having felt decidedly uncomfortable, by which he meant my counterpart had been placed in a state of readiness.

Back home, Brenda was very curious and jealous that the master had been invited to a snooty dance.

'What on earth made them invite you? I'd have expected that only public school boys would have been invited – there must have been some mistake.'

Came the summer, and all effort was directed at the A level exams. The master had little difficulty with biology, and made a creditable dissection and demonstration of the contents of the thoracic cavity of a pure white and heavily formalinised rat. Chemistry was OK, but physics was touch and go. But when the results came through with good marks for chemistry and biology, but a bare pass in physics, he felt relieved. One step nearer to the goal ahead.

Now it was time for the summer holidays, and Sol had booked them into a hotel in Blackpool. The five of them packed themselves into the Hillman Minx and set off. The roads were busy, and there weren't any motorways. David was very excited at the thought of swimming in the sea, having learned to swim just three months earlier. Brenda was looking forward to wearing her new bathing suit, which it must be said, was quite modest. She had qualified as a hairdresser, and had recently acquired a boyfriend, Derrick. He worked at the local bus depot as a mechanic, and was clearly smitten by her. She treated him like dirt, which had the effect of making him beg for every favour. By favour is meant deigning to allow him to meet her, despite her extremely busy social calendar, holding her hand was just about tolerated. He took her to the pictures a few times, but she refused to let him put his arm round her, and there was no, positively no kissing. The pain served merely to enhance Derrick's passion, which he could only assuage by the 'Wal' method. Poor Derrick.

And now Brenda was in Blackpool, with lots of eager lads about. The sleeping arrangements at their temporary home, 'Everest Guest House', consisted of Ma and Pa Bernstein plus David in one room, whilst Brenda had her own, and so had the master. None had en-suite bathrooms or toilets, there being two separate bathrooms situated at the end of the corridor. Ma and Pa's room had a 'sea view' provided one had a neck eighteen inches long, plus the ability to see round corners. The others overlooked a caravan site, which if anything was nicer than the aforesaid sea view. The caravans were of the static type with loads of families mainly with little children, some of whom were quite noisy. The noise was mainly of the 'whoops of delight' variety, the other less appealing sound being the ice cream van which seemed to lap the town every thirty minutes. Away in the far distance a golf course could be seen, which was of interest to Sol Bernstein who from time to time thought he might one day join the indigenous English by becoming a member of a golf club. Unfortunately, it was common knowledge at the time that some clubs were barred to coloured people and Jews, but that didn't put Sol off. Meanwhile, he and the family spent one fun afternoon at the putting green which was situated alongside the main entrance to the golf club.

That evening, they all dressed for dinner, which was the norm for the time. Sol wore a Burton suit, and tie, whilst Martha sported a dress recently acquired from a local outfitters. It was not exactly Norman Hartnell, or Balenciaga. But synthetic fabrics were the latest craze, nylon and crimplene being 'in'. Brenda, having secured permission to go to a dance in the town, wore a red halter neck dress, which the master had to admit, made her look just about passable. She also wore the *de rigeur* suspender belt plus nylon stockings. Kiss proof lipstick was applied, plus a dab of scent. She promised to be back by ten thirty, Martha having warned her about the ways of boys. And off she went. Little did she know that the master had taken it upon himself to follow, not on account of any sense of protection, but rather to gather evidence which might come in useful at a later date.

The *Palais de Dance* was about half a mile away and on the sea front. The master, having informed his parents that he would like to go out for a walk, and take in a film (*The Student Prince* was showing at the Odeon), followed his sister at a respectable distance. However, instead of going to the cinema, he bought a ticket for the dance hall, and trying to remain invisible to his sister, furtively made his entrance. The band was playing a quickstep, and the girls appeared older and far prettier than had been the case during the Friday afternoon dancing classes at Corrigans. As they twirled round, legs came into view and I engaged gear. This didn't please the master who felt it might impede his dancing abilities as well as altering his profile, so he ducked into the bar. 'Pint of Double Diamond please,' and to his relief no questions regarding age were asked. Out of the corner of his eye he could see his dear sister coyly flouncing as though she didn't care for any of the boys available. She engaged another girl in conversation, and then, to the master's surprise, began to dance the ballroom jive with her. It must be admitted, Brenda was no mean dancer, and shortly afterwards, was asked to dance by a tall, quite good looking youth.

'Where you from?' he asked her.

'New York,' came the reply.

'Well you don't sound American,' he answered.

'I know, I've only lived there for six months. I'm working for a recording studio,' she blatantly lied.

'Blimey, who'd have thought it? Can I buy you a drink?'

'All right,' she said, and they made their way into the bar. The master turned round in order to examine the bare wall.

'What'll you have?'

'I'd love a Babycham,' came the slightly suggestive response, mimicking a current advertisement.

As the two of them seemed pretty engrossed with each other, and the said wall was somewhat bereft of inspiration, the master ventured onto the ballroom. Spying a pretty girl sitting with her friend enjoying a cigarette, he wandered over, and applied his Corrigan's learned technique.

'I say, would you like to have a dance?' he innocently asked.

'Drop dead,' came the astonishing reply.

For this he was totally unprepared, it was as though he had suddenly entered a totally alien world. The next girl he approached said she was talking to her friend, and sitting this one out, then within a couple of minutes, was on the floor with a somewhat older youth, sporting sideburns, and tight trousers (I winced), plus winkle picker shoes. Meanwhile Brenda was to be seen dancing a waltz closely attached to a man with a moustache, who was wearing a cravat and sports jacket. He must have been about twenty-five years old.

The master's third attempt brought a terse reply, 'No thanks.'

The master decided a change of strategy was definitely required. So, instead of asking a girl who took his fancy, he decided he would try the opposite end of the spectrum, and approached a tubby tall girl, with pink-framed spectacles.

'How about a dance, sweetheart?' he asked, throwing caution to the winds.

She said nothing, stubbed out her cigarette, then grabbed him and swung him onto the floor. At Corrigans he had learned that the gentleman led, and the lady followed, but Dorothy, as he subsequently found out, hadn't been schooled at the same dance academy. In fact, she had left school at fifteen, to work in a sweet shop, and thought she knew how to dance. Except that she didn't, as the master soon found out, with one, then two, then three bruised toes. He bade a hasty retreat to the bar. Brenda was nowhere to be seen. He darted back onto the dance floor. No Brenda. 'Double Diamond please,' he ordered, as he considered what to do next.

As he gazed at the bar in deep thought, a voice at his side said, 'I could see you had a tricky dance with Dorothy. How about you buy me a drink?'

'Sure,' he replied.

The lady in question was undoubtedly older than his heretofore experiences, perhaps even hitting thirty. But she was quite pretty, her voice was rather husky, probably from smoking.

'Let's take a stroll onto the balcony,' she suggested, and before he knew what was happening, there they were, hand in hand en route, drinks in hand.

'There's a quiet spot over there,' she said, as they disappeared behind a huge palm tree stuck into an even huger pot.

The master was a bit uncertain what next to say. He needn't have bothered. Before he knew what was happening, she put her drink down and began kissing him on the lips, and pressing her body close – too close. He was clearly embarrassed, but I was galvanized into unwelcome activity. Hurriedly disengaging himself, he ran back to the ballroom only to see Brenda pulling down the head of her current dance partner, and kissing him with a degree of gusto. The master's brain was in a whirl, I didn't know which way I was going, down or up, on second thoughts, better down. He rushed out into the street, and began walking back to the hotel. He realised he had left his Double Diamond, and dashed back, explaining his predicament to the doorman. But his drink was nowhere to be found. Then he spied a tall slim girl, with pretty brown straight hair and peaches and cream complexion.

'Care to have a dance?' he enquired.

'OK,' she said, and together they walked onto the dance floor.

It was a quickstep, and she clearly knew how to dance, her feet and body closely following his action. Once more, I found I too was dancing, but not exactly contributing to the master's intended music and movement.

'Where are you from?' he asked.

'Skelmersdale,' she replied.

'Where's that?'

'Lancashire,' came the reply.

'And what do you do?'

'I'm a secretary at one of the mills.'

'Where are you from?' she asked.

'Shropshire, a village called Horton.'

'Never heard of it,' she said.

'I didn't expect you to have heard of Horton.'

'No, Shropshire,' the pretty uneducated mill girl replied.

The master realised he hadn't happened upon a local Mensa candidate, but she was pretty enough to look upon, and she could dance. They danced a few times, but when it came to ten o'clock, she announced she had to leave, as her parents expected her back.

'By the way, I said I was a secretary, but that's not strictly true. But I'm studying shorthand and typing which I'll need if I want to get on.'

'Well, that's good, so you can work for me when, if ever I qualify.'

'What do you mean, qualify?'

'Well, I'm going to study medicine, and hopefully one day, be a doctor. Can I see you home?' the master enquired.

'OK,' she replied. 'It's just about a mile down the road.'

So they walked, hand in hand. She and her family were ensconced in a guest house optimistically and unimaginatively called 'Shimla Palace'.

'Well, I'd better say good night,' she said. 'Oh, by the way, what's your name?'

'Harry, but they call me Pablo,' came the reply.

'And what's yours?'

'Maureen.'

'Well, Maureen, it's been nice knowing you, perhaps we'll meet up again later in the week?'

'That's not going to happen,' she said, 'because we're going back to Skelmersdale tomorrow.'

'Oh, I see, well can I have your address, I'd like to keep in touch?'

'All right,' she replied. 'It's 7 Station Road, Millers Bank, Skelmersdale.'

'Would you like to have mine?'

'Yes please.'

So the pair parted, not realistically expecting to correspond or meet again. But they were wrong. At which the master turned upon his heel and walked back to The Everest. It was now eleven o'clock.

The rest of the holiday passed uneventfully, the family returned home on a particularly rainy day, and were greeted by a pile of post. Amongst this was a letter informing the master of necessary arrangements for attending medical school, accommodation at the hall of residence, and recommendations for text books, all frightfully expensive. Also included were details of the Freshers' Conference, alias an introduction to university life. It would commence with a service in the Great Hall, followed by a tour of the medical school, and of the university in general. In the evening, the much trumpeted Freshers' Hop.

The master duly boarded the eleven a.m. steam driven train together with colleague, Robin Tees, who was reading chemistry, and they took the one-hour journey. As was the custom, the master proudly wore a duffle coat, Robin a grey mackintosh. Both carried sufficient baggage for two days, their remaining luggage being delivered by arrangement the following day. Robin was going to board with a landlady in the suburbs; the master was fortunate in securing a place at a hall of residence, situated in the expansive grounds which formed part of the estate of a well-known business magnate.

Upon arrival at the redbrick university, the eyes fell upon the large tower which resembled its counterpart in the Place San Marco in Venice. Then, the milling hordes trouped into the Great Hall. A seating plan separated Freshers of different faculties, and from that moment they went their separate ways. As the master shuffled his way along the tier appointed, he met two wide-eyed Freshers who would remain friends for life. Balmic's family lived in Nairobi (he was Asian as you will no doubt have guessed), and Jackson (a somewhat unusual forename), who had been adopted, his adoptive parents living in Mansfield. The master, Balmic, and Jackson were to be the three musketeers, who would battle their way through the extremely tough medical course.

Whereas students from other faculties had a relatively easy and enjoyable first year, medical students from the word go were to be subjected to a frenetic study of human anatomy that they would never forget. Unfortunately, in the case of the master, the thing he never forgot was the smell of formalin, but that was all. His knowledge of anatomy remained dismal, though the essentials were retained for the rest of his professional career. One thing was certain, he would never be a surgeon, as he would undoubtedly lose his way around the human body (when viewed from its interior), though he was already reasonable well versed in regard to certain exterior approaches.

The freshers' hop in the students' union was a beery affair. It was clearly part of the expected university culture for male students to drink beer and plenty of it. Most popular was Double Diamond, which according to advertisements of the time, would work wonders. The three musketeers had a couple, then went forth on the hunt. I received messages to the effect that now that I was a student, my services might at any moment be required (St Paul notwithstanding). I needn't have worried, this was not to be the case for another three years, as my master's height of five feet eight inches and weight of barely eight stones would hardly place him in the Mr Universe class. In fact, the advertisement for Mr Universe claimed that he had been a seven stone weakling prior to discovering the secrets of dynamic tension, which enabled him to put on muscle and attract the opposite sex. Of course one would need to subscribe in order to receive the details.

At this stage the master more closely resembled the seven stone weakling. Thus it came as no surprise that his efforts to impress the girls was not very fruitful. He would have to resort to another strategy. Jackson soon found himself getting on well with a young lass from a local teacher's training college. Balmic in no time was quick-stepping with a rather pretty blonde, with a strong West Midlands accent, and who worked as a secretary at Davenports brewery, their motto of the time being 'Beer at home means Davenports'. Came the last waltz, and the master succeeded in dancing with a rather heavily made-up girl rather plain but chatty. She was a nursery nurse, who hailed from Wolverhampton, but was staying locally with her gran. She explained she had to leave shortly, but agreed to a walk outside to say goodnight. The master sensed he was on to a good thing, and, finding a quiet spot around the back of the building, attempted to kiss her. I felt quite involved, which caused the master some embarrassment, and Sheila (for that was her name) some amusement. Nevertheless, a kiss was duly achieved, and repeated, but an attempt to reconnoitre her breasts met with a sharp rebuff. She said goodbye, and the eight stone weakling made his way back to the hall of residence, with Jackson who had managed to arrange a date with Evelyn, the would-be teacher. Balmic had a few steamy kisses with the blonde, then went back to his digs.

The first year of medical school consisted of dissecting a human body, for which purpose the students were divided into groups of four or five. The donated human bodies were all very old, and looked long devoid of life or expression. The first term's work consisted of the upper limb, whilst students also learned about the microscopic appearance of the various body tissues, in the histology class. Students also learned about the chemical changes that took place in life. The human body really was shown to be very complex. In fact a long way from the bottles of medicine dished out by doctors of the time, most of which tasted foul, and were in reality placebos.

The master's group of dissectors consisted of Howard, a young lad from Whitstable, Sonia a pretty thing from Lancaster, Jilly a seriously religious girl from Morecambe, and Tony, who hailed from Wolverhampton. Before commencing their odyssey of dissection, and over a pint at the Gun Barrels, they christened their corpse 'Malvolio'. Together, as a team, this intrepid fivesome cautiously navigated their way through the complexities of the arm and hand: bones (easy, only three, excluding the hand and wrist), muscles, nerves, arteries, veins, and lymphatics. At the end of the day, Ernie, a ghoulish looking character collected all the gubbins in a bucket, which was then taken elsewhere. Histology involved peering down microscopes at the various organs, which had been sliced professionally into very thin slices, and then beautifully stained. Thus individual body cells could be seen, and individual organs identified. The year would be spent doing upper and lower limb, abdomen, chest and skull. Teachers were known as demonstrators, who were surgeon-hopefuls, themselves studying for the primary FRCS. This stood for 'Fellow of the Royal College of Surgeons'. It was in a sense reassuring that surgeons had to know their way about in great detail. Maybe one day, there would be a bright spark who would invent a surgical sat-nav, so that anyone could hack away in confidence, but thankfully, not yet.

There were approximately equal numbers of male and female bodies. For most of the female medics, it was the first time they could study my ilk, though I felt squeamish at the prospect of what one day I would turn into. It must be said from the start, some senior gentlemen were possessed of extraordinarily long members, which didn't do much for my, or the master's ego. It did succeed, however, in attracting a considerable number of female medics whose interest it must be admitted, was not purely professional.

'Bloody hell, imagine one that big inside you – it must be agony,' and, 'Christ, I can't wait, but my boyfriend is so religious, I guess I'll have to,' was the range of student opinion. Biochemistry was pretty boring, learning all about the chemical reactions of the body, as it was nearly all theoretical. But boiling up urine to see whether, through disease, the kidneys were leaking protein, was fun, because the result was the appearance in the wee of a white substance resembling egg white, which in a sense, it was. And to diagnose diabetes, the presence in wee of sugar was demonstrated by heating with something called Fehling's solution, in this case a red colour change forming in the presence of sugar. But far more exciting was physiology. Students were told that the difference between anatomists and physiologists was that anatomists knew where to find it, but didn't know what to do with it, whereas physiologists didn't know where to find it, but if they did, they certainly knew what to do with it.

One weird lecturer had a clever way of demonstrating that when people swallow, it doesn't rely on gravity. In fact one can swallow even when suspended upside down. During the lecture, he had himself strapped to a bench which could be pivoted so that he was turned upside down. He was then passed a pint of beer in a glass beer mug. He proceeded to swallow the whole pint. He then was manoeuvred back into a normal standing up position. He then swallowed a rubber tube, which passed into his stomach. By applying a syringe to the tube, he was able to siphon back the entire pint of beer back into the beer mug. This brought a round of applause, which turned into horror when he calmly announced that it was a crime to waste a good pint, and proceeded to consume the entire contents for a second time.

Back at hall, he was surprised one morning that his pigeon hole bore a letter postmarked Skelmersdale. It had been re-addressed from his home. He opened it, and to his surprise found it was from Maureen.

I expect you've forgotten me, but I thought it might be nice to keep in touch. Life here is pretty boring, probably not half as exciting as yours. I've got a job in a local teashop. We get lots of different types. The best part is the tips. I made five pounds in tips last week. Most weekends we have dances in the local Palais, but the boys are a boring lot. All they talk about is work in the mills. Our dog has had some pups, they are so cute. How are you, what are you doing? We never had a chance to find out more about each other. Do write and tell me.

Yours sincerely
Maureen.'

What a surprise! The master recalled how pretty he had thought her, but recent events at the uni had blotted her out of his mind. And there was all that anatomy and physiology, and exams coming up. Sad to say, he never did reply. Such is life – tough!

By now, the anatomy dissection had reached the abdomen, which to the layperson meant the guts. This wasn't particularly difficult, the gut essentially consisted of a long tube with various different names assigned to it as one progressed along. The first station was the oesophagus, or gullet as commonly called, then the stomach, followed by duodenum, ileum, caecum with the appendix tagged on, colon, and last of all, the rectum. All very well, but the complicated bit was the omentum, or 'gatekeeper of the abdomen'. This was like a folded blanket which followed the twists and turns of the intestines as they developed before birth. It was there to stick to the intestine if it got punctured, because having a punctured gut could mean death from peritonitis. The blanket covered over the other organs, this part being the peritoneum, and things underneath it were called 'retroperitoneal', and included the kidneys. There were also lots of arteries and veins, and other channels called lymphatics. To add to all this complexity, were nerves, and lower down, the contents of the pelvic cavity. This was not specially interesting in Malvolio's case, since being male, there was little there of reproductive interest. Except one thing, or two to be precise. For some reason, Mother Nature had decreed that testicles, in this case, Bill and Ben, my neighbours, needed to be kept at a lower temperature than the rest of the body, so had to swing along outside the body. However, in order to keep in touch, they were connected by the testicular arteries which branched off the aorta nearly up to the arteries supplying the kidneys. And of course there was a structure about the size of a walnut, just in front of the rectum, called the prostate which was the gland that produced the fluid that was the stuff of (wet) dreams. That is why the master's prostate is called Old Walnut. I too was represented on Malvolio, but to be true, I was not a pretty sight. No admiring glances from the master's female colleagues, no pilgrimages were made to Malvolio.

Malvolio's me was about three inches long, and had clearly at some moment in history, been subjected to the same bullfight that I had endured in my first week of extra-uterine life. Having carefully dissected all the structures as instructed in the 'bible' (their dissecting manual), the medical students had to dissect me, in order to demonstrate the extraordinary muscles which, when distended with blood (in lay terms, an erection), could have more than doubled the size of Malvolio's me, though that was likely something of a memory from the far distant past. Finally, by an act that may, or may not have been as instructed in the bible, said member was with a swing of the scalpel, detached, thrown up in the air, to the accompanying exclamation of 'Olé,' by Sonia. At the end of the day, Malvolios's me was unceremoniously tossed into Ernie's bucket. Malvolio observed with a look of outrage, probably due to the shadow of the afternoon sun as it crossed the dissection room. Word of Sonia's performance spread like wildfire throughout the year, and was a source of chuckles for ages, in fact long after these students had qualified as serious doctors. To those readers who suspected a glimpse of future feminism in this, I can assure you, that it never arose, at least not to my knowledge. In fact, it must be admitted, I detected some signals when in her proximity.

Those students whose subjects were female, of course had a different perspective when dissecting the pelvic cavity. The wonders of the uterus, and ovaries were there beheld. It seemed amazing that this shrunken bag could have contained a baby in the past. Or that the external bits could have caused any interest or excitement to the likes of me, given their dark, shrunken and lifeless appearance. It was as though they were dissecting the pupal case from which the live insect had long emerged and disappeared.

Finally, the thorax, heart, and lungs, and a funny thing called the thymus. Noticeable in the lungs was that some corpses had very blackened lungs, whilst others were white and pink. The demonstrators explained that one could discern those that were city dwellers by their blackening, whereas those in the country had paler lung appearances. In fact the city-dwellers' lungs were the same colour as most of the older buildings in the city centre. Coal fires, and steam driven trains were still the norm. Whilst good old Blighty revelled in the knowledge that Britain's Mallard held the world's steam hauled speed record, and we were building Britannia class steam engines, the rest of the world was getting on with electrification. The master was interested in cars, and fervently believed that we also built the world's best cars, a dream that would be shattered big time, particularly by those countries he simplistically believed we had defeated in the war, one of which had resulted in him being born in Blighty.

And so to the summer exams. A typically hot sweltering summer, just when everyone was busy swotting. Then the first paper – 'Describe the muscles of the shoulder, in particular their origins and attachments, and nerve supply.' Dead easy, provided you knew it. Unfortunately, the master didn't, having instead done a bit of spotting, which meant taking a calculated risk on which questions would come up in the exams, based on previous papers. If the question had been on the hip, or knee, or ankle, he would have been home and dry, but it didn't. Anyway, to cut a long story short, by the time the exams were over, he along with seven others, was deemed to have failed. The end of his intended career as a doctor was now staring him in the face. He would have to re-take the exam in September, and if he failed again, he would be out. Fortunately, the university had laid on a revision course during the summer vacation, which he attended, and eventually passed. Whew! What a relief!

Came the summer of 1959. He went home for a couple of weeks where he was greeted by Brenda, who told him he would probably turn out to be a rotten doctor, as he had failed at first. She meanwhile was doing OK as a hairdresser, with a regular income of eight pounds a week, of which she paid her dad four for her keep. David was delighted to see his big brother, and together they walked to the local recreation ground to kick a ball around. Sol and Martha were proud of their son who was going to be a doctor (despite a temporary glitch). At the recreation ground, the two boys played football for about twenty minutes, when the master noticed a girl at the end of the pitch, looking at him. Could it be? No, impossible – but, yes it was! He went over, and was greeted by a knee-weakening smile. I received a million volt shock out of my past month's complacency.

'Hi, Carol. It's been a long time. How are you these days? Oh, David, go home, I'll see you later. Tell Mum and Dad, I'll be a while.'

Carol had grown into a most beautiful creature, blonde hair, blue eyes, and well-developed breasts which gave evidence of their existence by the rather tight sweater she was wearing.

'I'm fine,' she replied, 'been working as a switchboard operator at the local exchange. What have you been doing? I haven't seen you for ages.'

'I'm at medical school hoping one day that I'll be a doctor.'

'That's great, our doctor's ever so good. He comes round every week to see my granddad who's got diabetes and a bad leg. By the way, what exactly is diabetes?'

This gave the master the opportunity to impress Carol by his exposition on the functioning of the pancreas, control of blood sugar and the typical symptoms of diabetes as an emergency usually in young people.

'But granddad never had a coma, in fact he just complained of being thirsty, couldn't walk far because of pain in his legs which stopped him. When this happened, all he would do was stop, look in a shop window (if there happened to be a shop), light a cigarette (despite his doctor's advice), before going on. So is that the same disease as the one you're talking about with going unconscious?'

At this point the master realised his knowledge at this stage of his almost aborted career, did not permit him to give a convincing explanation, so instead, he changed the subject. 'Would you like to come to a dance at Sankey's on Saturday?' (Sankey's was the local factory which employed hundreds of people, making all sorts of things, including wheels.)

'Thanks, I'd love to. I'll see you there, about eight o'clock?'

'Fine,' the master replied. They chatted a little more about nothing in particular, both imagining the forthcoming dance, and the opportunities it might offer.

They parted and on arriving home, the master was greeted by Brenda with, 'So you've met that tart, Carol. She's a terrible flirt you know, been had by all the local lads. Couldn't you find someone better at that university you almost got chucked out of?'

This news rather upset the master, but he set it aside, as he decided he would try building a model aeroplane, a hobby he had made a preliminary attempt at when he was younger. Accordingly, he bought a simple kit and proceeded to cut out the various parts made of balsa wood. Somehow what had seemed very complicated a few years ago was now straightforward, and in no time he had cut out all the necessary parts. Next he glued them together with balsa cement. The next stage was to apply the tissue paper over the wings and fuselage, having included the elastic band which would turn the propeller. Finally, the plane was wetted gently in order to shrink the paper into a taut skin, having first pinned down the wings so that they wouldn't warp. Finally, he applied dope to coat the stretched skin with another strong skin, and the job was complete. He felt very pleased with the result, and together with David, went to the recreation ground for test flying. First he launched the plane by throwing it in order to find its centre of gravity by the addition of little weights. Having achieved this, he wound up the propeller fifty turns, then held the plane as the propeller spun. All correct. Now for the great moment! One hundred turns, hold steady, now launch! The little plane soared up into the air, watched by an admiring younger brother, then flew further away until after about twenty seconds the propeller stopped and it glided down to the ground making a pretty good landing. The next half hour was spent in more flying before the two returned home where Martha and Sol had prepared a pot roast. Sol was very pleased and proud of his (one day to be) doctor son, not for his airplane construction skills, but for the anticipated income that being a doctor would accompany. The master however had no particular interest in being rich, just enough to buy a big beautiful Jaguar Mark VII to ride in with Carol.

Came Saturday. The day of the dance. How would events unfold? I must admit the master was clearly somewhat excited, as far as I could make out. Cometh the hour, cometh the man. Morning, and a visit to the barber for a DA style, iron his shirt, splash on the Old Spice. Then off to the dance. He confided to David, who wished him luck. Brenda was also going out, but not to Sankey's, preferring instead to go to the Majestic, which was a purpose built dance hall for a slightly older clientele. The master paid for his entrance, then headed straight for the bar, and a pint of Double Diamond. There was a six-piece band, playing 'Unchained melody'. There were certainly lots of girls, mostly nothing to write home about, some that were OK, and for the most part guarded by chaps with long sideburns, slicked back hair, and winkle picker shoes. Some girls were dancing together, as though fellows didn't exist. Then he saw Carol, who was one of those who was dancing with another girl. It was a quickstep, and when it finished, the master went over to talk to her.

'Hello, Harry, this is Patricia, works with me at the hairdresser's.'

'Hallo, Carol, glad you could make it. By the way, most people call me Pablo. What are you drinking?'

'Mine's a Babycham,' promptly replied Patricia.

'I'll have one too,' added Carol.

The master made his way back to the bar where there was, by now, quite a queue. A few minutes later, when he returned, he found Carol was dancing with someone he didn't know.

'Tell me about yourself,' said Patricia.

'Oh, there's not much to tell,' the master replied, casting his gaze around, looking for Carol.

The master was somewhat preoccupied at this point, as he was worried that Carol was slipping away, but he needn't have worried. When the dance ended, she returned and began telling Patricia what a clever chap he was. Patricia was apparently very interested by now, particularly as she wished to know how to treat her grandmother's corns, a subject about which he didn't know anything. She ploughed on asking about low back pain, chronic headache, and lastly, her own problems with constipation.

'I'll tell you later. Carol, may I have this waltz with you?'

'All right, Harry, I mean Pablo,' and together they commenced.

Forwards, side together side, forwards, side together side. This sequence soon struck the master as somewhat boring, so he launched into his own variation. This involved holding his partner more tightly, before doing a sort of pirouette. As he did so, her breasts became pressed tightly to him, and I received the shock of my life – it literally shocked me rigid. This unfortunately upset the delicate balance of the dance currently being performed, in particular the anticipated silhouette was significantly deformed. The master realised this, and quickly made an excuse that he needed to fasten his still-tied shoelace. After this, he resorted to the intended routine which was less imaginative, but safer, as I detumesced.

'You know, you could be a good dancer, Pablo,' Carol observed.

The choice of the conditional tense implied a degree of uncertainty which the master found disconcerting. The implication that he wasn't currently a good dancer did nothing for his somewhat still embarrassed ego.

'Let's have another drink,' he said, and together they approached the bar.

'Do you think Patricia will mind you not being with her?' he asked.

'Oh no,' Carol replied. 'She's usually latched on to someone by now. Her problem is she likes talking about her problems, so that way she can ditch anyone who bores her, until she finds someone more interesting, when she asks them what they feel about free love.'

At this point the master recalled his conversation with Patricia, and realised what she must have thought of him. They sipped their drinks in silence for a while, as he reflected on his strategy. Clearly he needed to build on the assumption that he might possess the necessary skills to dance well, thereby impressing Carol, and thereafter, who knows. Carol meanwhile noticed a girl pal at the other end of the bar, and after a hurried excuse, went over to join her. The master pretended not to mind, and suddenly, espying Prodder Perkins, whom he hadn't seen for a long time, went over to him.

'Hi, Prodders,' he said.

'Well, if it isn't Doc Pablo,' came the reply. 'What have you been up to. Are the nurses all they're cracked up to be? How many have you had? I lost my virginity last week with Busty Betty. Not much to look at, but boy, could she go. A bit sore afterwards.'

'You brute,' the master remarked. 'You should have treated her like a lady, not an animal.'

'Not her, me, you fool,' said Prodder.

I felt a shudder of alarm. I'd never thought that the ultimate quest might turn out to be a painful experience. At this point they were rejoined by Carol.

'Hi, Carol,' said Perkins. 'I didn't know you had taken up with the doc. Be careful, you know what they say about medical students.If you can't be good, be careful,' and with that, he sauntered off.

'He's an idiot,' said Carol. 'Fancies himself something rotten. Let's dance.'

They returned to the dance floor, where the band were playing the hokey cokey, which was great fun for everyone. This was followed by a quickstep, during which the master tried to pull out all the stops, which unfortunately resulted in the pair colliding with two other couples.

'Better stop, Pablo, before we get escorted off the premises, let's walk home.'

They took a leisurely stroll around the sports ground which abutted onto the dance hall.

'Is it true what he said about medical students?' asked Carol.

'Oh no,' came the reply. 'Back at uni, where I'm in hall, we've often talked about it – you know, doing it the first time. One chap, reading politics, economics and philosophy, told us how he'd done it the first time at the Mostyn Hotel in Liverpool. He had a rapt audience, whom he ingratiated with all the gory details. For a short time he was regarded with more awe than the most learned professors at the university.'

'Well, I'm going to keep mine till I get married,' said Carol. 'I reckon lots of people who haven't really done it pretend they have because it gives them a kind of status. Mind you, I don't mind a little gentle exploring – come here, there's a gap in the trees.'

At which point the master found himself 'exploring'. I don't mind telling you, if I'd had a bone in my body (which I expect you will have surmised I hadn't), it would have been broken. Unlike the rest of the master's body, I remained faithful to the invertebrates, from which I guess eons ago, we humans had evolved. The master's expedition took him by way of the mountainous northern regions to the more temperate climate of the rain forest. A goodnight kiss outside her house, and the master walked home with a skip in his stride as he recalled the evening's events.

Came autumn, and he returned to uni for the next part of his studies. Unfortunately two of his colleagues hadn't made it in the retakes, and had sallied forth into the world of the pharmaceutical industry, from which one eventually would become chief executive, and be a millionaire. 'Physiology,' the master was reminded, 'is about knowing what to do with it once you've found it. Anatomy is about knowing where to find it.' This profound piece of information had a certain ring to it, and the master found physiology more interesting than anatomy. The physiology practical classes included some unusual experiments.

One included students having to strip naked one cold January morning, and spend half an hour on the roof of the medical school, recording their armpit and rectal temperatures every five minutes (not with the same thermometer). This demonstrated to the surviving students that whilst the armpit temperature fell (the outside temperature was one degree above freezing), the rectal temperature remained the same. It should be pointed out that all the students involved were male. If not, I'd probably have developed instant frostbite as I 'came out' to see how the lasses were faring. Another experiment involved drinking two litres of squash, then immediately going out for a two mile run at maximum speed. The control group of students would remain doing nothing. They had to pee into a graduated jug, and record their urine output. The runners on their return had, to everyone's surprise, not peed at all, nor did they need to. This was explained by the stress having made the posterior pituitary gland in the brain secrete something called anti-diuretic hormone.

But the most popular experiment involved drinking a considerable amount of very concentrated alcohol mixed with orange juice, and measuring the reaction time when pressing a button whenever a light flashed, or a buzzer sounded. The reaction times were then compared to those of the same student obtained prior to drinking the liquid. Wow, physiology was interesting! Certainly, the body moved in mysterious ways its functions to perform. Unfortunately, because they were mysterious, the master once again failed his Easter exams, and had to endure the same agony with the threat of expulsion. But hallelujah, thanks to the hand of fate, and some fairly vigorous workouts to which I was party, he passed. So now, a new field beckoned – exposure to the hospital wards, and real live patients. My time would come – perhaps.

Part 2
Summer

(Age twenty to forty)

The master was pleased, and relieved, that he was now regarded as a clinical medical student. This implied that he had graduated from books and laboratories, to patients, and wards. And of course, wards included nurses. I was increasingly letting him know that I wanted to prove myself in battle, but the mores of the time were such that this unveiling of the curtain was scheduled for the play called 'Marriage'. Additionally, although the female form in life was now professionally being revealed, (as apart from the formalin preserved specimens encountered in the dissecting room), they (the patients) were generally of an age that thankfully kept my temperature well below boiling. The students were all instructed in the art of history taking, and of examining the various systems. The mysterious noises revealed by the stethoscope were explained, and, with a bit of imagination, were heard by the students. Feeling the pulse, and measuring its rate was easy, but recognising whether when irregular, it was regularly irregular or irregularly irregular, took a bit more effort. The heart sounds were fine, 'lub dup' onomatopoetically expressed, but when to these were added, lub dup de oorr, and lush dup, and lush de oor, it all became rather complicated. The mysteries of rheumatic heart disease were assiduously learned by all. Common things like skin rashes and vague belly aches and 'gippy tummy', were ignored. High-powered cardiology, glimpses of heart surgery performed by the gods were the magic that held most students in thrall. Likewise, some of the nurses. Unfortunately, they regarded the medical students as akin to the dirt that was swept up twice daily, their attentions being firmly fixed on the registrars, and on occasion, the junior housemen – potential marriage fodder!

The consultants were the gods, who swept through the wards twice weekly. Students were allocated patients from whom to take a history and to examine. On the ward rounds, the students were expected to know the histories, and the results of investigations. All the junior doctors wore white coats to protect them from germs. Consultants, however, being gods, were immune, and therefore sported their Savile Row suits. The master's first patient was Mrs Mary Stevenson, who had rheumatoid arthritis. It had started very gradually, with painful hands and wrists, which became swollen. In the mornings particularly, she felt very stiff. She had been admitted to the hospital ward so that she could have physiotherapy, which included wax baths for her hands, lots of aspirin, and a new miracle drug called cortisone. The master noticed that her face appeared rather swollen and red, which he was told was officially known as a 'moon face', and was common for people subjected to the miracle drug. But to his amazement on the weekly ward round, the consultant announced that they would be giving her gold injections. Quite how this would help her remained a mystery to the master, perhaps she would feel more highly valued by all who came in contact with her.

The next patient, Mrs Birtwhistle, had an unusual type of face, with a large protruding jaw, called 'prognathism', and he was told, this was due to a tumour of her pituitary gland. He was told to practise his blood-letting skills on her. So, on the morning appointed, a Tuesday, and armed with a freshly sterilised syringe and needle, he proceeded. Unfortunately, the reusable needles of the time had to be sharpened, but this was not always assiduously carried out. Secondly, Mrs Birtwhistle was possessed of very thick skin (in the purely physical sense, a characteristic of her condition). This combination of misfortunes was the reason why the events that were to follow were more reminiscent of a joust than of a commonplace clinical procedure. Having failed on three occasions to thrust the needle through the chain mail skin, the master was full of apologies, and retired to the sluice to re-arm with (hopefully) a sharper needle. Mrs Birtwhistle was very considerate, she had been through this several times before, and was mildly amused, as well as contused and bruised. But eventually, blood was obtained, and then squirted into various bottles for the tests ordered by the medical registrar. Several other patients were seen, and at four o'clock, the students, having been fortified by coffee, went to the lecture theatre for the daily lecture.

That evening, the master and a few friends met up at the White Swan (known locally as the Dirty Duck), for a few beers. Also there were a few student nurses. They were conversing animatedly about the dishy new registrar, Dr Thornton, and studiously ignored the medical students. The master gallantly sought to enter their circle by asking them what they felt about cortisone. None of them had heard of it, which was not too surprising, as they worked on the ear, nose and throat ward, where at the time it had no use. They returned to their conversation, and the master was totally forgotten. Clearly he was making no progress, and I was in stage three narcosis.

The master at this time, I should comment, was sharing digs with three other students. Alan was reading Spanish, Joe,

Chemistry, and Phil, Sociology. The accommodation was on the first floor of a Victorian house. It had two bedrooms, equipped with single beds, a small lounge, a kitchen, and bathroom with toilet. Heating was by gas-fired radiators, with a gas meter in a cubbyhole in the hall. There was a record player, a Dansette, and a radio, but no TV. The master shared his room with Alan. Evening meals were generally taken in the university, either in the official student restaurant situated within the main building, or in the students' union. Most Saturdays, the master, along with Balmic and Jackson, would meet up in the union bar before proceeding to the Hop. At these times, many buses were parked outside the union building, having transported young ladies from numerous teacher training colleges, as well as nurses, in order to enjoy the prospect of drinking Babycham whilst being sized up by the beery male contingent. The master on these occasions would have little difficulty in securing a dance partner, but they were not particularly disposed to taking a stroll outside the building (ostensibly to inhale clean air unsullied by cigarette smoke of which there was an abundance inside). The best lookers were invariably snatched up by those chaps who were Cliff Richard, or Elvis wannabees. The master, as you will no doubt have remembered, was in neither of these categories. Then he met Doreen. She was training to be a teacher and came complete with a Belfast accent and a well-developed bosom. He gallantly bought her a drink, and consumed his third pint of Flower's keg bitter. After the last waltz, he walked her to her bus which would transport her back to the training college in a nearby town by 12.30. She permitted him a kiss, but a tentative foray towards said bosom was swiftly counteracted.

'Keep your hands to yourself – you medical students are all the same.'

Somewhat crestfallen, the master retreated, then perked up when Doreen said, 'See you next week.'

Unfortunately the master was unable to ascertain whether it was intended as a statement or a query. They never did actually meet again. Another of life's 'what ifs'. So for the next few days, life consisted of ward work, lectures, and reading from Davidson's textbook of medicine. This included lots of weird and wonderful diseases, but when the master was asked by a passenger sitting next to him on the bus, what was the likely cause of his (the passenger's) constipation, the master racked his brains to find an answer. Could it be an under active thyroid, or Chagas' disease, which he explained was due to *Trypanosoma cruzi*, a parasite commonly found in South America?

A somewhat bemused Bert Tonks, who had never ventured further afield than West Bromwich got off at the next stop, none the wiser.

Meanwhile, back at the master's digs, Alan was doing well in his Spanish course, and would be spending three months in Madrid as part of his studies. He had acquired a pretty girl friend, called Alice, who worked in the university library. As already mentioned, he shared his bedroom with the master, which meant that when he was entertaining Alice, the master was obliged to spend his time in the sitting room. This was fine, but one Friday Alan announced that Alice would be staying over until the next day, and would the master mind sleeping on the couch in the sitting room. Gallantly, he agreed, and wouldn't have minded too much had he been able to sleep. He couldn't at first fathom out why there was so much noise emanating from the bedroom after they had retired at the extraordinarily early time of eight thirty, the excuse being that they both felt very tired. The master exercised his diagnostic skills, and wondered if Alice was in pain, but hesitated about knocking on the door to offer his assistance. The moaning went on for ages, and was occasionally punctuated by Alan shouting, 'Viva Espania – yes, yes!'

Next morning he enquired how she felt. She looked fine, possibly a little flushed and bleary eyed. Alan looked worn out, and retired back to bed after consuming a hot cup of black coffee and a cigarette. The master offered to escort Alice to the bus stop as she had to meet a friend, Alan having to cry off on account of claimed mental exhaustion. She accepted his offer, and as they walked, he asked her whether she had been unwell the previous evening, as he had heard her moaning.

'Oh, it was nothing, just a little pain in my tummy, I often get it.'

'What seems to bring it on?' persisted the master, exercising once more his diagnostic skills.

'Nothing in particular,' came the reply.

'What kind of pain is it; is it constant or intermittent; where does it start; does it go anywhere else; is it worse or better after food; is it relieved by wind; have you had any trouble with your bowels or water works, or periods?'

Mercifully, for Alice, at this point the bus arrived, and she gratefully got on it. Later that day, in the Union bar, the master discussed this interesting medical conundrum with Balmic and Jackson. Balmic (who one day would become a consultant surgeon), felt that she was suffering from gallstones. Jackson (who would finish up as a rheumatologist) said it was probably nervous dyspepsia. The master tried putting all these facts and opinions together, all derived from the intellects of the nation's *crème de la crème*, and concluded that whatever it was, it was probably not serious, judging from Alice's sprightly step and relieved look as she leaped onto the bus.

Back on the wards, the master was coming into contact with all sorts of patients. The lecture on physical examination of patients stressed the importance of inspection (of whatever part of the patient was to be examined), searching for all sorts of clues. It was a bit like a detective thriller, the doctor (or student) being Sherlock Holmes, the patient being the victim, and the disease, the murderer. The analogy fascinated the master, but had the potential for unexpected consequences.

Wednesday, the 22nd June, he was allocated Cynthia Dodderidge. It was two thirty p.m. After a tasteless lunch of soggy white bread and cress, he sauntered across from the medical school to the hospital, which lay behind, but towered over it, into the students' room, and on the board his allocation of cases to study. The ward was in the Nightingale design, which meant it was laid out like a large long room, with about twenty patients down one side, and the same down the other. Privacy (of a sort) was provided by curtains between each bed. There were no televisions, but patients had their own portable radios. Smoking in the wards was forbidden, particularly as some patients with severe chest problems were in oxygen tents. Anyway, back to Cynthia. She was rather plain, well bosomed, wore spectacles, and had been admitted for suspected ulcerative colitis. The master introduced himself, and then took her history. This was followed by the examination, and naturally, he required a chaperone. His chaperone that afternoon was Nurse Pettit, who reassured Cynthia that she had nothing to worry about.

The master commenced. First, according to his lectures, he looked at the patient, in order to detect the likelihood of anaemia (pale-inner part of lower eyelid), jaundice (yellow where the eye should be white), cyanosis (blue-where the lips should be pink), overactive thyroid (poppy eyes) plus a swelling in the neck called a goitre, breathlessness, (looking at the chest to measure the rate at which the patient was breathing), hair loss (iron deficiency). For all of these he took his time, to ensure he would not miss anything. He thought possibly she was anaemic. All these were accomplished without incident with the exception of checking the respiratory rate. The master fixed his gaze upon Cynthia's chest, the view of which was dominated by her breasts. Although nothing could be further from the truth, this gave the impression to a fly on the wall that he was a dedicated tit man. And that is precisely the impression made on Cynthia. This was the first time she had been made so aware that a young man was interested in her bosom. Cynthia was excited. She began fantasising, which naturally increased her respiratory rate; she opened her mouth, moistened her lips with her tongue, and began sighing in a most unexpected manner. Nurse Pettit felt it was time to intervene.

'I think you'd better move on to the rest of the examination,' she said.

The master, somewhat nonplussed by Cynthia's heaving chest, felt that in view of her abnormal respiratory rate, the next appropriate part of the examination would be her unclothed chest. 'Inspection, palpation, percussion, auscultation,' was the mantra to be followed. Cynthia's chest was exposed, in its entirety. I leaped into action which immediately affected the master's respiratory rate. It was almost as though Cynthia's condition was now manifesting itself on the master. Inspection was to be followed by palpation. This was in order to ascertain that both halves of the chest were moving equally. The master placed his hands beneath Cynthia's breasts, compressing the chest gently, and noting by feel and sight the degree of movement of his hands. By now I was gearing up for action. This was it! Somehow, I don't know how, I received signals from HQ not to proceed, so I regretfully resumed my initial position of repose. Percussion, this involved placing the middle finger on the chest, and tapping it with the opposite middle finger. This technique could tell whether there was fluid in the pleural cavity (the membranes surrounding the lungs), and had originally been discovered by the son of an innkeeper, who measured the level of beer in a wooden barrel by tapping the outside of the barrel. Where there was air, the sound was resonant. Where there was fluid, it was dull. Medicine owes a sincere debt of gratitude to the providers of beer, as any medical student will contend. Auscultation involved placing the stethoscope over the chest, and listening for the breath sounds. The master studiously listened left and right, front of chest and back. All normal. Likewise, he examined the heart, as taught. From here he moved on to the abdomen. Nothing much to find except the pubic hair. Again I resumed battle stations, but as before, received orders to stand down. The master completed the examination by examining her reflexes. This proceeded uneventfully, though she wondered what the heck he was playing at when he tickled the soles of her feet. The master had been taught that in patients with her complaint a more intimate examination would be required, this being called a 'PR', which stood for rectal examination. However, Nurse Pettit had been told that medical students were not permitted to carry out such an examination unless instructed and accompanied by a qualified doctor.

'Thank you, Miss Dodderidge,' the master said. 'It's been a pleasure.'

'Mine too,' replied a somewhat flushed Cynthia.

After this, the master returned to the students' room to write up her case. He was also expected to test her urine, in order to complete the examination. This proved normal. So what (who) was the murderer? Sherlock went over the evidence. The victim had noticed the frequent passage of loose stools, with mucus and blood. It had persisted for over six weeks, during which she had lost about six pounds in weight. Clearly there was something wrong with her gut, and this would require further investigation. Two avenues suggested themselves. One was to look directly through some sort of optical instrument. At that time, there were no flexible instruments, only rigid chromium plated steel weapons, the lesser of which was called a proctoscope, which could peer inside the rectum, and then the most fearful, called the rigid sigmoidoscope which was about eighteen inches long, and came complete with a parallel tube down which air could be blown by a squeezy balloon. The sigmoidoscope had a central removable solid rod called a trocar, and having been introduced up to the hilt by a skilled consultant, was then withdrawn and the inside of the colon viewed by a lens with an attached light source. Of course, and without going into too much detail, the patient would have been prepared by means of enemas, in order to permit visualization of the lining of the bowel. This was carried out the following day on the ward round.

The consultant, a bit of a showman, was accompanied by five medical students, a houseman, and a registrar, plus the ward sister. Cynthia was asked to kneel on the bed, with her bum in the air. The students, naturally were agape, but before their imagination took hold, the consultant skilfully inserted the well lubricated device inflating it as it was inserted deeper and deeper. Cynthia said 'ouch' at one point, but a little more air blown in and she was again all right. All the students were invited to peer down the instrument, which revealed several areas of bleeding and ulceration, thereby confirming the murderer. Absolutely brilliant! Up to this point. But as the scope was being removed, Cynthia let out a sonorous fart, and deposited a sizeable lump of poo on the plastic sheet.

'What a striking experience!' remarked the theatrically inclined consultant, to the admiring audience.

The ward sister reassured and cleaned her, as the curtain came down and the audience dispersed. The master thought he had completed his task for the day, but on returning to the students' room, found he had been provided with a specimen of Cynthia's poo to be tested for blood. This involved taking a small dab with a spatula and placing it on some filter paper. A tablet called 'Haematest' was then placed on the filter paper and moistened with water. A blue colour on filter paper indicated the presence of blood. Job done!

Later that evening, the master was recounting the day's events to Alan, Joe and Phil. They were absolutely fascinated by his description up to and especially his examination of Cynthia's respiratory system, but asked to stop when it came to the next day's events. They went out to the Dirty Duck, where they met up with some medics and nurses. Nurse Pettit was there and recognized the master. She came over and casually remarked that she had been impressed by his interest in the respiratory system.

She would ensure, by chatting to the registrar (her current boyfriend), that he would have another case next day. Later that night I knew the master was excited and looking forward to this prospect. I had a trial run, as manually instructed, after which he slept well.

The day dawned, and the master headed off to the ward. Eagerly he perused the notice board looking for his patient. Sure enough, there it was, but to his chagrin, it was Brian Smithers. Mr Smithers had bronchiectasis, and additionally was a heavy smoker. A deadly combination. Not only that, but his teeth were dreadful. He had killer breath, and a sputum pot by his bedside copiously filled. The master went through his routine, but needless to say, took care not to allow his apparent interest in respiratory medicine to come to the fore in future.

Came the Easter vacation, and the master travelled home to see Mum and Dad (and Brenda), and David. Brenda was still working at the hairdresser's. She was currently going steady with Vic, who was a fitter and worked at the Castle works nearby. He was somewhat overawed by the master who was wont to impress him with gory tales of his experiences so far (most of which were fictitious). Brenda, as might be expected, tried repeatedly to drag him away, looking daggers at her dear brother, 'Dr Useless', as she named him. David was doing well at school, and into making model aeroplanes. He and the master went out to the recreation ground for another flight. Having given the propeller two hundred turns, and almost torn the elastic, the model was launched into the air. It soared upwards, and began circling in a wide circle, the tail rudder having been cemented at a slight angle to reduce the chance of the plane travelling away too far. After a while, during which the two had great fun, their peace was interrupted by Carol appearing on the scene. David realised he was no longer needed, and went home. The master greeted Carol excitedly, recalling his last experience (as did I).

'Fancy a walk over the Mulberry woods?' she asked.

'Sure,' replied the master. So they crossed the road, climbed over a stile, and set off across a field, keeping close to the path near the hedge. Birds were singing, the sun made a brief appearance through the clouds, an aeroplane droned overhead.

'That's an Anson,' informed the master.

'A what?' asked Carol.

'An AVRO Anson,' replied the master.

'Oh,' replied a totally disinterested Carol.

'Two Cheetah engines,' went on my oblivious master. 'Maximum speed one hundred and eighty eight miles an hour.'

'Oh really,' interjected Carol.

She linked hands with the master, and they approached the Mulberry woods. Apparently, there had been a few such trees here many years ago, now only one was left, but it was a magnificent example, yielding wonderful lush berries, many of which were claimed by the local avian population before any humans. On they went into the wood, until they happened upon a clearing, which afforded a clear view over the fields for a distance of about five miles. The wind, which had been pleasantly breezy, slowed, then ceased. A calm descended upon the scene, punctuated by the call of a distant wood pigeon. The master put his arm around Carol, drawing her to him, then slowly planted a kiss upon her lipstick-covered lips. They lingered for a few seconds, enough for me to get into gear. This unfortunately didn't please the master who was clearly somewhat embarrassed. He then began retracing the tour he had previously carried out, to wit, the northern hills, which on this occasion required a little more detailed exploration. To this end it was necessary to unbutton her blouse. He was then faced with the obstacle of her bra, about which he knew very little. How did one remove it? There seemed no obvious button or clip on the front. He gently caressed the region whilst pondering the problem. He tried slipping his hand beneath it, but this was not possible as it was wired and he would have required wire cutters, none of which were immediately to hand. At this point he felt that an alternative strategy was required. He recalled the idea of a pincer movement which was beloved of certain army generals, so transferred his efforts to Carol's legs. By now they were lying down on a grassy slope. She was wearing nylons, as was the custom at the time. He gently placed his hand on her knee, then whilst kissing, began his advance. So far, so good.

Meanwhile, as you can imagine, I was closing the lock gates of venous return, consequently placing the threads holding the buttons of the master's fly under considerable tension. At this point, the Avro Anson made a reappearance which diverted the master's attention for a while. Carol however was none too pleased, and placed his hand back where it had been. Called back to the intended pincer movement, the hand advanced until it came upon a suspender buckle, above which naked flesh was encountered. The home straight was now reached, but before the target could be palpated (or inspected, and certainly not auscultated), Carol gripped his hand and transferred it to her breast. She sat up, and quickly undid the clip of her bra behind her back. Now it was back to inspection. Pure unblemished skin, with pert pink nipples which seemed to rise as he stroked them (palpation). Percussion and auscultation were clearly inappropriate, so he decided to plant a kiss on the aforementioned target. Carol clearly liked this, and began breathing more heavily. The master looked up anxiously wondering what the cause of her respiratory distress might be. However, Carol then starting kissing him more vigorously, and to his surprise, he found his mouth occupied by two tongues. He had never experienced this before. Neither had I, but after a minute, I had the tension on the fly buttons released by Carol, who led me into the fresh air, and transferred her tongue from the master's mouth to me. This was the most incredible sensation, and one I had never heard about, though I hoped at the time she was not feeling hungry. The master retraced his steps to the home straight. This time, no resistance was offered, and his hand encountered nirvana, the soft warm mound separated only by her panty. Unable to hold back, I despatched one hundred and fifty million swimmers loaded with DNA in a sea of fluid (courtesy of Old Walnut), into the fresh air. Carol looked on curiously; perhaps she had never done this before. The master was profoundly embarrassed, and apologised.

'It's all right, Harry, I mean, Pablo, just letting nature take its course. But I'm still a virgin, and intend staying one until I marry. It's in the Bible, though the Bible doesn't seem to mind heavy petting.'

Later that evening, having seen Carol home, the master returned to his, somewhat flushed. Sol asked him where he had been, hinting that a fast walk in the country was very creditable and healthy, and he wished he could do it more often, but unfortunately his arthritic knees no longer permitted. The master saw no reason to inform him otherwise. But Brenda was more observant, noticing the tell-tale of lipstick on his collar.

'I know what you've been up to, and you don't get red marks on your collar from brisk walking. I think he's been seeing that Carol, Dad.'

But Sol wasn't interested, by this stage busily filling in his football pool coupon. He dreamed every night of winning seventy five thousand pounds on Littlewoods.

'Shut up, Brenda,' the master retorted. 'I've no doubt you get up to a thing or two. Who is the unlucky chap at the present?'

'It's Percival Mildmay, and he's hoping to be a priest. He told me that God would forgive everyone their sins, if they would believe that Jesus had died for them. So now we go the whole hog, knowing we are saved – it's a great religion, you should try it.'

'What is this hog thing?' asked Sol, pricking up his ears at what sounded like potentially sacrilegious food (and therefore interesting).

'Oh nothing that would interest you, Dad,' replied Brenda.

This was news to the master, it sounded great, and he had read the Bible. What was less clear was whether this belief would work if you committed the same sin repeatedly, say about three times a week, which he reckoned would just about deal with his cravings. It just so happened that young Percy called round the same evening to ask Brenda out. Before they could depart, the master introduced himself to the hopeful man of God, and asked him about sin and forgiveness. Brenda rolled her eyes, but the master persisted.

'So if God is so great at forgiveness, the pathway ticket to Heaven being Jesus' death on the cross, would the same forgiveness cover pre-marital, repeated sex?'

Percy went bright scarlet, mumbled something about the profound mysteries of the Holy Spirit, and words to the effect that 'God moves in mysterious ways his wonders to perform', before escaping with a furious Brenda clinging on. Meanwhile, later that evening the master retired to bed where he lay quietly thinking things over. He was not alone. I, together with Bill and Ben, plus Old Walnut held a committee meeting. We clearly had a potential crisis on our hands. Pre-marital sexual intercourse, which as we all know, was discovered in Britain about 1962, presented this profound religious conundrum. And if forgiveness was there for the asking, all one would need was the faith, and a condom. Or, to be safer, two condoms. And then, like a bolt from the blue, on 25th November 1962, on the Home Service (radio of course), was broadcast the Reith lecture, by an eminent psychiatrist George Carstairs. In the media, the nub of the lecture was of 'charity before chastity', and the fact that in certain societies, sex before marriage was the norm, and everyone was happy. This certainly held true for Samoa, but the master and his friends didn't live in Samoa.

The master returned to uni where he revisited the discussion with Alan, Joe and Phil. Alan said it didn't really matter, as he was an atheist. Joe said he hadn't given it much thought. Girls didn't really interest him. At this, the master, Alan and Phil expressed surprise. How could this be? They didn't entertain the idea of homosexuality, as this was regarded at the time as a rare perversion, as well as a crime. But they needn't have worried, as within a few weeks Joe would meet Alison and fall head over heels. The master took all this in, whilst pursuing his studies, and nurses (without much success), he would have to realise that qualified doctors definitely had the edge where the nurses were concerned.

The next major event was the master's twenty-first. Balmic and Jackson suggested that they would help organise it in their digs, which were larger than that of the master and his flatmates, who of course would also be invited. Preparations went ahead. They ordered a pin of Flower's keg bitter, plus crates of Ansell's bottled beer. Canned beer was not yet available. Jackson was the proud owner of an HMV radiogram which played records of all sizes and speeds, and was a cut above most small record players of the time as far as sound quality was concerned. Joe, Phil, Balmic and Jackson invited a group of physiotherapy students, a couple of nurses from the wards that the master was currently on, and a couple of the landlady's daughters. There was a small garden at the rear, with a barbecue. They rigged up a few lights, moved the radiogram to the opened French window, turned up the volume, and accompanied by Kenny Ball's jazzmen, the party got under way. 'Midnight in Moscow' was good for a ballroom jive, and Acker Bilk's 'Stranger on the Shore' just for listening (or smooching). The master was the proud recipient of some thoughtful gifts, to wit said Acker Bilk record from Balmic, a crate of Double Diamond, jointly provided and consumed by Alan, Joe and Phil, and a tie from Balmic. The master hadn't invited Carol because she would have needed to stay over, and the sleeping arrangements were, as yet, totally undecided. Among the guests however, he spied a rather serious looking nurse, who wore some unprepossessing glasses. Her hair was long and tidy, she had a willowy figure and nice legs (noted when she twirled round whilst jiving). She had a peaches and cream complexion, pink lipstick and a pretty smile. Perhaps it was the glasses which made her less desirable to the gathered ensemble, but the master prided himself on recognising quiet talent, and asked her to dance. Due enquiry, during the dance which was a waltz, revealed her identity as Josephine, and that she came from Shrewsbury, her dad ran a newsagent's, her mum was a trained nurse, and she hoped eventually to do midwifery. She had a nice perfume, and the master was quite taken. But when she took off her glasses and wandered off to powder her nose, on her return, still without glasses she was snapped up by Alan, much to the annoyance of Alice. The evening wore on, the pin of Flowers keg was emptied, the various drinks were consumed, Phil was sick in the loo, and all in all it was a pretty successful party. Alice succeeded in regaining Alan, and the master arranged a date with Josephine for the following week. Finally, by two o'clock, the partygoers dispersed.

Back at uni, the master came to the end of his three months of medical clerking, and this was followed by what was called 'surgical dressing'. This involved taking histories from patients as before, but the big difference was that they were due for an operation, and the students would go into theatre to watch. This was tremendously exciting, but a very strict protocol had to be observed. Students could actually assist in the operations. First they donned a cap, then pulled on a mask. Then they changed into theatre clothes, which were a dark green colour. White rubber boots were worn, and then they would have to scrub up. This involved washing their hands and arms very carefully before donning a large gown the tabs of which were tied up behind them by a nurse. Finally, came the donning of sterile rubber gloves. The whole process was time consuming, and initially technically difficult. Several times students were made to repeat the process because they had inadvertently touched something, and were therefore no longer sterile. But finally they were permitted into the arena, and observed the surgeon at work. The first operation was a partial gastrectomy, in which the surgeon was going to remove part of the stomach which contained an ulcer. The master watched fascinated as the scalpel was drawn vertically down slightly to left of centre. Bleeding was stopped by an electric cauteriser, which left the smell of singed flesh, much like grilled steak. To his horror, the master's sense of appetite was aroused. The master was asked to cut the stitches tied by the registrar who was assisting the consultant. The master found it a fascinating experience, but equally fascinating was looking at the nurses concealed behind their caps and masks. Thus concealed, and only their general defined shape, and eyes to be seen, they appeared sexy, mysterious and very appealing. However, with some exceptions, when, after the operations were over, and the same nurse removed her mask, the resulting impression was disappointing. There certainly appeared to be some rhyme and reason in keeping oneself hidden, and using the power of the eyes to entice, bewitch and ensnare.

At the end of the list was an operation to remove varicose veins. The surgeon would make a cut near the groin, then pass a long rod down the main vein, as far as just above the ankle. At the top end, the rod had a cone shaped attachment which rested just above the cut end of the vein. The student was then entrusted with the climax to this operation, which consisted of gripping the end of the rod which had emerged above the ankle, and simply walking away! The cone at the top gripped the vein and as it moved down, it concertinaed the vein which then came free as the student continued his walk.

Surgery was amazing, but also at times, exhausting. A session could last four hours or more, non-stop, and for large periods the student had to pull on a retractor to keep the incision wide open for the surgeon to see what he was doing. And this was under the heat of a powerful lamp. Then, one day, the last operation on the list was a circumcision. It was to be performed on a young man, because of recurrent inflammation in that area. The surgeon, under general anaesthesia would carry it out. Not a rabbi in sight! The master watched, but I was somewhat traumatised as it brought back old memories. However, I needn't have worried. Thanks to general anaesthesia, the patient had a painless rite of passage, though he seemed to be triumphant by sporting an enormous erection as he was being wheeled out of the theatre completely oblivious to the sideways glances of the nurses.

For two months the master pursued his surgical studies, always fascinated by the way the patient's body could be laid open, resembling a body ravaged by sword or axe on the field of battle, yet then be carefully reassembled layer by layer, stitch after stitch, followed by a puff of collodion spray, the application of a dressing, then to return to the ward. Unfortunately this required possession of a detailed knowledge of anatomy, which the master, try as he might, could never muster. If he were to be a surgeon, it would be like driving a car in a foreign city without a map – goodness knows where he would end up.

Came Saturday, and the master arranged to meet up with Balmic and Jackson at the Dirty Duck, before going for a curry in town. The Shah Bagh did a half decent biryani for ten bob, and then on to the hop at the student's union. By the time he arrived his bladder was bursting, so he paid a visit to the loos. I had a look round, Armitage Shanks as usual, but the VD sign had gone. Instead something alluding to 'Sexually transmitted disease', whatever that was. The usual short-lived dizziness as the master performed the ritual twiddle, put me back in my pouch, and back to the dance. The evening followed the customary ritual, as the stockmasters reviewed the stock, eying them up and assessing their potential, not as beef cattle, but more as bed rattle. However, nothing much was acquired by Balmic, Jackson or the master, and at the end of the evening, they went their separate ways. The master unfortunately was once again dispossessed of his bed by Alan who was entertaining Alice. This time he was able to diagnose with more precision the cause of the sounds that shortly after emanated from the bedroom, having been informed, after due enquiry, by Balmic a few weeks previously.

The next week, the three medical students began their 'specials'. This consisted of a few weeks of ear, nose and throat, known as 'ENT', psychiatry, gynaecology, ophthalmology and obstetrics. ENT consisted largely of patients having their sinuses washed out, and the occasional mastoid operation when antibiotics failed. The houseman on ENT appeared to have a permanently blocked nose, but clearly didn't have it seen to. The consultant wore a wing collar, dark pin-striped suits, and drove a pre-war Rolls-Royce. Psychiatry was an altogether different kettle of fish. The master read in depth all he could lay his hands on, struggling with the concept of neurosis and psychosis. And schizophrenia was extremely puzzling.

As part of the course, students had a week of psychiatry. The venue was Broadfields Hospital, a large forbidding Victorian redbrick institution. On day one, the master turned up at nine o'clock, and together with three other students was told he would have to interview a patient in the psychiatric ward. He was somewhat taken aback as the entrance to the ward was locked. However, the psychiatric nurse, Herbert Bolsover (known affectionately as 'Herballs') let the students in. What regaled them was truly horrific. Suddenly they were transmitted from the latter part of the twentieth century to an earlier age. The ward was huge, and some patients were walking about muttering and wringing their hands. Others were sat on the floor, rolling up their eyes. Some were drooling at their mouths. Some lay mute, staring at the ceiling. Some were grimacing in a most alarming way.

'He's been here since 1925,' announced Herballs.

All around was the smell of urine, and carbolic, and fresh paint on hot radiators. Most patients wore pyjamas, some with dark stains. This truly appeared to be Dante country.

'Right, Bernstein, you will be interviewing Mr Macpherson in the secure ward,' announced Herballs.

And so saying, another door was unlocked, and the master entered a single room.

'Good morning, Mr Macpherson,' said the master.

'Hello,' came the reply.

'And what seems to be the matter,' almost casually asked the master.

'I don't know, and I don't think the doctors know either. All I know is that I have this strong urge to kill someone whenever they mention Tyrone's tea.'

'Tyrone's what?' stupidly asked his lordship.

I cringed, and would have legged it if at all possible.

'My Uncle Tyrone, was very dear to me, but it's my belief my Aunt Rianna, God rest her soul, poisoned him so that she could marry that bastard Ronan O'Malley. Well anyway, I heard these voices telling me to avenge my dear uncle, so I took a bread knife to Rianna's throat. If only it had been a decent knife made in Ireland, it might have done the job, but unfortunately it was made in Sheffield and was as blunt as my nob.'

I took this as a sort of insult since, to the best of my knowledge, it was perfectly normal for me and my ilk to be blunt in form. I had no wish to be sharp, certainly not as sharp as an Irish knife.

'So, you're going to be a doctor?'

'Yes, hopefully.'

'Well, if I was you, I'd become a psychiatrist. You know psychiatry is very fascinating, and deals with all sorts of people, some are really mad. I know, because I've seen them – right outside this door. That's why I stay in my office here, it's to protect myself, but one day, when I get a decent Irish knife, I think I'll put an end to their misery. There's a new drug just come out, you might have heard of it. It's called Largactil, and believe me, that ward is much quieter now than it used to be.'

At this point the door was unlocked, and Herballs told the master his time was up.

'Thank you, Mr Macpherson, you've been most helpful. I hope you get better soon.'

'What do you mean, get better. I'm as right as nine pence, it's them out there.'

The next week, the students were to spend ten days, accommodation included, in a special institution which specialised in dealing with depression, eating disorders, and various neuroses. The students would take case histories, and discuss them at the mid-morning meetings, over coffee and biscuits. The principal doctor was a cheerful man, Dr Hartman. The atmosphere was altogether different from that of Broadfields. One of the doctors, a registrar name of Dr Sambrook, seemed a bit odd, possibly somewhat cynical about his role. Each week, there was a social evening, at which patients and medical and nursing staff intermingled. There was dancing to a record of the Victor Sylvester Orchestra, and for a bit more excitement, to Xavier Cougat. The master was somewhat hesitant about all this, because he had had impressed upon him the need to keep a professional distance between oneself and one's patients. So he was a bit surprised when Dr Sambrook suggested to him that he 'grab a hysteric, and dance the night away'. After the social, at which he did dance with a couple of patients old enough to be his mother, he left to go to his room. To his surprise, after a few minutes, there was a knock at the door. He opened it, and found a rather plain, intense nurse, whose room was next door, asking him to help as she had locked herself out. Would he mind getting out of his window and crawling along the ledge, then into her room and letting her in. The master went to his window and peered out. The ledge was only about one foot wide, and about twenty feet above ground. He weighed up the odds of carrying out her wishes, which no doubt would make him a hero in her eyes, or falling to his death or worse. He decided to play safe, and declined the tempting offer. To his surprise, she suddenly found that her key was in one of her pockets which she never usually used for this but had quickly put it there when her bedside phone had rung.

'Anyway, come in for a cup of coffee.'

The master accepted her kind offer, and entered. She told him she thought he danced very well, and would he like to dance with her. She had a Frank Sinatra 33rpm record, which she placed on the turntable of her Dansette, and reached out for the master. 'Strangers in the night', was soon followed by 'It happened in Monterey'. Soon it was happening right in her room, and I received the call to action stations. The dancing was slow and sensual, as the three of us moved in time to the music. The master started to kiss Marjorie on her neck, then transferred his attentions to her lips. She responded vigorously, and once again, he found his mouth contained two tongues. Without further ado, the master undid her bra, having found out from Alan that the trick was to grasp the buckle from behind, and give it a quick twist. Soon her breasts were being gently caressed, and his hand slid down to her thigh which was moving sinuously around his. Then, an up and under her dress, stocking, buckle, then bare thigh and panty edge. What now? The decision was taken from him, as she moved away, and quickly removed her dress. Her breasts were small but pert, with erect nipples which were just asking to be kissed. At this stage, the master was beginning to feel somewhat damp, and I suspected Old Walnut had jumped the gun, but I needn't have worried, he was just tuning up. Marjorie started removing the master's shirt. He quickly got nude, and she gave a clear look of approval at me. She lay down on the bed, and pulled the master onto her. Curiously she produced a condom which she applied expertly. He knew what to do, or so he thought, but found there was no entrance for me. In his mind's eye, it would be at the apex of the triangle (in a trigonometric sense) of her pubic hair, but after a bit of shufftying round, found it about two inches nearer the bed. This was rather awkward, but Marjorie obliged by adjusting her position, re-aligning the angles so that the rocket could attain a more effective trajectory. The way was now clear, and I was duly directed into the *avenue'd'amour*, or tunnel of love.

Now I had the opportunity to prove my worth. But the master didn't know whether he was expected to park me, job done, or adopt an in and out movement, or side to side gently. First he tried the last mentioned, but Marjorie said, 'Couldn't you be a bit more violent?'

So 'violent' it was! In and out went the piston, with Bill and Ben hanging on for dear life. Finally, Old Walnut provided the '*coup de grace*', and peace descended. Marjorie meanwhile had been making Alice-like sounds, which made the master look at her anxiously lest she be torn apart. But she appeared unharmed by the activity, if somewhat flushed. The master felt that a milestone in his life had been reached. At last he had joined the high plateau of manhood. Marjorie told him she was feeling tired, and thought he should go. She didn't make any comments as to the excellence or otherwise of the performance, which left the master somewhat unsure as to how he would be judged.

The next evening, whilst deeply involved in reading about hysteria, he heard the unmistakeable sounds of Alice-like noises coming from next door. Curious, he waited until he heard her door opening. He decided to 'coincidentally' go out to see what was afoot, only to see a somewhat breathless Dr Sambrook leaving.

'So, Nurse,' he said, 'I hope you understand the Freudian approach to bed-wetting.'

'Yes, Dr Sambrook, you have been most informative on that score,' replied Marjorie, ignoring the master, before closing her door. Life can be hard.

After psychiatry came gynaecology. Students were told to report to Lime Oak Hospital at nine a.m. Monday morning. They were allotted various clinics, the first of which was under the care of an elderly consultant with an Australian accent. He had a moustache and smoked continuously. The master watched in awe as he carried out an intimate examination, having donned a rubber glove. Having carried it out, he washed his gloved hand, and wrote up his findings in her notes. Meanwhile, he used the same hand to hold his cigarette. Next patient, and the same hand and the same glove were washed, lubricant applied, and an intimate examination performed. Thus went the morning, but then the master was told it was his turn to don a glove, and examine the next lady. Any thoughts in my direction were utterly extinguished in the cold light of clinical reality, plus the fact that said patient was aged eighty-five. She had a prolapse, which meant she needed to have her Hodge pessary removed, and replaced by a new one. The master inserted his two fingers, and was astonished how warm and roomy it was. He felt the pessary, gripped it and removed it as instructed.

'Well done, Bernstein,' said the consultant, Mr Seelig Parker, who then unwrapped a new pessary, and skilfully inserted it. He then turned to his group of three students and asked whether any of them had performed a vaginal examination before. At this point, Jeremy Halliday, who frequently boasted of his sexual exploits, asked Mr Seelig Parker whether the question referred to the social or clinical scenario. At this, Mr SP told him to perform a rectal examination, as well as a vaginal one. Young Parker began by inserting his gloved finger into the patient's rectum, and then, having stated that he thought it was normal, approached the vagina with the same glove.

'Don't ever insult the vagina by doing a rectal examination first,' he was reprimanded by SP.

Halliday turned scarlet, his earlier quip having made him the target of one of SP's popular aphorisms.

Students also had to assist in the operating theatre, where as previously, many mysterious nurses were viewed whilst wearing their masks. But gynaecology was only half of what was expected. Every student also had to deliver twenty-one babies. The course included lectures on the whole process which basically involved the clever way in which the mother manoeuvred her babe through a narrow tortuous passage, to emerge into the world. Such twists and turns made the master wonder why many women found difficulty in parking cars, and navigating. He surmised that perhaps their brains were hard wired to more important manoeuvres.

Another year passed with exams in pharmacology (drug prescribing, and their effects, both beneficial and harmful), psychiatry, eyes, ears, skin – it seemed never ending. Forensic medicine was taught by an amazing bald-headed professor possessed of eyes that could simultaneously look in two different directions, and register both images – much to the cost of any student whose attention wandered and assumed the professor's gaze was directed elsewhere. It was essentially a pretty gory topic, most of which held the students in thrall. The lectures were illustrated by ghoulish images in black and white (PowerPoint hadn't been dreamt of).

And then, with terrifying inevitability, final exams loomed. The medical school library was filled with students whose textbooks were opened and supported at forty-five degrees by other books. Surgery was studied mainly using Bailey and Love's text, whereas medicine was studied using Davidson's. Only the truly encyclopaedic personality would use Cecil and Loeb's huge tome. During this time, I and the other fifty or so in the master's year were hibernating. How to examine a heart, how to test for a hernia, how to elicit reflexes to the satisfaction of one's qualified mentors. By now I was deeply in narcosis.

Came the day. The written papers, lots of them, three hours each. One down, five to go! 'How would you manage a man of fifty-five years presenting in casualty with chest pain?' The answer: 'Go home and take a couple of aspirins,' would fail in 1962, but might not be so wide of the mark in 2013. Of course the master and his colleagues would by now have mastered the art of interpreting an electrocardiogram, and if it indicated a heart attack, then pain relief would permit the legal prescribing of heroin.

'How would you manage a lady of thirty years presenting with pain on the right side of the abdomen?'

'Just like I would a lady with pain on the left side,' might sound frivolous, but in fact would be correct. Or would it?

By now, I'm out of here. Haven't had a stretch in weeks, might as well sign up for the priesthood. And still it goes on.

'How would you treat a patient with pneumonia?'

'How would you treat an overactive thyroid?'

'What factors pre-dispose to peptic ulcer? How would you manage a bleed from one?'

Oh God, it's going on forever. And next, the clinicals. Real patients. A long case, and then three short cases. The master was assigned Mr Juggins, aged seventy-five.

'Good morning, Mr Juggins. What seems to be the matter?'

'Oh I do like a bit of a natter,' came the reply.

'Well, what have they been treating you for?'

'They said I'd got intestinal corruption, but before that I had gastric stomach, and last year, cardiac heart. It started after I was gassed in the war.'

Oh dear, things weren't going so well. Just then, a pretty nurse looked in.

'I see you've got Mr Juggins,' she said. 'How's he getting on after his stroke?'

This was the clue the master needed, and quick as a flash, he asked some pretty nifty questions, tapped a few reflexes, tickled his toes, and wrote down his findings. Finally, he tested the man's urine, and found some sugar. At this point, the examiners parted the curtain.

'Have you completed your examination, Bernstein?' one of them enquired.

'Yes, sir,' the master replied.

'All right then, tell me all about him.'

So the master set about the whole business, then when asked to demonstrate the signs, did a pretty slick exposé of his ability at eliciting reflexes. Finally, he scratched Mr Juggins' soles, and gratifyingly found that whereas one big toe pointed down, as is the case in health, the other shot skywards, as in patients whose same side has been affected by a stroke.

'Positive Babinski,' said the master confidently.

'Very good,' replied the examiner. 'And who was Babinski?'

At this, the master went pale

'A Russian physician of the nineteenth century,' he guessed.

'Actually, he was French, but you're right, he was born in the nineteenth century.'

And then, some short cases. First a young lady who seemed to be giving the master the eye. I felt a sense of revival for the first time in weeks, but all it was, was that she had poppy eyes, due to an overactive thyroid. Her fast pulse, and generalised excitability were not due to having the hots for the master. Oh well, go back to sleep. Then a lady with deformed hands due to rheumatoid arthritis. 'What would be the treatment?'

'High dose aspirin, sir.'

'Quite correct. And if that failed, then what?'

'Wax baths, and gold injections.'

'Excellent.'

'Now listen to this chap's heart.'

The master got out his stethoscope, and placed it over the left side of the patient's chest. No sound. Tried again. No sound. Felt the chest to see if he could feel the impulse of the heart. Nothing. The patient didn't look dead, nor like an alien with a robotic heart. The master felt at a loss.

'Try the other side of the chest,' suggested the examiner. Now the master could hear the heartbeat.

'Dextrocardia, sir,' he said.

'Quite right,' came the reply. 'His heart's not in the right place, but I'm sure he's a perfectly nice guy.'

Came the day, one week later, for the results. Balmic and Jackson both felt certain they had failed. Balmic hadn't heard a murmur of his patient's heart, because he had failed to switch his stethoscope on properly. However he then redeemed himself on another patient by hearing a murmur which the examiners hadn't been told about before, but which when they checked, was indeed there. Jackson had initially diagnosed a lump in the abdomen of his patient as cancer, but was corrected by the patient who told him that, as a result of his investigations, he had been told by his consultant that it was due to crap, not cancer.

A clerk appeared from the dean's office at precisely four o'clock. Groups of ten or so students came forward to read the results. Those that said anything preceded by 'Referred in -----' had failed in that particular subject and would have to sit again in September. But, judging from the whoops and screams (from the females), most had passed. And that included the master and his two mates. Two students, namely Oliver Anderson and Anne Catchpole had the word 'Distinction' after their names. They were clearly destined for greatness. Oliver would finish up a professor of anaesthetics, and Anne would found a hospital in Chad. Balmic had already been offered a house job in surgery in the marble halls of the teaching hospital, whilst Jackson would be doing six months of medicine in Mansfield. As for the master, he hadn't yet secured a job, preferring to see if he passed. Thus, all the most popular jobs were spoken for, and he finished up doing surgery in Wolverhampton. The hospital, known as 'The Royal' was situated on the Cleveland Road, a pretty dodgy part of town. However, all this was to follow. Today, they had passed their exams, and would be provisionally registered with the General Medical Council. All being well, provided they didn't blot their copybooks, they would be fully registered practitioners of medicine in one year's time. The master was excited, as was I, what with the prospect of marriage, now that the big hurdle (career) had been cleared. But to whom? That was the question.

However, tonight they were going to celebrate. Straight to the students' union bar, and a few beers. And then a few more. They got chatting to a group of nurses two of whom worked on a medical ward at the marble halls, and the other, a cousin of one was home on holiday visiting her parents, and worked in a hospital in Gateshead. She was possessed of a broad Geordie accent.

'Well, lads, noo tha you're doctors Ah expect you'll be looking fre a wifie.'

I leaped to action stations. She wasn't bad looking, generous lips, curly brown hair, nice northern uplands, legs a bit stout. But the master wasn't giving anything away.

'And what's your name, bonnie lass?'

'Jacqueline,' came the reply.

'What you drinking?'

'Ah'll ha a wee Babycham,' she said.

'What aboot a wee baby instead?' quipped the master. Action stations immediately, red alert, awaiting her response. What a dare? Obviously the alcohol had made him lose all his inhibitions.

'Ah'll ha the Babycham first, and then we'll see aboot that.'

And so the evening progressed, a quickstep, a bit of rock and roll, then a smoochy waltz. I could feel the proximity of Jacqueline's front, yes that part. The master's right thumb was gently approaching the foothills of the uplands, I was making a valiant step forwards to be recognised, which Jacqueline didn't seem to mind at all. I was quite enjoying this; in fact before I knew it, I was hard up against the enemy. Dancing at this point became technically rather difficult, so they decided to take a breath of fresh air outside.

'So what kind'a doctor do ya want to be? Are yer goin ter bee a famous surgeon?'

The master remembering his profound knowledge, or lack of, anatomy, informed her that this was very unlikely, as physicians and in particular consultant physicians were the supreme intelligentsia, whereas surgeon chappies were mere technicians. On the other hand, if she would like him to become a surgeon, she might consider helping him along with his knowledge of anatomy which was a little rusty at present.

'Ah might consider it. Which particular bit o'mah body might you be interested in?' she innocently asked.

The master considered this carefully. Some strategy was now required. To cut to the chase and say that he needed to see her whole naked body before deciding would appear a little obvious, so instead he said that the wrist was of considerable interest because a lot of people suffered from carpal tunnel syndrome. He thought he could work from there.

'What's so interestin' aboot a wrist?' she enquired.

'Well, the wrist contains a lot of interesting structures. Have you ever wondered what is involved in waving goodbye to a person? No, I don't expect you have, well now is your chance.'

And with that, the master turned on his heel, and walked away. He was feeling tired, and didn't expect much in the way of progress with the admittedly pretty Geordie lass.

MAUREEN

Maureen Aspinall had left Blaguegate Wesleyan Methodist School, Liverpool Road, Skelmersdale aged sixteen and got a job as an assistant in a newsagent's. Two years later, her life and that of Pablo had crossed when they met in Blackpool. Despite their intentions at their first meeting, although Maureen had kept her part, Pablo hadn't replied to her letter. Now five more years had passed. Pablo was a doctor, Maureen was unhappily married to a drunkard, name of John Robertson. They had married in haste, and Maureen delivered a little boy five months later, whom they called Cliff, no doubt as a salutation to Cliff Richard. John worked down the mine, but on pay day, in 1963, he would receive the princely sum of eight pounds which for the most part served to quench his thirst for John Smith's. Having consumed nine pints, he would stagger home with the intention of putting my counterpart to work. Unsurprisingly his three-inch torpedo remained a three-inch limp twig which wasn't going anywhere. Maureen tried to feign sleep on these occasions, as he could become violent in his frustration, and blamed her. Things went from bad to worse, and Maureen frequently explained her appearance by a propensity for colliding with fictitious doors. In desperation she wrote to Pablo's address which she came across as she was packing to leave. She went to stay with her mother in Skipton, together with

174

Cliff, now aged four. Her letter went to Pablo's home address in Shropshire, which he visited for a weekend prior to taking up his first house job in Wolverhampton. Sol at this time was unwell, having angina, and had been warned to stop smoking.

The master got off the train, and caught a bus to his family's home. There he was greeted with a whoop of joy from his mum. David asked him if doctors were rich, because if so, he would consider becoming one. The master informed him that his first month's pay would be an anticipated twenty-eight pounds, though admittedly there would be free board and lodging at the hospital. Brenda said that in her opinion all doctors were quacks, as none had been able to stop her having acne, which she blamed for her inability to get a handsome boyfriend. Instead she was currently being escorted by Bill Jameson, a pleasant enough chap who was happy enough to accompany Brenda when told to do so, buy her drinks when told to do so, kiss her when told to do so, but would not do any other of her bidding, being a staunch Christian, and strangely unaware of the get out of jail free card as stated in John 3 verse 16. He had become Vic's replacement, mainly out of Brenda's spite, in order to make Vic jealous. It would not last long however. Sol remained in his armchair, and gave the master a wan smile. He looked pale, and was breathing heavily. Clearly he was a sick man. The master asked him what the doctors had told him.

'They say I've got vagina, and it's due to my smoking Woodbines. I've always smoked them, and I've cut down to twenty a day from forty.'

His nicotine stained fingers told their tale.

'Actually it's angina,' the master informed his dad. 'You'll ruin your life if you don't stop smoking completely.'

'But, *mein Gott*, it helps me get rid of the phlegm every morning, really.'

There was no reasoning with him, he was a man on a mission to the hereafter. Later that day the master went for a short walk with his mother, in order to try and advise her how to advise Sol. But when they caught sight of Carol who was taking her dog for a walk, Martha told him it was OK for him to go over and speak to her.

'Hello, Carol, I'm just back for the weekend,' he informed her.

'Sorry about your dad,' she replied. 'He is such a nice man. I hope he gets better soon. What are you doing these days? Are you a doctor yet?'

'As a matter of fact I am, I'll be starting next week at the Royal in Wolverhampton. How about you, what have you been up to?'

'I've just got a job at the local newspaper. I deal with the small ads – not very exciting. I hope one day to be a reporter.'

'Would you like to go to the pictures, *South Pacific* is on at the Clifton?' asked the master (all thoughts of his ailing dad being ignored, and regarded as not keeping up with the times). The answer being in the affirmative, they arranged to meet outside the cinema the following evening at six thirty.

Back home the Bernsteins were being visited by the Goldfarbs who had heard about Sol's poor state of health, and had made the journey down from Liverpool. Martha had prepared tea for the visitors. 'Take this tray of sandwiches in, Harry,' said his mother.

As he was doing this, he passed through the hall en-route to the living room when he caught sight of a letter on the hall table. It bore the post-mark 'Skipton'. The master was puzzled, he didn't to his knowledge have any connections with Skipton. He picked up the letter and put it into his pocket, then proceeded to pass the tray of sandwiches round. David and Brenda were also helping, Brenda with bowls of crisps, and David with beef sausage rolls.

'Come on, Mrs Goldfarb,' said the master, trying to cheer her up.

'Oh, but your dad is such a lovely man,' she sobbed. 'He is a real gentleman. Let us hope, God willing, he will get better.'

Making an excuse that he had some urgent mail to attend to, the master went out into the garden, and took the letter out of his pocket. Carefully he opened it.

Dear Pablo,

I expect you'll be surprised that I'm writing to you after all this time. I often think of you, but unfortunately I made a terrible mistake, and now I am so miserable I just felt I had to tell someone. I'm married to a real monster of a man who gets drunk every Friday night and beats me up. I'm really desperate, and I've run away. I have a little boy, Cliff, who is four years old, and great. I'm staying with my mum, Elsie Cotter, in Skipton. I remember how nice you were when we met in Blackpool, I just feel the need to talk to someone. I expect you think I'm just a silly little girl who has got herself into a mess. Well you are right. But what can I do? Can we meet somewhere? Though I must admit, I've got very little money for travelling. Did you manage to be a doctor? Perhaps you could drive over – I know I've got a cheek asking, but I really am low. My address is: 45 Mill Lane, Skipton, Yorkshire. I would love to see you.

Yours truly, Maureen (and Cliff)

PS My mum has a telephone, and the number is Skipton 439.'

The master's head was reeling. On the one hand, he felt a need to comfort this poor lass (who he remembered was rather pretty), but on the other hand, she came with considerable baggage. He might be letting himself in for more than he could chew, and right at the time when he was setting out on his career. But there was the matter that he didn't possess a car. He had thought about it, but didn't have enough money. Perhaps he could buy one on the never-never, but the lenders might not be overly impressed by his annual salary of six hundred and seventy-five pounds. Anyway, he thought, it was worth a try. So next morning, he sauntered down to the Waverley Garage to see what was on offer. A cheerful salesman accosted him the moment he walked through the door.

'Nice morning,' the slick suited young salesman said. 'What can I interest you in? You look like you'd fancy a nice little sporty two seater, just the job for attracting the girls. We've just taken delivery of a lovely little Austin Healey Sprite.'

The master looked at it, and it seemed to be returning his gaze, with a cheeky smile. It really was beguiling with its two bulbous headlights, which were to eventually make it known as the 'Frogeye Sprite'. He sat in it, and imagined himself racing down a winding country road with Carol, the wind whipping up her skirt, his hand on the gear lever and likely to stray. I let him know that, in my opinion, this was just the car for him.

'How much are you asking for it?'

'Four hundred pounds.'

The master thought for a moment, then did the maths and found that with a bit of juggling, and with the increase in pay from six hundred and seventy-five to seven hundred and fifty pounds in his second job after six months, assuming he didn't get struck off the Medical Register by the General Medical Council, he might just stretch to it.

'OK,' he said, and eventually found himself planning a visit up north.

So the master agreed to buy the car on hire purchase. He had fifty pounds saved, and could just afford twelve pounds a month for three years. He completed the application forms, and was told the car would be ready the following Monday. When he told his mother and David, they were full of admiration. Brenda forecast that he would probably kill himself in it, and thereby save lots of patients' lives. What a little charmer she was!

Saturday evening, and he met Carol outside the Clifton cinema. Mitzi Gaynor and Rossano Brazzi were the stars. The film was very entertaining, and as they emerged, the master suggested they have a bite. The Wing Wang was the only place open, and they enjoyed their meal. They had to rush to catch their bus home, and the master walked Carol to her door.

'You can come in if you like. My mum and dad are away at her sister's in Hull this weekend.'

'OK,' replied the master.

She made him a cup of coffee and they settled on the settee. It was a brown leatherette version, circa 1946, well worn, but should last for ever. She snuggled up to him, and he pulled her close before planting a kiss on her cherry pink lips. She sighed and kissed him back passionately inserting her tongue inside his cheek and her little finger in his ear. It was as though an electric shock ran through him, and I was on fire. The rest was a bit of a blur, but all I can remember is a bit of fumbling by the master, followed by me being wrapped tightly in a latex suit. Now I couldn't see a thing, but I got the gist of it by the way I did the Cresta run, ricocheting from side to side, until after a relatively short time I was as about as hard as blancmange. It was all over. The master relaxed and closed his eyes. I was puzzled, and by now my previously tightly fitted suit was several sizes too large.

'Is that it?' she enquired.

'Is what it?' asked the master somewhat puzzled, under the illusion he had done what nature intended with consummate ease.

'Well yes,' he said.

'Pablo, I've no doubt you'll be a good doctor, but when it comes to sex, you've got a lot to learn. Anyway, I've got a headache, so you'd better be going now.'

'Why are you being like this?' asked the master.

'You obviously don't know how to please a girl. I've had far better before. Close the door behind you. Bye.'

The master couldn't believe his ears. I didn't know. Was it something I'd done? Was it something I'd not done? Was it something he'd done? It was time to hit the books.

He'd heard about a certain Dr Kinsey, an American doctor who did a lot of research, and later Masters and Johnson, who had researched just about everything known about sex, and a lot that wasn't generally known. Perhaps the master had *'ejaculatio praecox'*, whatever that was. Anyhow, whichever way you looked at it, I had clearly let him down. I felt really dejected. I wondered what was my history, as apart from the history of man and woman. What was my culture, as apart from that of nations and religions? What was my purpose in the greater meaning of Life? Why wasn't I represented in woman? Or was I, in some other guise? Of course, one assumed the master knew all about it. After all, he had graduated as a doctor.

The following Monday, the master hastened to the Waverley garage to take delivery of the Sprite. It looked really lovely as it reflected the sun from its red paint, its chrome grille, its bumper, but above all, it looked at him with its headlights, and it was love at first (well second) sight. He walked around it, marvelling at how smooth was its rear, and then realised this was contributed to by its lack of a boot lid. Nothing to interrupt the line. So how did you get anything into the boot? Answer, you stuffed whatever you had behind the seats. How clever! He started her up. The exhaust sounded crisp. Having completed the paperwork, the deposit having been paid from his savings account, he selected first gear, and roared away. The gear change was slick, and the handling sublime (at least when compared to the family's Hillman Minx which though very softly sprung always had its own mind about which direction it wanted to go). In no time it was doing sixty miles an hour. The soft top was folded behind, and he felt the wind in his hair. What would she do? He came to a long stretch of road and put his foot down. Eventually seventy miles an hour appeared, as did the next bend, so he slowed down.

Back home David was agog with curiosity and begged for a ride. Martha, who knew nothing whatever about cars, told Pablo he had been cheated because it only had two doors, no boot handle, and only a soft roof.

'Oh vell, I suppose you young men know what you want. Von day you vill see sense.'

Brenda refused to pass comment, and ignored the car totally, except when she needed a lift to the railway station.

'Not much of a car is it?' she said. 'It hasn't got a heater.'

'Well, anyway, it's got a radio, and I'll get a heater eventually,' replied the master.

'Bye,' and off she went without a backward glance having been delivered to the station. Later that evening, whilst David and his mum were watching *The Defenders* on the TV, he penned his reply to Maureen.

Dear Maureen,

It was nice to hear from you after all this time. I am truly sorry about your marriage. Life can be very tough at times. I reckon I've had it easy, and am now a doctor, but will soon be starting my first job. I feel quite terrified. It starts next week, but I could just manage to visit you next weekend if you are free. Perhaps you could phone me as there isn't much time for letters. My number is Trench 564. Hoping to hear from you,

Yours sincerely,

Harry (Pablo) Bernstein

He posted the letter the same day, and waited. It was Wednesday, his job started exactly in a week's time. What would he feel like when he met Maureen? And what if her husband was the jealous type. And what would be his reaction at meeting her four-year-old, Cliff? He felt very unsure about his feelings, especially by his failure to please Carol. Then his eye fell upon the Sprite which looked at him with its big eyes, seeming to say, 'please take me for a long drive'. And what better than a drive up to Yorkshire. Later that evening, he made some excuse to go out, and walked to the nearest phone box. He dialled O, and asked the operator for Skipton 439. He was told to place a shilling in the slot. Then he heard the number being dialled, and after a short while a mature lady's voice replied.

'Skipton 439.'

'Press button A,' said the operator, and the master heard the coin being swallowed by the black metal coin swallower.

'Hello, may I speak to Maureen, please? This is Harry Bernstein.'

'Maureen, a gentleman is on the phone for you.'

'Hallo, Harry, how nice of you to call me. How are you – you must be so pleased to be a doctor. You're really ever so clever. I expect you think I'm a silly girl, but I really would love to see you again. Just as a friend, nothing more.'

'Of course,' replied a slightly disappointed master. 'I could come this Saturday, and show you my new – well not really new, but new enough car.'

'You've got a car, how smashing. What sort is it?'

'It's an Austin-Healey Sprite.'

'Ooh, they're lovely, and you can let the roof down can't you? We could go for a ride in the Dales. I can't wait. When do you think you could get here? Auntie could cook us lunch.'

The master couldn't wait for Saturday to come. On Friday, at about eleven o'clock in the morning, as he was filling the car with petrol, he suddenly became aware of Carol standing close by.

'You never told me you had bought a car. It's lovely. Can I have a ride?'

'OK, hop in,' said the master.

Funny how her attitude to him had changed after his miserable failure to please her a few days ago. She got in, and he got into first gear, released the clutch, gave it plenty of throttle and away they went.

'Gosh it's really fast,' Carol said, 'let's go for a ride in the country.'

'OK,' replied the master, and soon the wind was blasting them both as their speed nudged up to sixty mph. The car held the road extremely well, and the master began really enjoying himself as he placed it precisely as he entered a bend. The steering was instant, and he had to caution himself not to turn the wheel too soon, as was his previous experience with the Hillman. He then noticed that Carol's stocking top was clearly visible, the wind having got under her dress. She wasn't paying attention, being entranced by the G forces as the little car went round bends as though on rails, the master playing clever tunes on the gearbox. It was at this point that his hand slipped off the gear knob and landed upon her thigh.

'You are a naughty young man,' she said, making no attempt to move it.

'I say,' said the master, aware of his opportunity, 'why don't we pull in here?' swinging the car down a farm track, which doubled back behind a hedge.

'I hope you aren't going to be a naughty doctor,' laughed Carol. 'I've heard about what doctors and nurses get up to.'

Before long, the master and Carol were, how shall I put it, behaving passionately, but within the confines of the car. Anyone who knows about the Austin Healey Sprite would know that, unless you happened to be extremely altitude challenged, sex would be well nigh impossible. And so it turned out to be. I had a most uncomfortable collision with the gear lever, as did Bill and then, after some wriggling Ben. Eventually, the pair gave up, and resumed their country ride. Seeing a country pub, they went in for a drink. After a few minutes, the master excused himself on account of the call of nature. I swung into action, aiming for Twyfords, but the master instantly registered an exclamation of pain. Something was clearly wrong, and it was plainly in my department. The earlier collision with the gear lever had caused some internal bruising, making peeing very painful. I felt extremely guilty, though it was hardly my fault. I shrank within myself. How dare I show my face after this? However, the master managed to complete his action, and went back into the bar.

'What are you drinking?' he asked Carol.

'I'll have a half pint shandy,' she replied.

The master had a pint of Watney's Red Barrel, and they shared a packet of Smith's crisps, Carol insisting on opening the little blue packet of salt and shaking the packet vigorously.

'Fancy another?' he asked.

'Yes please, make it a pint,' she said.

The master also had another pint, plus he ordered a couple of pork pies. Suitably victualled, they resumed their ride. This time he determined to see what the car could do, and on one long straight, managed to squeeze seventy-five mph out of it. Carol's hair was flying, as was her dress, but I dared not show my face. The master placed a comforting hand over his trousers, then we were going into a bend, quite fast. The car gave a little hop, but the master skilfully corrected it, then decided, wisely, to drive a little slower.

'You're a fast driver,' Carol complimented him. 'Are you doing anything special this weekend? How about we could go to the seaside. I could tell my parents I was going to see a friend, and come back on Sunday. We could stay somewhere overnight. We could have some fun. How about it?'

I leaped forward, then quickly retreated as I remembered my experiences when last I spied Twyfords.

'OK,' replied the master, then remembered his arrangement to see Maureen in Skipton next day.

'Actually, Carol, I've just remembered, I've got an interview for a job in Wolverhampton next week, and I'll have to do some preparation. Sorry, some other time, it would be great.'

Carol lapsed into silence, then said she needed to be home, as she had forgotten she had a hair appointment that afternoon at four o'clock.

Came Saturday, and the Sprite was pointed in the direction of Skipton, with the assistance of Mr Bartholomew, mapmaker extraordinaire. There were no motorways except the Lancaster bypass, and the so-called London to Birmingham motorway, which in reality went from north of Watford, to Crick in Northamptonshire at the time. But that didn't matter, as the Sprite wasn't really built for long high speed motorway driving, it was more at home on single carriageway roads, where a keen eye, a good gear change, and snappy acceleration were more important. The master was clearly enjoying himself, the radio was playing the yellow polka dot bikini song, and everything appeared to be going well, until the steering wheel decided it wanted to go left, even though this was at variance with the actual road. The car had developed a puncture. And it started raining. Nothing daunted, the master jacked the car up, and changed the wheel without any trouble. By about twelve o'clock, he arrived at Skipton, and began searching for Maureen's mother's house. After asking a couple of people he arrived at Mill Lane. The house was a pebbledash semi with a pretty front garden, and a white wooden fence. A toddler's tricycle was in the front garden. He knocked on the door, and shortly after was greeted by a jolly white-haired lady, with a teacloth draped over her arm.

'Welcome, Doctor, you're just in time for lunch. Maureen, the doctor's here.'

He heard footsteps on the landing, and as he turned to look at the stairs, became aware of two beady eyes watching him. He looked at Cliff, who shied away, clearly frightened. And then Maureen descended the stairs. She looked tired, but had lost none of her prettiness.

'Hello, Harry, I mean Pablo. It's ever so good of you to come all this way. Mum, this is Dr Bernstein, who I've told you about, and Cliff, say hallo to the doctor.'

'Hallo, Mister Doctor,' he said.

They all had a laugh.

'Pablo, this is my mum, Mrs Mattock. I'm Mrs Robertson unfortunately. Let's have lunch, Mum.'

Mrs Mattock had prepared a ham salad together with a large pork pie

'So, Dr Bernstein, I hear you recently passed your exams to be a doctor. You must be ever so clever. Our doctor, Dr. Ramsey, is very good. He treated Mrs Jellinek from over the road. She said he discovered she had a heart murmur, which no one had noticed before. Said it was due to her having had rheumatic fever when she was a child.'

'I expect it is a case of mitral stenosis,' offered the master, sounding very professional.

'Yes, something like that,' replied Mrs Mattock. 'Anyway, she's got to go to Leeds to have some special tests, then she might need an operation.'

'Oh, Mother, I'm sure Doctor Bernstein doesn't want to talk shop when he's off duty. Have some more pork pie, Pablo.'

'Thanks,' the master replied. 'It's jolly good. Is it local?'

'Our local butcher kills his own meat in his back yard. He always does us proud. I'm glad you like it. Now, when you've finished, I'll do the washing up, and look after Cliff. I'm sure you and Maureen don't want me around. Why don't you go out into the park for a walk. The weather seems to be brightening up.'

They crossed the road, and entered the park via a set of wrought iron gates. Maureen linked arms with the master. He thought this a little odd, but she really was pretty, and was wearing some form of scent which he found rather nice. Her complexion was very much English rose, her lips were nicely sculpted, if a little thin, and she had an alluring little mole on her right cheek. Her teeth were perfect, and she had small but clearly outlined breasts (this latter fact depending on his X-ray intuition). She had legs to die for, as he caught a glimpse when they were crossed as she sat on a park bench, and I felt a surge of electricity.

'Harry, I mean, Pablo. I hope you don't feel I've dragged you here under false pretences. I only want to talk. I've been through a lot. John, my husband, is a real brute. I thought he was a gentleman when we were courting, but after our wedding, he changed. On Fridays, he would go down to the pub, and then come back roaring drunk after closing. I told him I didn't want sex, but he took no notice, just tore off my clothes, and flung me on the bed. I struggled, but it was no use. And when he found he couldn't do it, because of the drink, he got angry and started slapping me about. We had the police at our council house twice because of the noise, which the neighbours could hear. Then of course, the inevitable happened, he managed it one Friday, and that's how Cliff came along. Poor mite, he's OK, but terrified of his dad especially when he starts shouting and pushing me about.'

The master listened dutifully, his mind in a whirl. What was he getting himself in for? Of course, he felt sorry for the girl, but he was shortly to start his career at a hospital in Wolverhampton, and couldn't contemplate a long distance and rather complicated relationship. And, of course, there was Carol.

'I'm so sorry you've had all this trouble, Maureen. What are you going to do about it? Have you considered seeing a marriage guidance counsellor?'

Instead of replying, Maureen pulled him close, and started kissing him passionately. He felt her closeness, her left leg half raised around him, Bill and Ben started rotating, and I swung into action. The master felt embarrassed, and gently prised himself away. All this was very complex, nothing he had had to contend with before. They walked further into the park, then entered a small café.

'What'll you have?' he asked her.

'Just a cup of tea please.'

The master ordered the same, and for a minute they sat in silence. He looked at her. She was looking down at the floor, a tear sliding down her cheek, moistening the tiny mole. The master placed his arm around her. She snuggled up to his shoulder, then started crying. At that moment, the hitherto quiet café was stung into awareness, as a voice shouted, 'So there you are, you little bitch.'

It was her husband, reeking of beer, flushed of face, and staggering towards the couple. He took a swing at the master, but missed by a mile, then fell over the table, sending the crockery, milk and sugar bowls flying.

'Call the police, Jenny,' shouted the lady at the till, to her assistant.

By this time, John Robertson had managed to stand up, grabbed a broken saucer, and was advancing towards the master.

'I'll teach you, you f****ing bastard, fooling around with my wife.'

He moved forward. The master by now was fully alert, and remembered his earlier schoolyard fighting experiences when he was about eight years old. He adopted the classical stance, right fist close to his chin, the left positioned forward, ready to punch. The drunk took a gigantic swing, which missed by a mile. As his chin passed by the master at a distance of about eighteen inches, the master let loose a right hook straight to the chin, which landed spot on target. John Robertson's intended lesson ended at that point, as he was out cold on the floor. The master was by now very worried, and wondering what to do. He felt for his pulse, which happily was good and strong. After about ten seconds, the loser sat up, looked around, and then realisation dawned. At this moment there was the sound of a police bell, and a black Ford Zephyr pulled up outside the café, having entered the park to the amazement of the Saturday afternoon strollers.

'Come on, time to go,' said Maureen, pulling on the master's sleeve.

They quickly left before any questions were asked.

'Where to now?' asked the master.

'Let's take a drive into the country,' came the reply, so, having retraced their steps they got into the Sprite and headed for the Dales.

The sun started shining, and the world took on a smiley face. With the hood down, and the wind rushing at her, her hair streaming out behind her, she looked quite beautiful. The master felt tempted to stop and start proceedings, I indicated my state of readiness, but at that moment another car which had been following decided to show off, by overtaking as they were approaching a bend. Wisely, the master slowed down, as the overtaking MG Magnette got back onto its side of the road just in time to avoid an unseemly end, care of a lorry. On they went, the countryside green and lovely, with undulating hills and farms, with patchwork quilt fields. Presently the master pulled in on an outcrop which offered a magnificent view. They sat on a conveniently donated bench, and contemplated their world. All memory of the recent incident faded, and Maureen's mind wandered into the land of 'what if?' What if she had never met John Robertson? What if instead she had lived closer to Pablo, and instead they had married? How different would her life have been? What if, even now, he decided to stay in touch? He seemed nice enough, not perhaps the world's most handsome, but OK, and kind. She reached out her hand, which he gently took. Then he put his arm around her, turning her to face him. Her pretty lips parted in anticipation, and he kissed her gently. She closed her eyes, to concentrate the feeling. I wondered if my services were soon to be required, but no instructions were forthcoming. I felt a bit puzzled, wondering what would be the master's strategy. He had a faraway look, as they retraced their steps to the car. Little was said as they returned to the house.

'Home so soon?' asked her mother. 'Yes, well I've got to be going, as I've got a job interview next week, and I need to prepare for it,' said the master.

'Surely you could stay for high tea,' persisted Maureen.

At this moment, Cliff appeared and asked the master to help him with his Meccano set. It was only a number one, with very easy to build models, so after a little hesitation, the master obliged. Cliff decided at this point that no way was he going to allow Mr Doctor to leave.

'All right then, I'll stay for tea, it's ever so kind, Mrs Mattock, but I'll have to leave after.'

Maureen then showed the master some of her family photographs, which were framed and standing on the sideboard.

'This was taken last year when we went to Cromer for our summer holidays. In the evening we went to the end of the pier show. It was brilliant.'

'Where is your father, Maureen?' asked the master.

'Oh, he died last year, he had stomach cancer.'

'Oh I'm ever so sorry,' replied the master. Mrs Mattock shed a tear, hurriedly disappearing into the kitchen. The master felt like kicking himself, he hadn't intended stirring the family's emotions.

'Grandad's died and gone to heaven,' informed Cliff, adding one further fact in case the deceased's eventual destination had been in doubt.

Maureen lifted Cliff onto her lap, and gave him a cuddle. After tea, the master duly thanked Mrs Mattock, promised Cliff he would come back some time and make him some more Meccano models, then walked outside with Maureen.

'Maureen, it's been great seeing you again. I'll try to come again, but it's going to be difficult because when you do your first hospital job as a doctor, you get very little time off.'

'I understand, but please do write to me. It would be nice to stay in touch.' They kissed briefly, and the master made his escape.

Came the following Monday, and at the time appointed, the master faced his interview in Wolverhampton. The consultant had a face reminiscent of a bloodhound, and informed the candidate that the work would be very hard, with little relief. If he wanted an easier time he should look elsewhere. The work would include general surgery, plus urology, which was this consultant's main specialty. There didn't seem to be any other candidates present with whom to compete, and during the course of the interview, the master was told he had got the job.

'You start on Saturday, the hospital administrator will give you all the details. We will need your National Insurance number, that is if you intend on being paid.'

This had been the master's intention, so out of mild curiosity, he enquired what his salary would be. His GP, who had impressed him with his Mark VII Jaguar, clearly commanded a salary of well over two thousand pounds a year. The reply was that his salary would be at the princely rate of six hundred and seventy-five pounds per annum, from which would be deducted thirty pounds a month board and lodging. The master's face fell, but then he brightened up when he realised this sort of hardship would all be over after one year, when all being well he would obtain full registration from the General Medical Council, could start practice as a GP, and order his Jaguar, and marry Carol, or someone similar.

Came Saturday, and he pointed the Sprite along the A41 direction Wolverhampton. Bye-bye Horton, hello the revered world of medicine. Wolverhampton, home of the admired Wolves football team, Billy Wright, captain of England, and many other stars. The Cleveland Road, not particularly elegant, a few run down pubs, a Chinese restaurant, and there before him, the elegant pillars of the Royal Infirmary. He finally found somewhere to park, then walked to the main entrance. A pretty nurse, blonde-haired and pink lipped greeted him on the steps. He couldn't believe his luck and asked her where he was meant to report. She told him that her boyfriend, the orthopaedic registrar, drove an MGB which was considerably larger and faster than a Sprite, had arrived the same day, and she knew where he had reported so offered to show the master. The clerk at the personnel office welcomed him, and explained the directions to his quarters (a prefabricated hut behind the main block), and gave him his keys. The room was pretty basic, but adequate, the bathroom and toilet was down the corridor and shared by two other doctors (both, as he would discover, male). Female doctors, a rare breed, were billeted in the nurses' home. A pair of white coats laundered and starched were laid out on the bed. He donned one, applied his biro, and tucked his stethoscope into his side pocket, then sauntered off in the direction of the wards.

The corridors smelled of recently applied polish, everything seemed very clean. He entered Scott and Twentyman Ward where he was greeted by the sister.

'Ah, so you're our new houseman.' She was a business-like woman of about mid-thirties, with striking ginger hair.

'You can start by putting up a drip on Mr Baines. The registrar left instructions, as he is stuck in theatre, and Mr Baines will be next on the list. He's having a prostatectomy.'

'Good afternoon, Mr Baines, and how are you feeling today?' asked the master.

'Bloody awful as a matter of fact,' came the reply. 'I'm starving, haven't had anything since last night, and I tell you, I'll be glad when this operation is over. Can you imagine what it's like not being able to pee?'

I gave a little shrug of sympathy and guilt.

'And it's not much fun having a catheter stuck up my doo dah.' I winced in agreement, hoping never to endure the same fate.

'Any more chores, Sister?'

'Yes, you need to clerk all the patients for Monday's list. It's on the wall, then you've to ring the anaesthetist on Sunday in case there are likely to be any problems. The list starts at eight thirty, and it's usually done by six o'clock. Then you do a post-op ward round, oh and by the way, you're on call on Monday from nine a.m. till nine a.m. Tuesday.'

The master realised after a very short time that he was going to be busy, too busy in fact for anything else. But although the work was tough and the hours long, the nurses were friendly, as were the registrars whose experience was what held the ship together between times when the consultants were not around. Oftentimes they would be at the private hospital. Lists were done twice a week for each of the other three consultants. The on-call rota was one night in three, there being two other firms. And weekend duties were one weekend in three, starting nine a.m. Friday, till nine a.m. Monday. Sleep was often in short supply, work was plentiful. But there were times of relaxation, like when waiting for a suspected appendicitis to arrive at three a.m., and ordering a fry up from the hospital night chef, which regardless of the hour, would be served in the doctors' mess.

There were parties on Friday nights in the doctors' mess, and were well attended by nurses. Few doctors were married. One Friday in November, the master found himself standing next to the pretty nurse he had met on arrival. She told him she had broken up with the orthopaedic registrar who was presently dating a nurse from New Cross Hospital, on the other side of town. Music was provided by a large Ferranti radiogram, courtesy of a grateful patient. 'Rock around the clock' by Bill Haley got the party into its swing. Cliff Richard added his touch as did Elvis. 'Unchained melody' was good to smooch to, as was the case with Pablo and the aforesaid nurse, name of Pauline. She had a good sense of rhythm, their bodies swaying in harmony, and close. I was clearly getting involved, at which point the master suggested they pause for a drink. The beer came out of a barrel donated by Mitchells and Butlers, from their Springfield brewery. One of their directors had expressed his gratitude for being relieved of his piles by one of the previous registrars. Pauline drank cider. The master was on duty, and therefore was not going home that weekend. Pauline had trained at the Royal, having started there three years previously. She hoped to specialise in orthopaedic nursing. The master was as yet unsure of what path to take, whether to go into general practice, or to specialise in hospital work. Unfortunately the latter would involve lots more exams, whereas, provided he didn't blot his copybook, in twelve months he would be able to apply for a post as a GP. With Pauline quite relaxed on her third pint of cider, the master decided to try his luck during a rendering of 'La mer'. He happened to be quite nifty on his feet, and following a dramatic spin, succeeded in almost planting a kiss on her pink lips, but unfortunately overbalanced (courtesy of Mitchells and Butlers), and finished up on the floor, with Pauline on top. Laughter all round followed, and the party really got going. Somehow he found himself smooching with a buxom brunette called Louise, who worked on the Ear, Nose and Throat Ward. He attempted to hold her close, but was prevented from so doing by the size of her breasts, but he wasn't complaining. Being of a mind for a little exploration, he suggested a pause for some fresh air, to which she agreed. They sauntered out of the back of the hospital, and approached the doctors' quarters. I could sense the excitement felt by the master, who asked her whether she might be interested in seeing his room, in order to compare the standard of accommodation provided for doctors with that for the nurses. Louise thought this would be an interesting piece of research, so they went into his room. They inspected the walls, then the door, then the wash-basin, then the curtains, then the carpet, then the lights, then the bedside table, and finally, the bed.

'It's not very big,' Louise noted. 'Look, you couldn't get two people onto it.'

'I don't know about that,' countered the master. 'Let's try.' And try they did.

The geometry of the arrangement required that if two people were to be accommodated, because of the size of Louise and of the bed, it would require a stacking arrangement; otherwise one party would be in danger of being ejected. Unfortunately, any activity of a promiscuous nature was threatened by a prompt fall onto the floor, which in fact is precisely what happened. The master planted his mouth on her lips, and encountered minimal resistance. He then informed her that he would like to practise his breast examination technique, as taught at medical school. She agreed it would be a good thing in preparation for the patients he would encounter. She duly removed her bra, and the master was enthralled by a perfect set of generous white breasts with pert pink nipples. He made the mistake of making a lunge at them.

'That's not how you examine a breast,' exclaimed Louise. 'Didn't they explain that the first thing is inspection, followed by palpation?'

'Oh, I'd already commenced the inspection bit while we were at the party, so I thought I'd get down to the nitty gritty.'

'All right, but be gentle.'

This was followed by an extremely comprehensive and thorough palpation. The master then transferred his attentions to her thighs, but was instantly met with firm resistance.

'Steady on, what do you think you are doing?'

I felt I had to protest, because by now I had been seriously stung into action, and I can assure you, any thoughts along the lines of varicose veins would never have had that effect. My head was screaming for air, as the master transferred his attentions to more gynaecological territory. Louise was now relaxing and started kissing more passionately. She then started transferring her attentions to more andrological territory, i.e. me. To my alarm, I thought I was going to be part of her supper, a latter day wiener, but the sensation was nothing short of ecstatic. Without further ado, nakedness was achieved by both parties, and I was given the shroud that precedes all shooting by firing squads. Next it was back to the Cresta run, ricocheting from wall to wall, with a final burst into the home straight. This was accompanied by Alice sounds, albeit somewhat muted. On a nought to ten scale, where Alice's original sounds were five out of ten, Louise's were about three. From here on, all such performances would be measured on the Richter, sorry Alice scale.

The happy pair then rejoined the party, to sounds of, 'Where were you, we thought you'd gone to bed,' probably not realising how near to the truth they'd been.

The party finally broke up at half past midnight. Next day the master, being on call for the weekend, did his ward round, and discharged about five patients, to be replaced on Sunday by those to be treated on Monday's operating list. The weekend was fairly busy, with an appendix diagnosed by the master, and confirmed by the registrar. Then they dealt with a perforated peptic ulcer, followed by a strangulated hernia. The afternoon was quiet, and the master caught up with some reading. There was a query ectopic pregnancy, for which he called in the gynaecology registrar.

Next morning, Sunday, he had to spend the morning in casualty, seeing anything that came in. He had to stitch some patients with cuts, including an old lady who had fallen down some stairs, and rearranged her face. In the afternoon, he admitted all the patients who were due for surgery on the list for Monday, then telephoned the anaesthetist describing the patients. Monday he was in theatre all day, then did an evening ward round to make sure they were all progressing satisfactorily. By now, fatigue was beginning to set in. Together with some colleagues they had a few beers in the doctors' mess. On Wednesday he happened to bump into Louise who was on her way to the hospital canteen for a coffee break. They arranged to meet later that evening for a drink at a pub just off the Cleveland Road. Afterwards, they had a Chinese before retiring to the master's bedroom. Alice four. I felt I was making slow progress, but that was better than no progress at all. After about a month, most of the job had become routine, but then the theatre sister dropped a bombshell.

'Mr Bernstein, you've got a circ list tomorrow. Mr Bozek will show you how it's done.'

'What's a circ list?' enquired the master.

'Oh it's all pretty straightforward. But it's important to do circumcisions well, otherwise there could be serious problems.'

This registered with the master, but as far as I was concerned, this reminded me of my greatest nightmare from all those years past, in fact, my first week after being born. The master didn't remember, but I jolly well did. The master was rather puzzled when he tried to pee on the morning appointed. I was nowhere to be found, having shrunk to almost invisibility. I didn't want to know. I was experiencing nightmares – the master didn't realise my suffering. And things took a serious turn when he attempted another round with Louise. Once again, I made myself scarce, which didn't particularly please her. The master couldn't understand what was wrong, and began worrying. He went to the hospital library to read up on erectile dysfunction, and decided that perhaps he had diabetes, but after testing his wee and blood, found no evidence to support this theory. Louise meanwhile had met up with Andrew, a tall West Indian chap, the ear, nose and throat registrar. She wasn't available to go out with the master, and appeared very content with life despite this fact. I think the master blamed me for these events. Came the time to do the 'circ' list. Mr Bozek was an excellent instructor, and soon the master was quite proficient at the job. Came the weekend, and the master headed the Sprite for home.

Arriving at the family house, his mother flung her arms around him, so happy to have her boy back. Sol looked up from reading the *Daily Mirror*, pipe in hand, and graciously accepted his son's kiss on the back of his head. David was out at the time, doing some shopping. Brenda asked the master what the score was.

'There isn't a match on today, but I expect Wolves will thrash Everton.'

'Not football, stupid, how many have you killed so far?'

A real charmer. The master ignored her – what a sour puss. Came Saturday, and he arranged to meet Carol for a dance at Sankey's. Unusually, the firm possessed a beautiful cricket ground, and the aforesaid *Palais de dance*, where an enthusiastic six-piece band played every Saturday night. This was to set the pattern for the next four months, the master working hard and taking every available weekend to go home to meet Carol. She likewise couldn't wait for him to come, despite his previous poor performance on the Cresta run, and their relationship felt as though it was becoming serious. To the master, the thought of marriage to Carol seemed to be the crowning of his dreams, only the Jaguar was outstanding, but there was no way of achieving that unless he won the pools. Or became a GP, but he wouldn't be eligible till he completed his second six months' house job. He had applied for and been successful in obtaining a job at a busy hospital in Birmingham, Dudley Road.

But first, came Christmas, the end of his first job successfully completed, though it was clear to him he would never make a surgeon. This was brought home to him when the consultant surgeon one day in theatre said, 'Bernstein, in your six months working for me I feel you have the makings of an excellent physician,' i.e. not a surgeon.

Not to worry, the master never did see himself as a surgeon. But now Dudley Road beckoned after Christmas – perhaps medicine would be more to his taste than surgery.

Came Christmas, he took Carol to a dance and, as he had five days' leave left, invited her for a weekend away. This caused a few eyebrows to stir, but he made it clear they would have separate rooms. They stayed in a country hotel in North Wales. There was a dinner dance on the Saturday night. Carol looked stunning, her blonde hair swirling around her as the master whisked her around in a quickstep. Then, rock and roll, and a smoochy waltz. She was butter in his arms, and all thoughts of separate rooms were fading fast. That night it was all hands to the deck. Bill and Ben did a twirl, I presented arms, standing to attention before being launched down the Cresta run. Alice seven. Then came the encore, and to the master's amazement Carol took the initiative in a hitherto untried manner. To wit, she decided to straddle the master, as a result of which all the angles were wrong and needed readjusting, but once achieved, the result was again Alice seven. By now I was pretty tired and assumed it was time for what the bed really was designed for, but Carol had other ideas. Where a short time earlier, she had been butter in the master's arms, now I was jelly in her hands. But not for long as the jelly transformed into the kind of vegetable commonly used by night pilots during the war. By this stage I was lying back and thinking of England, all thought of sleep having been banished. It became clear that Carol was no stranger to the teachings of the *Kama Sutra*. By next morning I was comatose, and the happy couple remained asleep, their arms entwined until eleven o'clock, when they were awoken by the maid knocking on their door. So I suppose it will not come as a surprise that within a month the master had proposed, been accepted, and the date of the wedding agreed for after the master had completed his six months at Dudley Road Hospital. Carol chose a sapphire and diamond ring from H Samuel's in the High Street.

The Dudley Road job was totally different. Medicine was obviously more interesting to the master than surgery had been. He had to deal with heart attacks, strokes, pneumonia, cancer, in fact just about anything. He gained in confidence far more rapidly than in knowledge, because in medicine, as in life, familiarity can, if one is not careful, breed contempt. Magical drugs included digitalis, aminophylline, mersalyl, butazolidine and lots more. Some of these would in later years be shunned or superseded, but in those days, it was 'heigh-ho, and on we go, some you save, some you can't'.

Preparations for the wedding went ahead, the date chosen was August 1964 at the local parish church. Brenda offered herself as matron of honour, two other bridesmaids being

Carol's younger sisters. Sol and Martha didn't mind the wedding service being carried out in a church as they had long given up regular Jewish customs. Perhaps memories of the Holocaust perversely led them to wish no more to be 'different' though their German accents would remain with them for their lifetimes. David was chosen as best man, and did a good job. On the day the morning started with rain, but brightened up by eleven o'clock in time for the service. The reception was held at the Forest Glen, at the foot of the Wrekin, and went without a hitch. For their honeymoon, they decided to travel to France in the Sprite, and possibly beyond. The usual confetti and pranks followed, and they were off.

That night was spent in a hotel in Dover in readiness for the early boat to Calais next morning. Where once the wedding night was the culmination of young lovers' dreams, having test driven the love machinery, post-wedding fatigue set in, and their first night was a celibate affair. However, the next week was a blissful combination of the freedom of the *routes nationales,* baguettes, brie and pate at the roadside for lunch washed down with the local *vin rouge.* They stayed overnight in pretty basic hotels, some with very creaky beds, on which I contributed the conductor's baton in the symphony of love. And so it was that, upon arrival back at the master's parents' house, a letter was waiting for the master. He had decided a month previously, that general practice appealed, and therefore he had applied for a city practice in Highfields, in Leicester. The letter informed him that his application, subject to interview, had been successful. At the interview he was asked a few routine questions, including where had he graduated (already stated on the form), where had he done his pre-registration jobs (already stated on the form), and did he have any special areas of interest. To this he had to reply that as yet he had none, but was looking forward to the experience this job would offer.

His application having proved successful, he and Carol rented a flat in Oadby, and settled into married life. Carol had succeeded in gaining shorthand and typing qualifications, and had no trouble securing a job at a solicitors' in Leicester. The city itself was quite 'forward looking', insofar as many of the elegant Victorian buildings had been demolished in order to embrace sixties modernism. High-rise flats were the order of the day. The city possessed three hospitals, the Royal Infirmary, the General, and Groby Road, an old TB hospital, eventually to be replaced by the Glenfield Hospital. General practice was very busy, with many night calls, and frequent patients with coughs and colds, demanding a 'bottle of medicine' like the old doctor i.e. the now retired Dr Jacobson used to prescribe. The master initially found the job demanding but gradually became worn down by the routine. And the money, though not bad, was unlikely to provide the Jaguar of his dreams. Speaking for myself, life was becoming a bit of a routine, once or twice a week, Alice score varying between zero and two. Carol didn't seem to mind, though gradually, almost imperceptibly, she evaded the master's attentions.

He didn't register annoyance at first, as he was still preoccupied with his work, and considering a career change, because he was finding the routine boring. He found an advertisement in the *British Medical Journal* for a ship's doctor, for the Union Castle line. He felt he should discuss it with Carol first. After morning surgery, he was told that there would be no afternoon surgery, as there was a burst pipe which had caused flooding in the examination rooms. So, instead, he headed for home, with the new job in mind. Parked outside the block of flats was a Jaguar Mark VII. This seemed to him to be a sign that the master's master was looking out for him. Or so he thought, but fate was about to play a cruel twist.

He entered the flat, but hearing no welcoming call from Carol, assumed she was still at work. He made himself a cup of tea, and settled down to watch *Crossroads* on the TV. After a while, he thought he might visit the local golf club on the off chance someone would fancy a round. He went upstairs to change. As he opened the door of the bedroom, he knew instantly his marriage was over. Carol was oblivious to his presence, as was the lady closely entwined, the scene being a compilation of arms and legs, with writhing bodies, and moans, Alice number eight. The shock was profound for all concerned, performers and audience alike. The other lady was rather stocky with a gamin hairstyle, strangely clad in nothing at all except riding boots, and clutching a whip. There is no doubt that had the mammal beneath her been a horse, she would have been a serious Derby contender. The master shouted to Carol.

'What the hell's going on? Is this what you get up to when I'm away? What's the other bitch's name?'

'Lavinia,' answered the jockey, turning round. 'Fancy a ride?'

To my intense surprise I was at attention immediately. This was something totally unknown, and never even dreamed of. A threesome, including the master's wife! Unbelievable! And incredible! The master didn't know which way to turn. All roads led to the Cresta run. I didn't know if I was coming or going, or both coming and going. After about half an hour of vigorous debauchery, all three participants lay back resting. Lavinia offered cigarettes all round, and a kind of peace descended.

One month later, having resigned his GP job in Leicester, and agreed on a legal separation from Carol, the master was comfortably ensconced on board the *Athlone Castle*, of the Union-Castle line, heading out of Southampton en-route for Cape Town. He had undergone a short cramming course on seaboard survival, and brushed up on maritime medicine. It wasn't long before he himself felt he had need of a doctor as the ship ploughed across the Bay of Biscay. Thereafter, the voyage was pretty uneventful. He had to stitch a few people who had suffered falls, none serious, treated two cases of asthma, and sent a suspected appendicitis ashore in Madeira. It was quite soon apparent to him that there were several predatory ladies aboard, and one man, Felix Adamantis, who was having protracted conversations with the young male waiters. The ladies were invariably over forty. The fit more youthful bunch already appeared to have husbands, fiancés, or in one instance, the boyfriend. One of the predatory ladies was a vivacious widow, lately separated by nature from her loving husband who had left her very comfortably off. He had been a 'name' at Lloyds, and they lived in Weybridge. The lady in question was a Mrs Travers, who happened to consult the master at evening surgery, the day after the ship had departed Madeira.

'What seems to be the matter?' was his routine question after the usual formalities had been completed.

'I'm worried in case I've got a breast lump – well not exactly what you could call a lump, more a sense of fullness, well not exactly a fullness, perhaps a sense that something might not be right.'

Armed with this collection of symptoms so clearly described, the master proceeded to ask the usual questions regarding family history, of which none was relevant.

'Well, aren't you going to examine me?' the good lady asked.

'Certainly, I've just got to ask Nurse Shakespeare to chaperone,' said the well-trained master. Unfortunately Nurse Shakespeare was nowhere to be found, (in truth she was 'busy' with the purser in his cabin, in a snatched moment of animal frenzy). The master weighed up the situation, and decided it would be safe to proceed with the breast examination. As he did so, Mrs Travers sought to guide him to the suspicious area, which strangely was well away from her breast. In fact it was far south, palpation of which elicited a peculiar sighing which, in the clinical situation, was somewhat unusual, unexpected, and not a little worrying. In fact, she was making Alice noises. The master completed his examination of the breast, and hastily reassured her that there was nothing to worry about.

'Well, Doctor Bernstein, why don't you come to my cabin later, we could drink some champagne?'

I knew full well what she meant, and what was promised. In truth, I wasn't entirely up for it. OK, she wasn't bad looking, but I sensed it might get the master into trouble. But the master was clearly missing any fun, having been celibate (apart from a few practice runs) since the Carol debacle.

'OK, what time shall I come?'

'Why not now, unless you've got any more patients to see,' came the reply.

'As a matter of fact I'm through now, so let's go,' he said.

Mrs Travers had a stateroom plus a balcony on the top deck, which must have cost a bomb. As they walked along the corridor, they bumped into a rather flushed Nurse Shakespeare.

'Where have you been?' asked the master.

'Oh, I wasn't feeling too well and had to go to my room for a short while.'

'So, how come you're here, when your room is in the opposite direction?'

End of dialogue. Proceeded to Mrs Travers' stateroom. Champagne duly taken out of fridge.

'Just open it, Doctor, whilst I freshen up.'

It was *Cristal* champagne, which the master had never had before. In fact, he'd never had anything remotely similar, the nearest being Cava. He carefully opened the bottle, and poured some into each flute. He then turned round, and I received a high voltage shock. Mrs Travers was wearing a black teddy, high heels, and elbow length gloves. She was in truth, a most attractive example of the vintage, as was the champagne (1957). They both took a sip, then she de-trousered the master expertly. The next moment I, not the master, was in her arms, and then her mouth. Oh Cresta, Cresta, Cresta, what champagne lubricated bliss, what exquisite torment, what a premature finale, and how embarrassing.

'Don't worry,' she said, 'we've got time for the next round. Have another glass, you're probably dehydrated.'

The couple then indulged in small talk, with which I will not bore you, but presently I sensed my powers returning.

'You know, you're pretty well endowed,' she commented. 'Let me see, I've got a tape measure here.'

And with that, I was reduced to a mere object to be measured. I tried to put on a brave face. The answer was seven inches.

'Not bad, but do you know what the world record is?' she asked.

'Not a clue.'

'Well, it's alleged that an American has one that is thirteen and a half inches long. What about that? It would terrify me. I think yours is just fine.'

And with that, I was back in action again, and again half an hour later. More champagne, the master was beginning to feel rather tiddly.

'One more for the road,' beckoned Mrs Travers.

Then a strange thing happened. I couldn't explain it. It was a kind of paralysis, the sort that no ways of the laying on of hands could overcome. The master was clearly embarrassed, and apologised.

'Don't worry, Doctor, even the medical profession cannot claim immunity from the brewer's droop.'

Apart from this, and the death of a nonagenarian two days before Cape Town, the rest of the voyage was uneventful. The master, despite several entreaties, kept his distance from Mrs Travers, claiming pressure of work.

Entering Cape Town harbour as was to be anticipated, was a spectacular sight, with Table Mountain as always, bearing its cloudy tablecloth. The master was looking forward to an evening with some of the officers, when an urgent telegram was brought to him. Puzzled, he opened it. The message read: *'Fly back as soon as possible stop Your father suddenly passed away last night stop Mum'*.

He felt he had been slugged. The shock was profound. He couldn't grasp it at first, then arranged to speak to the purser, with the news. The purser expressed his sympathy, and said he would communicate it to the other officers including the captain. He would arrange for a locum doctor right away. A cheque for his services would be transferred telegraphically to his bank. The master then telephoned BOAC, and was booked onto a direct flight to Heathrow from DF Malan Airport leaving next day.

On arrival home he was greeted by (surprisingly) a warm hug from Brenda, as well as a mighty crush from David. His mum was weeping continuously, but still managed to give him a hug and a kiss.

'Tell me what happened to Dad,' he asked.

'He was reading the newspaper, and Mum asked him whether he wanted a cup of tea. Getting no response from behind the paper, she repeated the question. Still no reply. Then she pulled the paper away, and to her horror, saw him apparently staring into outer space. Then she said, "Sol, what are you playing at? Trying to frighten me are you? Sol, Sol! Oh my God, he's dead. No. No. No!"'

The funeral took place five days later in the village church. The eulogy was delivered by the vicar, having been informed of Sol's past. He described how Sol and his wife had escaped their fate from the Holocaust, their arrival in England and the prospering of their family, of which he had been justifiably proud. They were a highly respected family despite having initially had to contend with being regarded as aliens. Then the burial followed, Martha weeping uncontrollably.

Fortunately the family's income, though modest, was assured, as the German government, out of a profound sense of guilt, was paying restitution to many who had suffered the same fate. Brenda was still working as a hairdresser, and was by now engaged to Vic. David was studying technical drawing at the local technical college. But now the master was in a bit of a quandary. Which direction should he follow? Was his marriage irretrievably destroyed, or should he approach Carol, to see if it could be salvaged. And what about his career? He decided against calling Carol, as she had not contacted the family, and hadn't turned up for the funeral. That relationship was dead. He glanced through the *British Medical Journal*, and *The Lancet* looking for posts. To his surprise there was one which appeared very attractive, a GP locum in Skelmersdale. He could look up Maureen.

BRENDA

Brenda awoke to the sound of her alarm clock. It was July 1965. She remembered she had an important client that morning, Mrs Vera Hunter, the wife of a local landowner, and gentleman farmer. Mrs Hunter always had a blue rinse, and was a demanding woman. She wasn't very popular, but usually gave a generous tip, which kind of made up. Brenda snatched her breakfast, and just managed to catch the ten to nine Midland Red bus, which got her to work by a quarter past nine. Chloe, her colleague, had already got the tea on, and was sitting reading *Woman's Own*, smoking. She offered Brenda a cigarette from the packet of Kensitas, which was accepted. The radio was playing 'Music while you work' and a typical routine day beckoned.

'What's on today?' enquired Brenda.

'Oh, nothing special,' replied Chloe, 'but the delightful Mrs Hunter is scheduled for eleven o'clock, and you've a couple of wash and rinses before. How's Vic?'

'Much the same, nothing much to say, nothing much to write home about, pretty reliable, pretty boring, can't get excited.'

'Sounds ideal for marriage then,' quipped Chloe.

'All right smarty pants, and how's your love life?'

'Met this chap last week at the Majestic. Taking me to the pictures on Friday. Don't know what's on – doesn't really matter, you know what I mean.'

It seemed crystal clear to Brenda that Chloe's plan was to get it on with whoever it was. She wished she could feel that way about Vic.

As the morning wore on she got through the wash and rinses, and awaited the demanding Mrs Hunter. She saw the Bentley draw up, driven by Mr Hunter, and to her surprise, he came in with his wife.

'Good morning, ladies,' he said. 'Do look after the little lady. I'll call back for her in an hour.'

She sat down in the appointed chair. Chloe wrapped a towel around her neck in readiness for the wash, when Mrs Hunter noticed she had left her gloves in the car.

'Oh dear, I've forgotten my gloves, do fetch them, there's a dear,' she said to her husband. Mr Hunter was a robust man, ruddy complexion, and carrying a slight surplus of weight. He had a twinkle in his eye.

'Actually, I'm in a bit of a hurry, perhaps one of you ladies could come outside to the car, and I'll hand over the missus' gloves.'

'You go,' said Chloe. 'I'll mix the shampoo.'

So Brenda accompanied the farmer to his car. To her surprise he seemed quite leisurely considering the urgency of his alleged hurry. To her amazement, he put his arm around her, and asked her whether she would fancy dinner on Friday at a posh restaurant in Shrewsbury. She was aware of his after-shave, and admired his barefaced cheek.

'But what would your wife think, Mr Hunter?'

'Well, she's not going to know, and anyway, Friday is her bridge night.'

Brenda felt a thrill at the promise of a clandestine meeting, in total contrast to a predictable evening with Vic. She knew it was going against the grain, but the thought of going out with a married man, the thought of going to a posh restaurant, the thought of being driven there in a posh car, touched her.

'All right, Mr Hunter. Where shall we meet?'

'I'll meet you right here, at seven o'clock. The shops will all be shut, and the streets quiet. All right?'

'Yes,' was all the blushing Brenda could muster.

Her head was in a whirl. She was entering the world of loose women, brazen hussies, scarlet would be her colour. In fact, scarlet was her colour as she returned with the gloves. She felt covered with confusion, but somehow managed to compose herself, and get on with Mrs Hunter's hair.

'How's life, my dear?' asked Mrs Hunter. 'Have you got a young man?'

'Oh yes, Mrs Hunter, his name is Vic. Works at the Castle, as a fitter. Hopes to pass some exams so that he can apply for promotion. He works very hard.'

'Sounds nice and reliable,' replied Mrs Hunter with an ill-concealed tone of boredom. She opened a copy of *Woman's Own*.

'Oh look, here's a picture and story about Victor Mature. I think he's gorgeous, don't you? He was terrific in *The Robe,* and *Samson and Delilah.*'

Brenda agreed that he looked great, quite out of her league. She couldn't remember the films though. Why couldn't she meet chaps like that? Vic Teague was nice enough, but the sparks didn't exactly fly. And Percy Mildmay, (having assured her of

God's forgiveness beforehand), had relieved her of her virginity, but nevertheless had left her with a sense of disappointment about the whole process. Now she was facing an evening with Mr Hunter. She didn't even know his first name, he was at least ten years older than her, and she was about to administer a blue rinse to his wife seated in front of her. She wondered at this point how Sweeney Todd would have felt. A wealthy farmer, who drove a Bentley. All sorts of visions flashed before her. As for Mr Hunter, well he was of passable appearance, he didn't reveal any killer breath, so let's wait and see.

'Oh, sorry, Mrs Hunter, I hope these curlers didn't hurt.'

Brenda didn't mention the incident to Chloe, though she was quizzed as to what had kept her so long. Her response was that the gloves had proved hard to find, as they had slipped down between the green leather seats. Brenda's gaze at the time had ignored all the aesthetic beauty of the car, an S type, with a magnificent walnut fascia, but instead had marvelled at the roominess of the back seat, and the possibilities it offered.

Came Friday. The last client was booked in at five fifteen, a wash and set. Chloe had left earlier, excited about her date at the pictures with the chap she'd met the previous week at a dance. Brenda caught the bus home, told her mum she was going to the pictures. David hadn't yet come in. She bathed, soaking in a sea of bubbles, fantasising about Victor Mature. For some reason that I can only guess, she eventually started making Alice noises. But no-one heard, as the extractor fan was switched on. She wore ruby red bra and matching panties, a white suspender belt, and her best nylon stockings. Her dress was dark blue, and to this she added a gold-plated necklace. Martha thought her somewhat overdressed for the Clifton, and happened to ask what picture she was going to see. Damn! She was temporarily caught out, as she didn't know, so she invented a title.

'It's *The Robe*, with Victor Mature, I think, though I'm not sure.'

She alighted from the bus, and hurried to her rendezvous, arriving five minutes late. The Bentley was there waiting, its owner seated smoking a cigar.

'Good evening, my dear. My, you look fabulous, by the way, we haven't been introduced. Funny isn't it? My name is Bernard. What's yours?'

'Brenda.'

He took her hand, and gallantly kissed it. She blushed furiously, never having experienced anything like it before. She was enveloped in a world of leather, cigar smoke and expensive aftershave. The car proceeded rapidly gaining speed, as it swished along Watling Street, passing near the Roman town of Viroconium on its way to Shrewsbury. A table had been booked at the Lion Hotel. The head waiter greeted Mr Hunter remarking how pleased he was to see him again. Brenda was briefly perused, and ignored. They were ushered to a table in a corner, with a small table lamp. It was all very comforting. Yes, she would like a drink beforehand, and feeling quite grown up, she ordered a dry Martini. Bernard had a pint of Wrekin ale. And a second pint. And a second Martini. The menu was scanned, Brenda ordered chicken in the basket, Bernard, a fillet steak. And as though they both hadn't drunk enough, a bottle of Pommard, which went down extremely well. Both by now were very relaxed. For sweet, Brenda ordered a knickerbocker glory, Bernard cheese and biscuits. This was followed by Irish coffee.

As might be anticipated, by now Bernard was shall we say, fairly well oiled, Brenda was unsteady on her feet, but felt good, very good. This was the life! Posh car, good food, lots of booze. The only thing missing was Victor Mature. She looked again at Bernard, and attempted to fantasize, but no-way could he be mistaken for Mr Mature. He fitted the mature bit however, being all of forty-five years old. They left the hotel, and went for a walk along the River Severn, St Chad's Church high on the hill, and Shrewsbury School on the other side. He put his arm around her. She didn't resist. Then he turned her towards him, and kissed her neck. She found this rather amusing, fancy an old man doing this to her. The next thing he was pressing his lips to hers. She felt an intuitive feeling of wanting to respond, then good sense prevailed, and she told him to stop.

'I don't kiss on the first date, and anyway, we hardly know each other. Let's just keep it nice and friendly, no more.'

Bernard wasn't too pleased. He was used to getting his way, although admittedly this was more with ladies of older vintage. The return journey in the car was quiet, little was said, though much was thought about. Bernard liked this young lass of under thirty, he surmised she had a nice body, if only he could get to it. Brenda thought him old, but there was probably considerably more mileage in the relationship, provided she played her cards right. The car dropped her off about a hundred yards away from home. Bernard said goodnight and gave her hand a gallant kiss.

'We must meet again, mustn't we?'

'Yes, Bernard, that would be nice. And thanks for a lovely evening.'

Brenda carefully inserted her key in the lock, hoping to enter unobserved, but David caught her tiptoeing up the stairs.

'Oh, been out on a date, have we?'

'Yes, what about it?'

'Anyone I know?'

'No, no-one special, just someone I met at work.'

'I thought you only met ladies at work, you don't get too many men sporting blue rinses round here. Come on, give give give.'

'Oh all right, it's just some bloke I met, one of our client's brothers,' she lied.

'So where did he take you? Did you go to the pictures, I don't think there was a dance tonight.'

'Well, as a matter of fact, he took me out for a meal. Then we chatted, and he dropped me home in his car.'

'Oh, so he's got his own car. Must be pretty well off. Well done, Sis. Goodnight.'

Brenda heaved a sigh of relief. Telling them of the enormity of what had happened would be lighting the tinderbox. But the next day, she was dying to tell Chloe, who listened to her with her mouth agape.

'But he's married. And he's much older than you. Did he try it on?'

'Well, just a bit, but I told him to stop. I think, if I play my cards right, it could be a load of fun, and be ever so exciting. Forbidden fruit and all that.'

Chloe felt very envious. Her evening at the pictures had been pretty routine. Half cinema watching and half snogging. She wondered when Mrs Turner would be booked in again, and playing bridge. Well, to cut a long story short, Brenda and Bernard went out twice more, and then he invited Brenda to accompany him to a farmers' fair in Hereford, on the pretext that he was going to buy some beef cattle. It would involve a night at a hotel, but she needn't fear, he would arrange separate rooms. He booked in at the Green Dragon, a traditional sixteenth century coaching inn. Brenda enjoyed the day at the farmers' fair, with all the hustle and bustle, the noise and the smells, the good-natured banter. Bernard seemed to be pretty popular, and when the other farmers saw her, they gave him a knowing wink. She guessed he was probably a bit of a lad, but she didn't mind, as she was having a good time. Her room was delightful, and had its own shower and toilet. The bed was a double one, which she hadn't expected.

They dined in the hotel's restaurant. By now she had picked up the routine of a drink before, a drink or two with, and another after the meal. Feeling very daring, Brenda allowed Bernard to check her room, as he had expressed interest in seeing she was being well looked after. Obviously, his true motive was otherwise, and Brenda knew. The usual choreographed procedure began, and Bernard realised he was onto a good thing. The only problem was me, or shall I say, another of my ilk. It never ceases to amaze me how many men paralyse the nerves involved in getting us into combat, by liberally bathing them in alcohol. Poor Bernard was very frustrated, and Brenda was insufficiently experienced in the wily ways of the professionals, who no doubt would have been successful in creating a Ben Nevis out of a Wrekin. Before long, both fell asleep. Next morning however, Ben Nevis made its appearance, and the Cresta run was once again in use, with a few Alice noises, but no better than it had been with Mildmay. Bernard delivered her home safely that day, and then lost interest. He decided in future to leave it to the professionals. Brenda recounted her experiences with a few embellishments to an awestruck Chloe. In future she remained faithful to Vic, who hadn't the faintest notion of what had transpired.

DAVID

David was doing well at the Shrewsbury Technical College, and managed to gain an apprenticeship at Dowty Boulton Paul, in Wolverhampton. This company had built aircraft, the most famous being the Defiant, which rivalled, but never quite achieved the immortality of the Spitfire. They also worked on jet aircraft, including the Canberra and the Vampire. David was very excited, and passed all the necessary exams. He would travel up to Wolverhampton every day on the seven forty-two, and was employed on the production line of the Balliol, which was a training aircraft. He became an ardent supporter of the Wolves, and attended the Molyneux ground whenever he could. 'Out of darkness cometh light' was the club's motto, though quite how this applied to soccer would only become clear when floodlighting was installed. He was a very loyal chap, and supported his parents to the best of his ability. Always, however, he felt that he was in his brother's shadow. Biology and disease had never interested him, whereas building and flying model aeroplanes had wetted his appetite, and now he was happily involved in real aircraft production. Religion didn't really influence him, and he hadn't much time for the opposite sex, until he met Vera.

Vera worked in the drawing office at the factory, and was quite petite, with red hair, and freckles. She lived in Darlaston, and was a typical Black Country lass. Her laughter was infectious, and they got on like a house on fire, but romance wasn't on David's mind. He seemed immune to the stresses and strains imposed on others by their hormones. One day, they happened to meet in the works canteen at coffee time. Lots of people were smoking, and as David entered, he saw Vera being offered a cigarette by Jake Dawkins, a well-known Wolverhampton Lothario. He managed the drawing office, and felt a little jealous of David's relaxed attitude when in Vera's company. He had already bedded two of the girls in the typing pool, and rather fancied a stab at Vera. Vera politely declined his offer, saying she had never started smoking and didn't intend to.

'Thanks, Mr Dawkins, but I'd rather not, thanks all the same.'

'Come on, Vera, what about we go out for a drink and a bite of supper after work on Friday?'

Vera had heard about Jake's reputation, and didn't want to risk hers. And anyway, thus far she had kept her cherry, despite a pretty determined attempt to rid her of it at last year's works Christmas party. This had occurred after she unwisely accepted a lift home from one of the managers in his MG sports car. She owed her virginity not so much to her moral fibre as to the geometry of the cabin layout, and in particular, the gear lever. The manager's manhood was no match for the size and stubborn resistance offered by said gear lever. When he attempted to lever himself over it, the car countered by the size and position of the steering wheel. Any attempt to recline the passenger seat was resisted by the lack of this facility on this particular car. All in all, the design of the MG owed a lot to the teachings of St. Paul, whose views on chastity had subconsciously been transmitted to the design team at Abingdon.

'Well, that's really a tempting offer, but it just so happens I'm going to the pictures with David on Friday.'

'Well, just tell him you've had a better offer.'

And with that, he put his arm around her, and half lifted her towards him. David saw that Vera was clearly embarrassed, and came over.

'Mr Dawkins, I think Vera isn't feeling too well. I'd rather you left her alone.'

'Oh, so you're the gallant Sir Galahad,' countered Jake, 'buzz off or I'll make it the worse for you.'

'What exactly do you mean by that, Mr Dawkins?' bravely asked David.

'Well, let's put it this way. I suppose promotion is something you've thought about at some time. Well, I could relieve you of your ambitions, so you'll have a quiet life in a dead-end job.'

'Thanks, Mr Dawkins, but if that's what I have to do in order to help Vera, then so be it. Come on, Vera, let's go out for a little fresh air.'

And with that, they walked out of the canteen, leaving Dawkins aghast. He wasn't used to resistance, but soon forgot this when he spotted Busty Betty coming in for her break.

'Gosh, David,' said an awestruck Vera, 'that certainly was brave.'

'Oh, it was nothing much,' replied David, 'he's just a loudmouth. Tell you what, how about we go out on Friday night? Max Bygraves is on at the Gaumont.'

'Why, David, that would be lovely,' said Vera.

From that day, their relationship blossomed, and a year later they got engaged. They got married in All Saints Church in

Darlaston, the church having been bombed in the war and rebuilt in 1950.

*

Now to return to Pablo.

He telephoned the surgery, and on the following Monday set sail in the Sprite for Skelmersdale to be interviewed by Dr Horatio Evans, the senior partner, who was in need of an assistant on account of the other partner, Dr James, having developed cancer of the bowel, and whose return was uncertain. Dr Evans was a typical no-nonsense Yorkshireman who told the master the job was, 'Bloody hard, most of the patients are lead swingers, or have incurable chest disease as a consequence of having spent their working lives down the pit or in the cotton mills. Either that or lung cancer since most also smoked at least twenty Woodbines.'

Armed with this cheerful information the master accepted the post that was offered, and agreed to start work the following week. Then he telephoned Maureen, who was clearly delighted to hear from him. He told her he would be back the following week to start his locum job. Dr Evans told him he had arranged temporary accommodation for him at Mrs Watkins, who ran a small but homely B & B.

The following week he started his job, with morning surgery on the Monday. As predicted, the waiting room had a selection of coughs and colds, with two little children with runny noses, who were busy arguing and crying. His first patient was Mrs Joan Ellimore, who was troubled by her piles. Next, a sore throat, then painful varicose veins, then angina, then a breast lump, and coffee arrived served by Mrs Machin. Plough on to the end of the morning, then off on home visits, mainly to the elderly, as a routine, not requiring a special request. After that, he had a couple of hours free, before evening surgery from five till seven o'clock. By the first weekend, he was feeling quite tired, but had to be on call, as Dr Evans was going away for a golfing weekend. Despite this he was able to meet Maureen and little Cliff for afternoon tea on Sunday. She appeared wearing a pretty flared dress with a pointy bra, high heels and stockings. She wore a cheap necklace and pink lipstick.

'Hallo, Pablo, it's lovely to see you. Cliff, this is the doctor, don't you remember?'

'No,' replied Cliff, disinterestedly. 'Come on, Mum, let's go, this is boring.'

He clearly was a case of premature teenager-hood.

'Cliff, behave yourself,' she said.

'Would you like an ice cream?' asked the master.

'No,' came the reply. Things weren't going particularly well. Afterwards, the master drove them back to Maureen's house, Cliff perched on her lap in the Sprite. This he clearly enjoyed, and tried changing gear without prompting.

'All right, Cliff, you can do it when I tell you,' said the master.

'Right, now, pull the lever down,' and this permitted a fairly acceptable gear change. Now Cliff was a changed person, and performed several more changes, two without prompting, resulting in a grating noise

'Do you ever have a baby-sitter?' asked the master.

'Yes,' replied Cliff. 'Mum often has the baby-sitter, for when she goes out with my uncles. Sometimes they bring me chocolates, and allow me to watch telly while they go upstairs to have their discuss – discussions.'

The master turned pale – it was immediately obvious that Maureen was on the game.

'Well, what do you expect me to do? I've got to provide for Cliff, and my mother.'

'Maureen, I never thought that of you,' said the master judgementally.

'Well, in that case you'd better go.'

And that was the end of the Maureen affair, though in fact there never was an affair though there might have been. The master however felt sorry for her, and tried to recover the situation, but to no avail.

'All right, Maureen,' he said, 'I will, but don't think I feel any the less for you. I realise it's a difficult situation.' And so Maureen faded out of the master's life.

To be perfectly frank, the next couple of years passed uneventfully, the master being very busy, and there were no ladies who took his fancy. I was beginning to feel quite redundant, because with the exception of the odd training run, my services weren't required. Until one morning after surgery, he was asked to see a drug rep. To those not familiar with the medical profession, this was not a drug pusher, at least not in the criminal sense, but a representative of a pharmaceutical company whose job it was to persuade the doctor to prescribe its particular brand. In truth, the master didn't take in a lot of the facts with which she regaled him. The slope of the graph indicating the duration of onset of clinical response to the drug was less fascinating than the slope of her thighs. The bell-shaped curve of a normal distribution, in a statistical sense, was outweighed by the dual bell shapes of her breasts. At the end of the ten-minute session, she asked him if he had any questions. He said no, but she then invited him to a meeting the following week to be held in an Indian restaurant, where other GPs would also be present, and where there would be a short presentation and discussion about the product, before the meal. Although the drug in question could hardly be regarded as revolutionary, the master agreed out of interest in the attractive lady in question.

Came the evening, and Bella gave a ten-minute presentation to an audience whose interests were in truth, more gastronomical than pharmacological. At the end of the meeting, the master, gentleman that he was, offered to help her carry the screen and projector to her car. Bella was a curvaceous lady of twenty-four, with long glossy black hair, generous lips as well as her other attributes previously hinted at. She was very matter of fact and quite jolly.

'I suppose you'd like to catch me up, and ask me out?' she said.

The master was quite taken aback, as he knew this sort of thing went against the usual professional code, but he was prepared to give it a try.

'Well would you like to come out for a meal sometime?'

'Sure,' was the reply, 'on the understanding that you're not married.'

I stirred a little from my state of slumber, and two years of disuse. They arranged to meet at a country pub out in the Dales the following Friday. The master found himself looking forward immensely to the possibility of throwing off the mantle of celibacy, but additionally, she seemed a most attractive person. Perhaps she had some sort of past history. He called for her in the Sprite. She had an apartment just outside the town. It was a pleasant summer evening, and he put the hood down. Luckily she had a headscarf, and away they went. She clearly enjoyed being driven with some panache (not much panache because it was only a Sprite, and not capable of more than seventy-five miles an hour, but it cornered beautifully), which led to the master showing off a bit. The evening star made its appearance. This was noticed by Bella, who asked whether the master knew what the evening star was. He replied that he didn't, but was duly informed that it was Venus. He wondered if this was some portent of what was to follow, and I thought the same. The evening went well, the food was simple but good, as was the beer. There was no worry about drinking and driving, as the blood alcohol was not routinely measured in those days. If there was doubt, the police would ask the suspect driver to walk along a straight white line. Sometimes they also asked the driver to repeat, 'The Leith police dismisseth thee'. The master dropped her off outside her flat, but there was no invitation to come in. She permitted a small peck on the cheek, and they exchanged phone numbers.

Over the next few months, they met on average once every two weeks, and gradually their feelings for each other developed. Bella was single, and had been engaged previously to another doctor called Harry Shipman. She dropped him because he had some strange views on euthanasia, which she found quite disturbing. The master asked her if she would fancy a weekend in London. She agreed, and the following weekend they were London bound in the Sprite. The master had managed to get seats for *Oliver*, at a theatre in Shaftesbury Avenue. They had a post theatre supper at *'Le jardin des gourmets'*, which cost a bomb. Then, to a little private hotel in Ebury Street, and bed. One double bed. They undressed, switched off the lights, but left the wall gas heater on, which threw out a warm glow. They undressed. Bella was exquisitely lovely, her lips moist with passion. The master could hardly believe his luck, and they kissed, first tenderly, then with ever increasing passion. By now, I was getting into overdrive, which clearly came to Bella's notice, as she (literally) took me in hand. It was as though she were examining an interesting antique ornament, which I didn't find particularly flattering.

'Not bad,' she murmured. 'Now let's see what it can do.'

I must admit, I didn't perform badly, unaware that my perception of performance was in Bella's view, merely the overture to the opera. Reprise followed reprise, the Alice score rising from an initial four, to nine, which resulted in a polite tapping on the ceiling from the incumbents on the floor above. In the course of the aforementioned activities, the bed had migrated across the floor, and was knocking against the opposite wall. At last, passion requited, the lovers lay back, and, bodies still entwined, sank into a deep sleep. I think I can, without fear of contradiction, say that was the busiest night of my life. The following day, after a traditional English breakfast, the lovers went for a walk in Hyde Park.

From that weekend in London, they continued seeing each other regularly, until eventually, after six months, the master proposed to Bella and provided a pretty diamond and sapphire ring from an upmarket jeweller, which cost him a month's wages. Together, they saved as much as they could, in preparation for their honeymoon, to be spent in Tenerife, and the wedding which was to be a registry office affair. Bella's father was a travelling salesman in the hosiery trade, and with an amazing collection of funny stories, oft repeated. Her mother was rather quiet, and wrapped up in gardening. She had no siblings, so it was a bit of a wrench seeing their little girl joining another family. Speaking of which, David, the master's brother, was best man. Balmic and Jackson, his student pals also attended. Neither was married, Balmic was by now a registrar in surgery, hoping to pass the FRCS exam, to eventually become a consultant surgeon. But job interviews were hard to come by, so that eventually, in the future, despite attaining the exam, he would emigrate and become a surgeon in Canada. Jackson was destined to become a rheumatologist, with a passionate desire to find the cause, as well as the cure for rheumatoid arthritis. Martha was smartly dressed in a costume with an embroidered veil. Brenda and Vic were also there, Brenda by now being six months pregnant.

The wedding passed without incident, and the happy couple flew to Tenerife, to commence their honeymoon. The weather was hot and sunny, and the master lazed on the beach taking in the sun. He hired a little Fiat, so they could travel around, and marvel at Mount Teide. He wore some shorts in an attempt to attain a more generalised tan. Unfortunately, the Fiat's seats were of poor quality plastic, as a result of which Bill and Ben and I suffered terribly in the heat, bathed in sweat which had no hope of evaporation. Bella by some good fortune escaped this by wearing a dress. At first, things seemed OK, but by the third day, Bill, Ben and I together would have passed as a lobster had we been paraded on a fishmonger's slab. Any thought of me standing up for England vanished quickly. The master suffered terrible irritation, and Bella had to purchase some calamine lotion, with which to bathe those parts she had intended putting to a different use. Despite this setback, the honeymoon was very enjoyable, paella and Rioja were generously partaken of, and the happy couple returned to England. Alice sounds were not to be heard for about a month, due to the protracted healing process, and the master and Bella being very busy at work. Life was fine, they had time to go out frequently to enjoy themselves, until one day, Bella gave the master some news that was destined to change things radically. She was pregnant! In the course of the next ten years, they were to have, in all, four children: Nathan, Michael, Ronald, and a daughter Elise. They bought a fine Victorian four-bedroomed house, and watched their family grow. They moved the family about in a Ford Cortina, bye-bye Sprite, and those halcyon days in which it had played so important a role.

Part 3
Autumn

(Age forty to sixty)

I was still occasionally needed, but it somehow wasn't the same any more. Life had slipped into a kind of routine. I couldn't muster the same kind of elevation, and Alice sounds became a thing of the past. And so time passed. The children grew up, Nathan secured a place at university to read law, Michael went to an agricultural college studying animal husbandry, Ronald also went to university, but dropped out after a year, and joined a rock band. Elise went to a dance academy. Now the master's fiftieth birthday was imminent, and a celebration was arranged to take place at the local cricket club.

The master had, by now put on quite a lot of weight, and had developed borderline diabetes. Bella was also a bit overweight, but struggled valiantly to keep fit. The master had developed a penchant for red burgundy, and whisky, particularly Bushmills. I felt totally neglected, as my sole duty had now been relegated to that of peering at Armitage Shanks, or Twyfords or Duravit. I was incapable of attaining ninety degrees elevation without being lifted, and that only for the aforesaid purpose. I was feeling thoroughly pissed off. The master was becoming increasingly disenchanted with the state of the NHS, and still having to make home visits, including nights and weekends, although it was on a rota with six other GPs. Bella kept cheerful, and was a good mother, and an excellent cook.

Came the day for his fiftieth birthday celebration. Bella had bought him a Longines watch, having dug deep into her savings. Nathan had secured a bottle of vintage port from Berry and

Rudd, who also supplied the royal household. Michael presented him with a Lowry print. Ronald provided a Jimmy Hendrix record. Elise had found some cufflinks made from half-sovereigns. Outside caterers were brought in, and the meal was very good, especially the roast beef. Next day, he and Bella flew to Milan, hired a car and drove to a delightful hotel beside Lago Maggiore. All was apparently well, except that I wasn't. Bella said it didn't matter, but deep down, it did. The master found it hard to understand how something which once upon a time, worked well, at times embarrassingly so, now was a limp caricature of its former self. They toured the other Italian lakes. Lake Como, and in particular Bellagio, was the highlight of the visit.

The following week, life was back to normal, the weather was drizzly and dull. Where life abounded the previous week, the Lancashire world was grey, dull, and utterly miserable. As were the patients, huddled in the waiting room with coughs and colds, and demanding antibiotics. It was difficult to dissuade them of the futility of antibiotics for these ailments which for the most part were due to viral infections, for which antibiotics were useless. Better, far better, to have stopped smoking (ash-trays however were still provided). At morning tea break, the three doctors of the partnership would, when convenient, foregather. The other two comprised Audrey Phipps, a plain plump lass of fifty something who had graduated from Sheffield, and Piers Hannigan, who was aged thirty and was a Guy's Hospital product. Piers was a somewhat flamboyant character, blond-haired and rather handsome and drove a Jaguar E type. The younger and not so young female patients were usually pleased to make an appointment to see him. The master didn't mind, he had no particular aspirations in that direction, his main interests being Bella's cooking, and his collection of burgundy wines.

One Thursday, Bella awoke feeling ill and professing a raging throat, and a high temperature. The master gave her a couple of aspirins, and advised her to drink plenty of fluids, but not alcohol. That morning during the tea break, the master happened to mention about Bella. Audrey said she would pop in and give her a once over if the master didn't mind. He said he was sure it was nothing serious, but thanks, by all means, and he would be very grateful that she was putting herself out. He was very busy himself, and had been requested to make several home visits, including seeing Matthew Weaver, who was dying at home, of lung cancer. But just as Dr Phipps was getting ready to visit Mrs Bernstein, she was asked to attend another patient who was possibly suffering a heart attack. Dr Hannigan said he would deputise and visit Mrs Bernstein. The master expressed his gratitude.

Later that afternoon, he saw poor Weaver, who was coughing continuously, and bringing up blood. He declined the master's suggestion of being moved to hospital, preferring the company of his dog to help him see out his last days. An injection of morphine settled his cough, and he fell asleep. On the way back to the surgery, the master felt that perhaps he should pop back and see how Bella was. By now it was half past two, and to his surprise Dr Hannigan's Jaguar was parked outside the house. He was instantly worried in case Bella was more ill than he had assumed. As he entered the house, the TV was on, quite loud, with Coronation Street. He went upstairs, and as he stood on the landing, his blood went cold. From the bedroom came the distinct sound of Alice noises. A cacophony of moaning with the

237

occasional interjection of 'Yes, yes, yes'. He opened the door. Bella had clearly made a remarkable recovery, and was riding young Hannigan as though her life depended on it. Hearing the door open, she gave a muted scream, and ran past the master and locked herself in the bathroom. At this point things moved very quickly. I was the silent witness. The first punch knocked out Hannigan's two front teeth. The second broke his nose. Then the master backed off, and went downstairs. He poured himself a double whisky, and agonised. After about five minutes Hannigan appeared with tissue paper stuck all over his face.

'Look here, old chap, I'm frightfully sorry. I just felt she needed a bit of the you know what. Clearly she wasn't getting enough. I suppose I was helping you out. A fine way to show your gratitude.'

He was lucky the master didn't knock out his remaining teeth. Instead he threw him out of the front door, then went upstairs to confront Bella who by this time had showered and pulled on her dressing gown.

'Pablo, I know "sorry" isn't enough. I don't know why I did it. But there has been a void between us for some time now. You can divorce me if you wish, and I'll go quietly. We can arrange to see our solicitors when we've had some time to think things over.'

'Bella, what exactly do you mean when you say there has been a void between us?'

'Well, Pablo, it may have escaped your notice, but you have performed abysmally in the bedroom department. You have been totally unaware of how I feel; you've always avoided the subject whenever I've tried talking to you. You go on about pressure of work, and you are clearly drinking too much. No wonder things aren't functioning.'

I felt a pang of guilt. But what could I do about it?

The divorce was quick and relatively amicable. Bella admitted adultery. The house was put up for sale, with the proceeds divided equally. The master initially rented a flat, and after three months, secured another job, in Shrewsbury. In the evenings he went for walks along the towpath of the Severn, in an attempt to sort out his life. He was still drinking quite heavily, and I might as well not have existed.

The shock of the event had a profound effect on him. Things became a struggle – even getting out of bed, even eating, and drinking. He gradually began sinking into a deep depression. He considered suicide, but simply didn't have the energy. He was getting late for work, which prompted comments from the staff at the surgery. Dr Hannigan remained for four weeks, and then by mutual agreement had to leave on account of non-professional conduct. A locum was obtained, Dr Jamir Khan, who had qualified in Islamabad. Fortunately his English was acceptable, and he was eventually well received by the patients who initially made it clear they preferred to see a doctor whose first language was English. But within a couple of months, he became quite popular. His wife was English. They had met when he was doing a senior house officer job in midwifery, as a consequence of which, he secured the necessary qualifications to oversee pregnant patients. Dr Bernstein came to rely more and more on Dr Khan, and continued drinking heavily. He found he couldn't sleep through the night, frequently waking at three o'clock, and being unable to fall asleep again. Naturally, he soon felt totally worn out, and had to take sick leave. He decided it was time to end it all, and purchased a couple of bottles of aspirin. He then took fifty tablets, drank half a bottle of whisky, and went to bed, hoping to die. Fortunately, his stomach rebelled, and he rushed to the toilet, where he was violently sick. He then returned to the bedroom, and fell asleep on top of the duvet. At eleven o'clock next morning he was awoken by loud knocking on the front door. He managed to stagger downstairs, opened the door, and found the postman carrying a parcel for him. It was a mail-order catalogue which Bella had ordered, and which he promptly binned. He then showered, and told himself how stupid he had been, and went out for a walk. Gradually he pulled out of his depression, and was able to return to work.

BALMIC

Balmic satisfactorily completed his house-surgeon's job at the local teaching hospital, and then did a six months' job in medicine out of town. This didn't matter to him, as he was intending to be a surgeon, so it was mainly prestigious surgical jobs that would count. After his job in medicine, he applied to the medical school, for a demonstrator's post in the department of anatomy, whereby he hoped to gain sufficient knowledge to pass the primary examination for the Fellowship of the Royal College of Surgeons, (FRCS), which he felt would guarantee him a position as a future consultant surgeon. Unfortunately what he had failed to realise, was that there existed in fact, if not in theory, a colour bar. Thus, having eventually passed the primary FRCS, and proceeded to a surgical registrar's post, he could not get such a post in a teaching hospital. Instead it was in a local city some forty miles away, where he gained considerable experience treating all manner of conditions which his Caucasian colleagues in the marble halls could only marvel at. Nevertheless, he ploughed on, and eventually passed the final FRCS examination. In theory now, he needed to obtain a senior registrar's job, and with good luck after a further four or five years, he would stand a good chance of getting a consultant surgeon's post.

But it didn't happen that way. OK, so he didn't get an interview for the first two senior registrar posts for which he applied. Then, at his third attempt, he got an interview for such a post at a district general hospital which had close links to the local teaching hospital. He kissed Urmila (his wife of two years' standing, and their son Balmic junior), before setting off in his Beetle.

'Well, Mr Punja, tell us about your range of experience. Have you done any partial gastrectomies?'

Balmic laughed. What a question! He had done scores, whereas colleagues at the teaching hospitals hadn't done many, because they were done there by the senior registrars.

'Actually, I've done thirty in the last eighteen months, plus loads of cholecystectomies (removal of the gall bladder), thyroids, prostates, colon resections, and three aortic aneurysms.'

'Come come, Mr Punja, you can't expect us to believe you've had this amount of experience.'

'Well, actually, I've got a testament to that effect from my boss, Mr Horrobin.'

'Ah, Horrobin, I remember him. Yes. Well we won't go into that. By the way, haven't you considered applying for a job in, where is it, oh yes, Kenya? I'm sure there is a great demand for chaps like you. Well, Mr Punja, I suggest you wait outside till we've finished interviewing.'

And so the hopeful Balmic waited in the corridor. There were two other candidates waiting, both caucasian, and one, Mark Lessing was from the same medical school as Balmic. They greeted each other, and chatted about their previous experience. The other wore a pinstripe suit, and had a striped shirt with a detachable plain white stiff collar. His hair was brushed down to one side, and he had half-rim spectacles. He had qualified at St Thomas's Hospital in London. He did not speak, but buried himself in *The Lancet*.

'Mr Fitz-Hugh Robinson, please come this way.'

He smiled and walked past the other two, his black shoes with shellacked toecaps emitting a squeak.

"He can't be for real,' said Balmic.

'Bet he gets the job,' replied Lessing.

Lessing's father was a GP, who had trained at the same medical school, and Lessing had secured a registrar's job at the teaching hospital. However, he had had far less surgical experience than Balmic, in fact he could hardly suppress his envy at the range of Balmic's experiences.

'I reckon you'll be a cert for this job, Balmic. I don't come close. Of course that other chap might just walk away with it. He even looks like a Harley Street consultant.'

After a quarter of an hour, a smug looking Fitz-Hugh Robinson emerged, and, ignoring the others, resumed reading *The Lancet*.

'Mr Lessing, would you come this way please.'

Balmic tried to engage Fitz-Hugh Robinson in conversation, but with little success, so got out a copy of *The Times*, and attempted the crossword. After twenty minutes, Lessing emerged.

'Well, how did you get on?' asked Balmic.

'Not bad, they seemed more interested in reminiscing about old times when they were at medical school with my dad. Then they asked what experience I'd had, and had I done any aortic aneurysms. I told them that was the province of arterial surgeons, and that I hadn't performed any myself though I had assisted at a couple. They seemed satisfied.'

After a further fifteen minutes, the clerk appeared. This was it! All three interviewees looked up in hope. Balmic felt confident that, based on experience, he would be the outright winner.

'Mr Lessing, please come this way.'

An unbelieving Lessing got up and followed her.

'Well, that's it then I suppose. Didn't really want the job. Got an interview at Guy's next week,' said Fitz-Hugh Robinson.

And with that, Fitz-Hugh Robinson got up and left. Balmic wondered what he had done wrong. He asked the clerk if he was still required. She told him he was free to go, and better luck next time. None of the interviewing panel was going to see him.

When he got home he told Urmila of his experience.

'Oh, Balmic, I'm so sorry. But you must realise, there is still colour prejudice here, whatever they say. We could go to Canada and try our luck.'

'Don't worry, darling, I've got three more applications in the pipeline.'

But he didn't get any more interviews. His hospital was delighted to keep him, as he was carrying out sterling service, and taking much of the pressure off the consultants. One of them, Mr Cheeseman, took him aside one day.

'Punja, I don't like telling you this, but as you may be aware, you'll never get a consultant job in this country, despite your ability. You know the reason, I dare not say it. But I promise you, the best possible references.'

And so it was that the Punjas flew to Winnipeg the following autumn. Balmic applied for a post at St Boniface Hospital, and was duly interviewed. All went well, but then came the bombshell.

'Of course, Mr Punja, you do realise that your FRCS isn't recognised in Canada, so you'll have to complete two years' further training here before you are eligible to take the exam. After that, we look forward to receiving your application.'

Balmic broke the news to an unbelieving Urmila.

'Well, darling, you'll just have to get on with it.'

And so he did, and two years later, complete with the Canadian FRCS he secured the equivalent of a senior registrar's job. A year after that, and no doubt helped by his previous experience, he became the equivalent of a consultant. Two weeks earlier, Urmila had been delivered of their second child, a healthy boy whom they named Suru. Balmic, no doubt building on his earlier experience, soon became head of the arterial surgery division. Apart from the fearfully cold winters, life was looking up. Then, in 1975, he made a successful application for a job at the Vancouver General Hospital, which was affiliated to the university, in effect, a teaching hospital appointment. Vancouver's gain was the United Kingdom's loss. Lessing never succeeded in gaining a consultant's appointment on account of a drink problem. Fitz-Hugh Robinson obtained a job in plastic surgery at a hospital north of London, but used this as his launch for rooms in Harley Street. Here he became a society doctor, the Arabian brethren especially admiring this caricature of Englishness. But it would all fall apart when he was found guilty by the General Medical Council of incompetence after a patient died under the knife whilst undergoing cosmetic surgery, in an attempt to out-do Jayne Mansfield, who was well known for her bow wave. The unfortunate patient was found at post-mortem to have a serious heart condition, which had gone undetected prior to surgery at a prestigious clinic. He was sadly missed by the aforesaid Arabian brethren for whom, at a grossly outrageous price, he would surgically restore virginity to certain noble ladies born into a culture for whom this really mattered. Fitz Hugh-Robinson was suspended, and was last heard of working at a clinic in Saudi-Arabia. Balmic and Urmila meanwhile were to have two more children, making four boys in all.

JACKSON

Jackson Annesley after his graduation did his pre-registration medicine at a busy hospital in Mansfield. His six months of surgery were at the same hospital, but it became clear to him that he would rather be a physician than a surgeon. He obtained a senior house officer's post in Stratford, and studied hard for the membership of the Royal College of Physicians examination. This was the equivalent for a would-be physician as the FRCS for a would-be surgeon. The dreamed of accolade was MRCP. The exam was notoriously difficult with a pass rate at the time of little over ten per cent for the first part. Nearly everyone failed first time. But Jackson sailed through, and was thus placed at a distinct advantage in applying for a teaching hospital registrar job.

He had obtained considerable experience in treating a multitude of conditions, but was particularly fascinated by rheumatoid arthritis. It was a disease for which the cause was unknown, and like many others of unknown cause was termed 'autoimmune'. Someone had discovered that the body's immune system could sometimes actually cause harm in addition to protecting against and fighting infections. Indeed, lots of diseases whose cause was unknown were stated by doctors to be 'autoimmune', at the same time being accompanied by a facial expression of wisdom so profound that no mere patient could begin to understand the complexity. In other words, the profession was hiding its ignorance. It was at about this time that cortisone was being tried and at first the results were remarkable. Patients who had been confined to their beds could suddenly get up and dance – at least that was the picture conjured up in the United States. And a Nobel prize was not long in coming to be awarded to two doctors over there. But all was not well. Many patients developed serious side effects, and quite quickly the drug fell into disrepute. Gold injections, originally tried in the treatment of tuberculosis, were found to be of benefit, but again, side effects were the problem. Jackson felt that everyone was trying to find a cure, or at least a quick fix, but no-one seemed interested in finding the cause. There were several false dawns.

It was at a hospital dance, he met a pretty girl called Marilyn who was training to be a teacher at a college near Camberwell. She originally came from Shropshire, but her parents had moved to the Midlands, and she had tagged along with a friend called Jean who had come to the dance with Godfrey, her boyfriend. Jackson began dating Marilyn, and the relationship blossomed. Before long, my counterpart was called into play, and performed acceptably, if not remarkably. A year later they got engaged.

One evening in December, Jackson was on his way to accompany Marilyn to a dinner dance in London, arranged by her teacher training college. Unfortunately, his car had a puncture, so he was late. To his surprise Marilyn was very annoyed at his lack of punctuality, though it was nothing he could have avoided. And then, promptly at ten o'clock, she announced she was leaving in a taxi. Jackson followed the taxi in his car, then entered the college just behind her, and chased her up to her room. She told him the engagement was off, and removed her sapphire and diamond ring, and gave it to him. He was distraught, having no idea what he had done wrong. But Marilyn could not be reasoned with. Jackson was deeply hurt, and for a while, his work suffered. He became acutely depressed and considered ending his life. For a while his work suffered, and his consultant called him aside one day.

'Jackson, there's obviously something wrong. Up to now, your standard of work has been exemplary, but yesterday we received a complaint that you had been rude to a patient.'

'It's just that my fiancée has broken off our engagement, and I've no idea why.'

'Well, apart from the fact she must be mad, I think she's probably done you a favour, though you may not think so right now. Try to concentrate on the part two of the membership exam, that should be your priority right now. You shouldn't have any trouble, after all you passed the first part first time.'

A few months later, having come to terms with the situation, he presented himself for the second part of the membership at a prestigious London teaching hospital. He had a short while previously sat the written paper which had gone well. Now he had to deal with a long case, followed by several short cases. The examiners he faced all looked like Fitz-Hugh Robinson clones. During the short cases the examiner, without comment walked out, never came back, no explanation was given, and he was left to wander home in his misery. Unsurprisingly he found he had failed. He wondered what sort of Royal College he was trying to become a member of. But he persevered at the exam, taking it on no fewer than two more occasions, until eventually he was successful.

Now he knew his career would open up, but first he had to come to terms with the fact that jobs in general medicine were the hardest to come by, whereas physical medicine was much easier. He wondered what physical medicine entailed, and was put off by the fact that it seemed to concentrate on physical methods of treating patients, especially those with arthritis, but also some with neurological disorders. Many of the existing consultants hadn't passed the MRCP, instead possessing a diploma in physical medicine. In fact, many were dedicated physicians who had been trained in army hospitals, and who had done sterling work during the War. However, change was afoot, with the incorporation of rheumatology as an up and coming specialty in its own right. And soon it was attracting the best doctors, who recognised the fascination of the various conditions it encompassed, especially rheumatoid arthritis, but also mysterious complaints like lupus.

One day, he saw an advert for a registrar post in the same hospital where he had had the unfortunate experience when first attempting the membership exam. By a twist of fate, his application was successful, and soon he was enjoying the delights of London. As an aside, but nevertheless applying his heightened powers of clinical observation, he noticed that the nurses were by far prettier than any he had seen before. Could this be a coincidence? His social life blossomed, his unfortunate experience with Marilyn was soon forgotten. Although his pay was modest, he was able to secure a mortgage on a one-bedroom apartment in Camden Town. And before long, he had met and married Connie, a pretty medical secretary to a consultant gynaecologist at the hospital. His career advanced such that three years later he was upgraded to senior registrar by due process following interview. This was the springboard for a future consultancy. Another four years, a few papers published, and he was successful in obtaining a consultant rheumatology post in the Home Counties. He and Connie had three children, two of whom went into teaching, and one into the priesthood.

*

The master, meanwhile, found that his work was much the same as it had been in Yorkshire, but there were some patients who, reflecting the relative affluence of Shrewsbury, requested private care. One such was Veronica Middleton, a thirty-year-old solicitor, with a practice overlooking the Quarry. She was worried about a mole on her arm, about which the master was quickly able to reassure her, as it had none of the features of cancer. There being no need to see her again, the master discharged her. To his surprise, the following week he received a call inviting him to join Veronica for a small dinner party at the Prince Rupert restaurant. The master was happy to accept, as in truth, his existence had become rather lonely. He was introduced to two other couples, who were married, both of whom were solicitors, husband and wife teams. Naturally the conversation was somewhat biased towards the law, but the master's opinion was sought on the legality of abortion. The master could tell that he was being scrutinised as potential marriage fodder for Veronica who was under the wing of the others. He wasn't too worried, as she was strikingly elegant, five feet seven inches tall (he estimated), bust thirty-seven inches (he estimated), and hips, probably thirty-five inches. He felt that he would, should the opportunity present itself, be able to verify his estimates. She had a long slender neck, with a few wisps of dark hair over the nape. I felt a jolt – was this to be the grand awakening? The meal over, they all retired to the lounge for coffee and brandies. He walked Veronica back to her flat which was situated just a couple of streets away. She invited him in possibly for another coffee.

The flat was elegantly furnished, with some fine Stubbs reproductions on the walls. Clearly she was into horses. Over coffee they chatted into the early hours. She gave him her life history, he his. She was a widow, her husband having sadly died of leukaemia about a year ago. There were no children. She told him she had not had any relationships since the death of her husband, but felt in need of support on the anniversary of his death. Then she burst into tears, and the master took her into his arms to comfort her. He gently kissed her on the cheek, then the side of her neck, then the nape, and then on her lips. She responded gratefully and they clung together. At this point, she asked him if he would like to go further. He was clearly keen, and had already undone her bra. I was screaming, 'Hold on a bit, I'm nowhere near ready,' but my pleas fell on deaf ears. Well, the rest can be imagined, two naked bodies entwined, but something missing. And that something was me. Try as I might, and as the master might, I was in total repose, not in the least ready for action. Veronica for the first time in her life, attempted oral resuscitation, but to no avail.

'Never mind, Pablo, it affects lots of men. I expect it's all the stress you've been through.'

Despite this shortcoming, their relationship flourished, and they became an item. They sampled the delights of the Shropshire hills, and trips to Snowdonia. The big problem however persisted. The master finally plucked up enough courage to take medical advice. He attended a private surgery in Harley Street, and was told he probably had the male menopause. He was prescribed testosterone, which made no difference to me, but gave him acne, something he hadn't had since his youth. He did not welcome it. He tried strangling me with some peculiar rings, but this didn't work either. He modified his diet lest he have diabetes – again, no dice. Thus he became resigned to a life of celibacy. Veronica was very patient. They got engaged, having established that what was not to be would continue thus, but should there be some breakthrough in medicine, then normal service could be resumed.

In the United States of America, a drug called Viagra was being tried for patients with angina, and blood pressure. It turned out to be useless, not because of side effects, but because it just didn't work. However, it had a most peculiar, and wholly unexpected side effect. And that side effect was that it breathed new life into me. It was as though Viagra was the handmaiden of Venus, the goddess of love. She was to be joined a few years later by her sisters, Levitra and Cialis. Now everything promised to be hunky-dory, or so the master thought. So, one evening, having primed me with said Viagra, and having wined and dined Veronica, we went into action. But, sad to say, Veronica had decided life was fine as it was, and didn't feel any need for me. The master tried every trick he could think of, plus a few he had read about, but, no dice! Veronica was determined to remain a chaste lady. Thus it was that the engagement was broken off, and the master emerged, once again a free man. Then he received the sad news that his mother had died suddenly. The funeral was held in Shrewsbury as she lived about twelve miles away, and the whole family attended. Brenda and Vic by now had three children. The master had become a grandfather through the action of Ronald, whose rock band career was doing well, though he was still not married.

The master had heard of massage parlours, and that they were in effect brothels, so he decided he would give one a try. But he didn't want to be seen in his home town, so decided to travel to Wolverhampton for the purpose. Whilst there, he went into a pub, and struck up a conversation with a man of about thirty something, who unfortunately thought he was being chatted up, and gave short shrift. Finally he asked a taxi driver, who transported him to the nearest den of iniquity.

'Gentlemen's Massage' advertised itself in the early evening, with a red sign. Nervously, he opened the door, and walked in. He climbed some stairs, and was greeted.

'Hallo, darling, have you been here before?'

'No,' he replied.

'Well, take a seat and the girls will see you shortly. That will be ten pounds please.'

He handed over the money and waited, his heart pounding. Presently a pretty girl of about twenty-five appeared, and said her name was Natasha. She led him into a small room, in which there was a bench, with a paper roll covering it. She told him to undress, so that she could massage him. He did so, and laid on his front. She applied some oil, and proceeded to massage him. This he found quite pleasant, and had to remind himself why he was really there. After half an hour, she said the massage was now over, and did he wish for anything further. At this moment, he realised he hadn't taken any Viagra, but after a list of options, and their respective prices, selected hand relief. In this I was involved, but only to a very limited degree, but the expected result occurred, which wasn't much cop. Then the master bid farewell to Natasha, thanked her, and said he might return some time.

The following weekend, and having taken the blue pill, the master was once more in the massage parlour. But it was Natasha's day off, and instead it was a plump, blonde lady of twenty, with large breasts and a very muscular bottom, named Mary. He guessed she worked on the land, and needed to supplement her income. So he asked her. 'Actually, I'm a medical student at Cambridge, and I come here weekends to supplement my meagre existence. And what do you do?'

At this point the master was taken aback, but told her he was a GP.

'Oh, that's very interesting, I'd like to be a GP when I qualify. What's it like?'

So, for the next twenty minutes, the conversation was about the current state of the NHS, and how general practice compared with hospital practice. At the end, he enquired about the massage.

'Oh, I'm sorry, I forgot. Yes, let's get on with it.' After about five minutes of vigorous pummelling by Mary, the master felt he had had enough, and didn't have the courage to contemplate sex with this strong automaton.

Third time lucky? The following week, Natasha was back, and I am pleased to report I earned top marks. I performed impeccably, and achieved, an albeit contrived, Alice score of ten. The master departed with a smile on his face, and fifty pounds poorer. Thanks to Venus' handmaiden, the fair Viagra, I and my ilk could now return to fulfil our biological role. There is no doubt, the world was from hereon forward, a happier place. Viagra, we salute you!

But life goes on. The master regained a spring in his stride, started drinking less, and took a daily walk. His physical and mental health improved. He began to enjoy his work more, and looked forward to the next regional meeting of the British Medical Association. There was to be a session on rheumatoid arthritis, which he found to be a real challenge amongst the few patients he had with this condition. After the meeting, he attended the dinner and found himself seated next to a most attractive lady of forty something. They introduced themselves. He learned that she was a widow, with a son who worked in banking, and that she was a director of nursing at her hospital. Their conversation ranged over a number of medical topics. She told him she had attended the session on rheumatoid arthritis, having a personal interest in this disease, because her mother suffered from it. Her name was Samantha Bellingham. She had red hair, and a few freckles, a slim body with smallish hips. Her face was strikingly pretty. The master felt things happening, as did she, and so did I. The pheromones were definitely working, perhaps having been kicked into action by Natasha who had been ministering unto the master on a fairly regular basis. In fact the master did wonder whether sex could one day be prescribed on the NHS, because he had no doubt, it made him feel a lot better, and, wisely taken, in moderation, was probably safer than Librium. Well, eventually these two (the master and Samantha that is) decided to take their relationship to a new level, and found it mutually satisfying, care of Viagra. Sam was quite demonstrative, and surprisingly inventive. Let me put it this way. Why stick to A roads when you can use a dual carriageway? And the number sixty-nine came to mean more than the consequence of multiplying twenty-three by three. In the summer they went on a Caribbean cruise, which was fabulous, though self-restraint had to be exercised to the full in the presence of so much delicious food. And then it happened.

He woke up on a medical ward in Southampton. He had apparently been taken ill on the last night on board, as the liner was rounding the Isle of Wight. He became aware of a discomfort in his chest, which he attributed to the meal he had just partaken. Over the course of the evening, however, it became worse, and he realised this was not simple indigestion. Then he collapsed, his head falling into the *crème brûlée*, and knocking over his glass of Sauternes dessert wine. He was treated with oxygen and morphine in the ship's sick bay, an electrocardiogram having shown an acute heart attack. Once on the medical ward, he recognised Sam and gave her a wan smile. His recovery was slow, but he was eventually discharged after a fortnight, with instructions to take things very easy from then on. He noticed that he was short of breath when walking up hill. Occasionally his ankles would swell. Sam understood all the signs of heart failure, and carefully nursed him back to a kind of health.

Part 4
Winter

(Age sixty to seventy-two)

U pon return from the cruise, the master started taking more exercise in an attempt to regain some form of physical fitness. Initially he walked about a quarter of a mile, then gradually built it up, until he could manage three without too much difficulty. After three months he was able to return to work on a four-day week. Sometimes he felt angina pain on walking faster, but a glyceryl trinitrate pill under his tongue soon gave relief. But he was determined to get better, and pushed himself to exercise, angina or not, even when he had to pop the pill. So eventually, it all came good, and he could walk five miles without turning a hair. Sam was delighted. He was happy at work, and his patients welcomed him. Then fate took a turn.

Miss Virginia Harcourt was unmarried, and working as an accountant when she attended the practice. The master pressed the buzzer, and she entered the consulting room. She was aged thirty, dark-haired, and fairly attractive, if a bit on the plump side. She said she had recently become troubled by tummy pain. The usual questions followed, when did it occur, how often, whereabouts was it felt etc etc. She was then asked to undress exposing her abdomen for the master to examine her. As usual, the master went back to the office area to ask Miss Warburton, the practice nurse, to chaperone him. But she was busy with Dr Benedict. The master returned to his consulting room, explaining the situation to Miss Harcourt, who understood, and said she had no objection to him examining her without a chaperone being present.

The master then inspected her abdomen, and followed this by gentle palpation, asking whether she was experiencing any discomfort or pain. She was slightly tender under her ribs, in the centre. He then pressed a little deeper to see if there was any mass that was palpable, but there wasn't. The master diagnosed it as indigestion, and prescribed a bottle of magnesium trisilicate. She thanked him, and left the consulting room.

A fortnight later, the master received the shock of his life when a letter from the General Medical Council arrived, saying that this patient had told them he had indecently assaulted her during the examination. In fact, she alleged he had explained that it was necessary to examine her intimately, and to her surprise, had utilised my services in so doing, and that she had been so shocked, she had not protested at the time, but had left in a state of distress and disarray. He was aghast. What could he do? It was something he had known ever since a medical student was professional suicide. It could, if proven, be the end of his career, and social disgrace. Unfortunately, even if disproved, there was no guaranteeing it wouldn't leave a stain on his character, such is human nature.

That evening, he told Sam. He had to pop a pill on account of another angina attack. He had to reply to the General Medical Council. But what was he to say? Unfortunately he had had no chaperone as witness to use in his defence. Before responding to the GMC, he contacted the Medical Defence Union, and at their request, submitted a full account of his recollection of events. They wrote to the GMC, but the GMC said they had no option but to suspend him pending a full enquiry.

His whole world was turned on its head. He became very depressed, even contemplating suicide. What a way to end one's career! And then, horror of horrors, the police called, and told him he had been accused by Miss Harcourt of rape. She had delayed this length of time because she was so distressed, and didn't know what to do. Clearly, by this time the master needed a solicitor, and quickly. He decided to give Veronica Middleton at her solicitors' office, a call seeking advice. She was very helpful and sympathetic.

'Lovely to hear from you, Pablo. What a bitch this woman is! I've heard of her sort. Sad in a way. Do you know any more about her? How long has she been a patient of yours? Have you seen her before? Tell you what, I'll have a word with a barrister friend, and get back to you.'

A week later.

'Hi, Pablo. I've had a word with Jason Hutchins. He's a hotshot barrister. He suggested finding out whether this patient has made any previous similar complaints.'

'Thanks, Veronica, that's a great idea.'

Back at the practice, the master chased up Miss Harcourt's file. She had only recently registered, having moved from Surrey, into the Shrewsbury area. The Surrey records hadn't yet been received. So he decided to phone the previous practice in Wentworth. He was put through to the senior partner, and explained the situation.

'Miss Harcourt? Don't tell me. She's made a complaint? Well, what a surprise. She did the same here, and when we went into it, she had done the same at two previous practices. Don't worry old chap, her case wouldn't stand up in court. She's a fantasist. Sad really.'

And that was the end of the matter. Once the information was passed to the GMC, the Medical Defence Union, the police, and finally to Miss Harcourt, the allegation was dropped.

This was a great relief to the master as well as to Sam. She knew he would never do anything so foolish. And he realised he would always insist on a chaperone in similar circumstances. Unsurprisingly Miss Harcourt took herself off the practice's list.

MARTHA

Martha was born in 1909, and had grown up in Upper Silesia, the daughter of a chemist, who owned a pharmacy in a town called Beuthen. Her childhood was happy, the family was fairly affluent, and her ambition was to teach remedial gymnastics to children with disability. The family adhered to Jewish custom, but trouble, big trouble lay ahead. Anti-Semitism was rife, but tolerated as something to put up with. However, in November 1938, after the infamous *Kristallnacht*, Goebbels came to Beuthen to preach hatred against the Jews. Before this, Martha and Sol had met and married in 1937. They lived in Sol's home town, Katowice, a few miles away. The Bernsteins were a fairly well-to-do family, Sol having graduated in engineering in Darmstadt. Sol's father had died of an ear infection in 1936, so Sol looked after his mother. In 1939, just before the outbreak of war, Sol, Martha, and Sol's mother travelled by train to Gdansk, and caught a boat to Harwich. Martha's parents stayed behind, to help organise visas for others wishing to escape. They themselves never would, suffering their fate in Auschwitz in 1942.

Once in England, Martha lived the life of a refugee, hoping that one day, she would see her parents again. But that was never to be. Sol was interned on the Isle of Man, but afterwards released, and conscripted into the British Army Pioneer Corps, based in Catterick, Yorkshire. After the war, Martha busied herself bringing up her family, and after Sol's death, in charity work. She remained an attractive widow, and surprisingly had two proposals of marriage. One was admittedly from a somewhat inebriated (and still married) family member, the other from a retired army colonel. Both were refused.

She was a proud and popular grandmother, much respected in her community. Martha was eighty when she fell and broke her hip. At the time she was living alone in Shropshire in a nice two-bedroom bungalow. The combination of sherry, and Librium did it. Afterwards, although she was operated on and returned home, she was never the same. And it became noticeable her bungalow was not very clean, and all sorts of horrors were found in the fridge whenever she was visited by the master. Eventually she was found a place near Shrewsbury, in a very friendly and well-run care home. The master would visit occasionally, but the conversation became repetitive after about five minutes, so therefore he would chat to some of the other residents. Then he would return to his mother, who greeted him as though she hadn't seen him for ages. She gradually descended into a deeper degree of dementia, which was very painful for the master, when she failed to recognise him, but nevertheless made polite conversation asking him in a formal way, how his career was progressing, and was he married. One cold night in November, she had a stroke, and passed away a week later.

At her funeral, Beethoven's 'Ode to Joy' was played and tributes to her charity work, and culinary skills were made in the vicar's eulogy. She was cremated, and her ashes interred beside Sol's grave in a quiet Shropshire village.

The master's sixtieth birthday was a somewhat muted affair. Dr Phipps and Dr Bernard Benedict took him and Sam to a Michelin starred restaurant in Ludlow, where they enjoyed a brilliant meal. The master and Sam stayed overnight at the Feathers Hotel, for which Ludlow was famous. Next day, they drove out to the Clee hills, and walked a little. But it was a cold and windy day, so they returned to Shrewsbury. Arrangements had been made for the master's retirement, much against his will, but his ill health demanded it. He had been diligent in saving for his pension which was very reasonable. A comfortable, if unexciting retirement beckoned. Then, one day, at 11.31 a.m., he had an epiphany!

Sod old age! Sod infirmity!

So he decided to buy a motorbike!

But he needed to pass the test, as his car licence didn't suffice. Everyone, including Sam thought him mad. He contacted a local driving instructor, and rode pillion to a local car park where, after due explanation, he was able to ride around in ever decreasing circles before stalling and stopping. His training sessions were carried out on a 125cc Honda which was relatively easy to control. Then he went out onto the road, fifty yards ahead of his instructor with whom he was in radio-contact. Of course it was compulsory for him to sport L plates. His certificate of basic training required him to demonstrate adequate control, including starting on a hill. He passed and was allowed to ride anywhere on a motorbike up to 125 cc but with L plates. This was fine, but hazardous on busy trunk roads, where lorries gave him a hard time. He realised he would need something more powerful. The way to achieve this would be by passing the full test for bikes up to 125 cc, and then gaining experience over two further years.

After that, he would be permitted to ride bikes of any size. Alternatively, one could go for the direct licence, which was quite difficult because the transformation from 125 cc to 500 or more was considerable, as these bikes were far heavier, and once past a certain angle, would simply drop, and be extremely difficult for a small person to lift.

The test needed adequate knowledge of the Highway Code, and far more difficult, to pass the hazard awareness test. In this, he had to watch a video, and press a button whenever he spotted a hazard. It soon became apparent that what he considered hazardous was not in agreement with whoever had constructed the test, and vice versa. Next he went out with some others, one of whom was a slender lady in her twenties, who clearly found the extra weight of a 500cc machine too much for her. The extra power at hand was quite intimidating at first, but he soon adapted, and got the hang of things. The most difficult part of the test that was to follow was the one hundred and eighty degrees turn round across a fairly narrow road. If one needed to put out a leg onto the road to steady oneself, one would automatically fail. Came the day, and to everyone's surprise, he managed to pass. The next excitement was which more powerful motorbike to buy. He perused the several offerings from the likes of BMW, Honda, Suzuki, and even Harley-Davidson. Unfortunately his chest wasn't hairy enough to justify a Harley. The modern Japanese bikes were very good, and fast, but didn't evoke in him the true spirit of a British bike. Therefore, and after much thought, he opted for a Triumph Bonneville. Sam, when invited, agreed to ride pillion, and found it almost as exciting as what she had been missing now for some time. Where previously every uphill slope had caused the master to feel short of breath, now all he had to do was twist the throttle a little more, and roar up whichever hill beckoned. There was the ever-present thrill of leaning into corners and accelerating away from them. Overtaking was a doddle, you went out facing death, and were back into your own safe side of the road in a trice. But you had to be careful, and get it right. Any mistake might be your last. Right hand bends threatened immediate decapitation. Day trips to North Wales, the Isle of Anglesey, and east into Yorkshire were challenging, but immensely satisfying.

One evening they discussed trips further afield, and realised they needed to add panniers and a third pannier over the rear of the bike. They purchased bike leathers with protective padding. Then off they went, bound for Europe. The first night they spent in a hotel in Dover, then caught the six o'clock ferry to Calais. By lunchtime they had reached Paris and found a cheap hotel in the Montmartre district. During the afternoon, Sam decided she wanted to look at some shops, so the master decided to explore Paris on foot. After about half an hour, he found himself in Pigalle, an area well known for nefarious activities with ladies of the night (and day). He knew his (serious) limitations in this department, but couldn't help being tempted by a strikingly pretty dark-haired lass, possibly of Moroccan origin, who asked him if he wanted some fun at a very reasonable price. I was appalled – how could he? It was bound to end in (expensive) failure. The agreed price was two hundred francs. They walked a short distance, then entered an old building and climbed a steep staircase. I was worried, hoping his heart would cope – perhaps the stairs would kill him, but if not, then what was to follow might. Somehow the master summoned up inner strength, and went up the stairs as if they weren't there. I was amazed! Next thing, Zola (for that was her name), asked him to take off all his clothes, she kept on her black lace bra and panties. Then she turned her attention to me, having clearly spotted me desperately trying to hide. But there was no hiding place! She fished me out and by a process of well-practised manoeuvres which I shall omit to describe, succeeded in creating a miniature rival to the Eiffel Tower! Next, we were back on the Cresta run, shortly followed by Alice noises which sounded surprisingly genuine. What a minx! An hour later, over aperitifs at a café on the (hideously expensive) Champs Elysées, Sam asked him how he had spent his afternoon.

'Oh, just meandering around, dear. Isn't Paris beautiful?'

'Well, I hope you've behaved yourself, you know what they say about Paris. It's as wicked as the red light district in Amsterdam. You know, I'd love to visit Pigalle, just to see what goes on. Let's go this evening.'

And so the master found himself once again, this time arm in arm with Sam strolling the streets of Paris' red light area. He hoped to goodness they wouldn't bump into Zola, but she had obviously finished her shift.

'I feel so sorry for these girls,' Sam said. 'You know they are riddled with diseases, which they are bound to pass on to their clients.'

The master visibly flinched, realising he had been unwise. He remembered his training at university, having spent a week following Dr Winkelstrom in the VD department. The images he recollected were none too pleasant. I felt OK, so far, but wondered whether Zola had repaid the master's fee with a free donation of bacteria. A week later, as their motorcycling tour reached Nice, the master found that in fact there were some changes. Peeing was painful, and he noticed a slight discharge. He decided to treat himself with some antibiotics, but was unable to persuade the French pharmacists to supply him. His fame and prowess as a doctor had not reached their shores. And then the symptoms cleared, and the couple continued their holiday. Their tour took them on to Monte Carlo, and a brief flutter in the casino, before heading back. Four days later they were back in England.

The next weekend, they visited Horton and the master's old stamping ground, this time using the Cortina. They had had sufficient of motorcycling for the present, it really was quite tiring, albeit very exhilarating. Things had changed quite a bit. The dance hall where he had frequently taken Carol had by now disappeared, the cricket ground had been replaced by a football pitch. He showed Sam his old school, now a Sikh temple. They visited Michael, their second son, who lived in Newport and worked at a nearby agricultural college. He was delighted to see them arrive unannounced, and introduced them to his partner Valerie.

'I'm delighted to meet you, Dr Bernstein. Hello, Mrs Bernstein. Oh, by the way, this is my little boy, Kevin. Come here, Kevin, don't be shy. They won't bite.'

Kevin was a little boy of four, the offspring of a previous relationship. He was tousle-haired, and quite impish. Everyone had to like him. Valerie put on an impromptu tea, having nipped out and returned after ten minutes with a tasty fruit cake purchased in the high street. After about an hour, the master excused himself, in order to answer the call of nature.

'It's upstairs, first on the left,' said Michael. I saw the light of day. Armitage Shanks, nothing special. But then things changed.

The pee wouldn't come at first, then barely a trickle. A few minutes later, and after some rather hasty goodbyes, Sam and the master headed back to Shrewsbury.

'I've got a problem, Sam,' confided the master. 'I think it's my prostate.'

He didn't know that Old Walnut was protesting his innocence.

'I'll have to go to casualty at the infirmary.'

Sam drove him, and they waited in casualty. Presently they were seen by Dr Patel. The master was asked to undress, and wait in a cubicle. He was given a robe, and given a bottle into which to pee. No joy. Then taps were turned on, but still no luck. The next thing Dr. Patel was explaining that he needed to perform a rectal examination to assess the size of Old Walnut. To his surprise, it was normal.

'I told you so,' hissed Old Walnut. 'Why does no-one ever believe me?'

But its protestations fell on deaf ears.

'That's odd,' said the doctor. 'I'll have a word with the registrar.'

Half an hour later, the registrar appeared, a ginger-haired chap called Mr McNally. Surgeons by custom are addressed as 'Mister'. James McNally told the master that he would need to catheterise him, in order to release the wee. Sam was asked by a very nice staff nurse to wait in the corridor, and was provided with a cup of tea. Eventually a trolley was produced containing the equipment. I felt distinctly ill at ease. Up to now the only people who had handled me were the master, and various ladies for you know what. Oh, and of course, the rabbi who had circumcised me all those years ago. McNally approached with a sterile rubber catheter. To his surprise, he couldn't advance it within me. I felt affronted, but was nonplussed as to what was going on.

'I think you've got a urethral stricture,' he explained. 'A stricture is a narrowing of the passage of the tube through which you wee. It can happen when there has been an untreated infection in the past. Have you ever had any infection in this neck of the woods?'

The master thought hard, then remembered his visit to Paris, and explained to McNally. Zola must have given him the clap, and now he was paying a different price.

'We'll have to perform a urethral dilatation in theatre,' the registrar explained. Anyway, to cut a long story short, and to spare you the details, this was carried out successfully, but had to be repeated approximately every three months. Sam was very understanding when eventually he confided in her.

'You men are all the same. Paris or Amsterdam, or Bangkok, your brains all migrate south. You never grow up. There's more to life than sex.' (That's your point of view, thought the master.)

Years passed and the master, by now aged sixty-five was having to live life at a slower pace. At times he felt tired, and on hills, short of breath. He could still climb the Wrekin slowly. He wouldn't attempt Snowdon. Thanks to the contributions of Venus' handmaidens, first Viagra, and in later years, Levitra and Cialis, I was still brought out of the cupboard on special occasions, when with a little assistance, I could still give a good account of myself. I had seen many sites in my peregrinations:

Twyford's, Adamant (the Philharmonic pub, Liverpool), Armitage Shanks, Charlotte, Geberit, Twyfords, Allia (Paris), Porcher, Shires, Duravit, Rotter (Berlin Airport), McAlpine

(Luton Airport), Kohler (Little Chef), Vortic, Valadares, Laufen (Crown Plaza, Nottingham), and many more, some more difficult to decipher, but all having had homage paid them by me and my brothers.

The motorbike was still ridden, albeit infrequently. Brenda and Vic were to have three children. Brenda had turned out eventually to be quite pleasant, but no more than that. David was employed in the design section of the British Motor Corporation, based at Longbridge in Birmingham. Unfortunately, the whole firm was destined for collapse and ignominious failure due to Red Robbo and his trade union savages, combined with weak management. David then moved on to work for Toyota in Derby. Nathan was a barrister, in chambers at one of the Inns of Court in London. He had married Fiona Smith-Carpenter, and lived in Highgate. He was rarely seen. Ronald had gone into computers which were still in a developmental stage, the BBC B model having just been launched. Elise was a dance teacher in Chester, having married Terry, an accountant. All turned up for the master's funeral a few years later.

However, a funny thing happened as he was being laid out by the mortician. I had not yet received the attentions of said mortician when the phone rang and he was called away. He obviously forgot that his task of laying out the body had not been totally completed, and went off as it was five o'clock. Thus, I, unlike the rest of the master, was not restricted from the subsequent actions of *rigor mortis*. The next day, and an hour before being placed in the coffin, the funeral director was himself mortified at the sight that greeted him. I had the final say. A triumphant farewell.

As they say in the Royal Air Force, 'Per ardua ad astra.'

And so it was. The greatest erection ever witnessed, at least in that part of Shropshire.

A hole had to be hastily drilled on the lid of the coffin to accommodate me, and an inverted metal flower vase placed over. And on top, secured by super glue another vase, carrying some roses.

Bye bye world, as the coffin, to the accompaniment of Chopin's funeral march bore the master horizontally through the curtains, and me vertically, beneath two flower vases and a rose.

So now, with my master's life extinct, it falls upon me to reflect on my life, and what I have learned. One week after my master was born, I was subjected to a procedure demanded by tradition. All through life, the master was aware he had been born to parents who had been forced to flee their homeland because they were Jewish. The master when living his childhood in the English countryside where Judaism was unknown, and where a German name meant one was regarded as an alien and therefore subject to playground violence, felt a strong urge to conform, to admire all that was English. However, open to future criticism these experiences were, it was nevertheless an inescapable fact that this country offered a safe haven, and it was also out of a sense of gratitude that conformity was sought.

This urge to conform was also felt by others in his family, even to the extent of converting to Christianity. It took many years before the master took the opportunity to ask what was the purpose of religion. One feature of all religions seemed to be a desire to be good and do good, though revenge was also hinted at. The epiphany came when he realised what science taught. The realisation of the infinity of the universe, the existence of solar systems, galaxies, black holes, fundamental particles, nuclear energy, evolution, genetics, medicine, and lots more, led him to question why any God, of whatever name, gender, or spirit, would not, being of course possessed of such knowledge, have chosen to reveal it through any or all theisms. Theism, it seems, was a device whereby advantage and power would fall to those professing it, and the promise of reward in the hereafter would rein in vast sums of money, which no doubt accounted for, for instance, the beautiful cathedrals and churches admired by the master in his lifetime, and in one such, I now bid England goodbye.